THE SPY WHO SEDUCED HER
The Brethren Series

Copyright © 2017 by Christi Caldwell

For more information about the author:
www.christicaldwellauthor.com
christicaldwellauthor@gmail.com
Twitter: @ChristiCaldwell
Or on Facebook at: Christi Caldwell Author

For first glimpse at covers, excerpts, and free bonus material, be sure to sign up for my monthly newsletter!
Printed in the USA.

Cover Design and Interior Format

© KILLION
THE   GROUP, INC.

Brethen #1

The Spy Who Seduced Her

THE BRETHREN
THE SERIES

USA TODAY BESTSELLER

CHRISTI CALDWELL

SINFUL BRIDES
The Rogue's Wager
The Scoundrel's Honor

THE THEODOSIA SWORD
Only for His Lady

DANBY
A Season of Hope
Winning a Lady's Heart

BRETHREN OF THE LORDS
My Lady of Deception
Memoir: Non-Fiction
Uninterrupted Joy

CHAPTER 1

The Brethren of the Lords comes first:
before everything and everyone.
Article I: The Brethren of the Lords

Spring, 1820
London, England

NATHANIEL ARCHER, THE EARL OF Exeter, had gone from a once battered, beaten, and bruised spy captured by an Irish radical to leader of the Brethren of the Lords.

Shaped by his imprisonment and two years of torture, he'd become a man who'd no time for anything or anyone outside the Brethren. His work filled his days and nights, and had become the family he'd never had nor would ever have.

Where other noblemen were content with a carefree life, taking part in mindless *ton* events, Nathaniel despised those frivolities as much as he had as a young man just out of Oxford. He'd always preferred the purposefulness that came in ensuring England was secure and its people safe.

The twelve hours he'd spent seated behind the great, mahogany desk examining a list of potential future members of the Brethren for the one vacant post, stood as a testament of his devotion to his work.

Opening the next file, Nathaniel quickly passed his gaze over the top sheet.

…No field experience. No military experience…

"This is what we've become, then," he muttered under his breath as he continued reading. A secret agency under the discretion and direction of the Home Office that the King sought to fill with indolent lords; peers who put favors to him for a role within the Home Office for their equally indolent sons.

Ultimately, however, Nathaniel, in his role of Sovereign of the Brethren, had the final decision. It did not preclude him from having to go through the motions, all to appease the King. And though he'd simply toss out those lords who would not suit, the task drained time and energies away from the organization.

"I take that as a 'no' on Lord Hammell," his assistant, Mr. Lionel Bennett, drawled from the same seat he'd occupied for the better part of the day, opposite Nathaniel.

"A firm no," he groused as he set aside the sparse folder. Leaning back in his chair, he rolled his stiff shoulders. "Surely there are more qualified candidates than *this?*" He stretched his arms out before him, giving a slight shake to strengthen the blood flow to the limbs.

With a droll smile, Bennett handed over another. "I present Lord Sheldon Whitworth."

His lips twitched. "*You*, present?" he asked, taking it from the younger man.

His assistant widened his grin. "Rather, the *King* recommends Lord Sheldon Whitworth."

Lord Whitworth: a rogue and a rascal in dire need of reform. "Of course," he mumbled. The Brethren had more than enough of those types in their midst. The manner of men Society would never take for anything else but reprobates. A familiar annoyance stirred. He'd tired long ago of being tasked with maturing the King's hand-selected nursery of lords.

Bennett chuckled.

Nathaniel had to hand it to the other man. After half a day at the task, most would be rumpled, fatigued, and disgruntled. Bennett, however, who'd served the Brethren since his days at Oxford had an unruffled affect that only a man of his five and twenty years could manage. *To be young again.* But then, having been born the child of a former agent, the Brethren coursed through the younger man's veins.

"He is six and twenty," Bennett was saying. "Second son of the Duke of Sutton."

All the lords of London with second and third born sons who'd disavowed the clergy and military, thought to foist their spares upon the Home Office, as a way to both exert and expand their influence and *importance*. "I can read as much," Nathaniel said dryly, not lifting his focus from the next *illustrious* candidate. In defense of those peers, they could not know the same offspring they sought posts for would be considered for field agents of the Brethren; that secret organization known only by the King, its members, former agents, and the Home Office.

Lord Sheldon Whitworth:
Served in His Majesty's Navy
No field experience
No sea battle experience

He made quick work of reading through the file. Another military upstart with a *right* to a position in the Home Office.

"There is a letter of commendation attached at the back," Bennett volunteered.

Flipping to the next page, he skimmed the praise-laden letter from… "The Duke of Sutton," he muttered under his breath. Yet another powerful peer exerting his influence on behalf of his kin.

"It makes one wonder, if those same lords knew the risks their spares would take on if selected for the post, whether they'd volunteer their names to the King," Bennett mused aloud, in echo of Nathaniel's earlier thoughts.

"Your own father did," he felt inclined to point out. When Nathaniel had received control of the organization and been tapped by the King as Sovereign, one of the first requests for employment had come from a previous member of the Brethren.

"My father was clever enough to know that nothing could stop me from taking up work for the Home Office." Bennett flashed a half-grin. "I simply did not know of his ties to the Brethren."

Lord Lucien Bennett was one of those to serve as Delegator, handing out assignments to agents. He had gathered precisely the manner of work he'd submitted his son's name for.

Despite Nathaniel's initial reservations, he'd learned almost

instantly the young man was far more than his familial connection. With a sound of disgust, he abandoned yet another folder. He
stared expectantly back at his assistant.

Obligingly, Bennett held out the next.

Opening it, Nathaniel surveyed the file. He lifted his head,
unable to keep the incredulity from his query. "Quimbly's spare?"

His assistant nodded.

The Duke of Quimbly had petitioned the King no fewer than
two times on his son's behalf… and that was only in the two years
that Nathaniel had been appointed the Sovereign. The meticulous
records kept indicated there had been four previous requests put
before his predecessor.

"Is there a role in the Home Office for him?" Bennett ventured.
"Not the Brethren, necessarily," he spoke on a rush. "But some
other assignment, elsewhere."

Stitching his eyebrows, Nathaniel scrutinized the younger man.
Methodical, efficient, and wholly dedicated to the Brethren, he'd
never before shown a weakness. "You know the gentleman?"

Bennett turned his palms up. "He was a classmate at Eton. Clever.
Mocked by other classmates for being too clever. Quiet."

"And yet, he was interviewed by the Home Office and found
unsuitable for a post within that division?" Dismissively, he set the
file aside. "If they are not fit for the post of agent, they are not
suitable for any role within the Home Office." Nathaniel grabbed
his pen. Dipping it in the crystal inkwell, he proceeded to cross off
the twelve candidates he'd reviewed that day.

Bennett drummed his fingertips on the arms of his chair. "You
rule solely by the articles of the organization."

"There is no other way." Nathaniel sprinkled pounce upon the
wet ink and then blew. He had given more than two decades to
the Brethren and then inherited the rank of leadership within it.
The secret agency was more than just another division within the
Home Office. Where other men had sweethearts, wives, or children, the Brethren had come to be his everything—his life. His
skin pricked with the feel of the other man's eyes on him and he
looked up.

"Sometimes… there is… more to a person, a case," Bennett
nudged his chin at Quimbly's discarded file. "A candidate."

His assistant spoke with a candidness Nathaniel appreciated, and also an experience of an agent twenty years his senior. Those attributes had shown through at his interview and were the reason he had made Bennett his assistant. "There may be," he acknowledged. "But duty before all. The organization—"

"Comes first," Bennett supplied. It was a credo that had been passed down for centuries. "Oh, lest I forget. I have another candidate for you to review." Leaning down, he fetched a folder from under his seat and rested it on Nathaniel's desk. "He is *not* one of the King's picks. I came across his credentials at the bottom of the pile."

Intrigued, Nathaniel looked to the folder in question. After Bennett had taken his leave, Nathaniel stacked the folders of rejected candidates; countless men whom the King would exert his influence to see staffed within the Brethren. He flexed his jaw.

A once elite organization that had existed for too long with outdated rules of governance, when he'd taken over the helm, the Brethren had been nearly defunct. It had been a group within the Home Office in dire need of restructuring and modernization. And that is precisely what he'd spent these past two years doing: rebuilding so that his influence was everywhere. From the manner of missions undertaken by agents to threats to the Crown and crimes against the peerage to the rules of governance. He'd rewritten the articles that guided the organization, systematically interviewed, and then dismissed agents who'd proven unreliable over the years, and kept on only the finest—a handful of men and women who'd not a single mistake to their career. Hiring and keeping on agents who were clever-minded, unswervingly loyal people with a like drive to ensure the security and prosperity of Crown and country.

His work would not be complete until the Brethren was restored to its former glory.

Nathaniel sighed.

Removing his reading spectacles, he tossed the wire frames down and they landed atop that stack of leather folios with a quiet thump. Time inevitably changed all: everyone and everything. However, it had been vastly... easier when the King had not interfered with the business of the Brethren.

Nathaniel again rolled his stiff shoulders and, donning his glasses, examined the file left by Bennett. He proceeded to read through the accolades and accomplishments of Mr. Colin Lockhart.

One of London's finest Bow Street Runners and a bastard-born son of a duke—a duke who'd not written a letter on the man's behalf. Intrigued for the first time since he'd begun his evaluation for future members of the organization, Nathaniel leaned forward.

Not long ago, the only men and women afforded a place within the noble ranks of the Brethren had been lords and ladies born to power and privilege. When he, the first man born without a title, only having been bestowed one for acts of heroism, had ascended to the head of the organization, he'd instituted a shift within those considered for the vacancies that arose. The men working as Runners demonstrated far more grit, and a greater grasp of the types of cases the Brethren undertook.

Wetting the tip of his index finger, he turned to the next sheet of vellum that enumerated Lockhart's impressive list of closed cases.

A knock sounded at the door.

"Enter," he called, not bothering to look up from his examination of Lockhart's credentials.

"My lord," Bennett's voice slashed into the quiet. "Fergus Macleod arrived a short while ago."

"Macleod?" Silently cursing, Nathaniel glanced over to the longcase clock. *Bloody hell.* Forgetting a damned meeting. He was getting old. There was no other accounting for it.

His assistant coughed into his hand. "Would you rather Lord Fitzwalter see to the appointment?"

"No. No," he said hurriedly. Lord Fitzwalter had been appointed by Nathaniel as the Delegator. There were few men he trusted more. Regardless of how many hours worked or appointments seen to, Nathaniel's duty and responsibility to the Brethren always came first. Why did that leave him oddly restless? "Show him in," he instructed. Mayhap it was the parade of younger men, all who served as reminders of the passage of time, and the expectations he'd once had for his own life… after he'd retired from the Brethren.

The nearly silent fall of Bennett's footsteps, and the click of the door, indicated the other man had gone.

Macleod was the most recent addition to the Brethren. A young man born the third son of a Scottish earl, he had spent the better part of a year undergoing training in the Bristol countryside.

Today, he'd receive his fourth task and would enter the world as a member of the Brethren, carrying out assignments for Crown and country. When Nathaniel had taken over the role of head of the Brethren, that had been the first change he'd implemented: in addition to the regular meeting with all agents of the Brethren, he demanded private appointments with his youngest recruits. It was then that Nathaniel was able to ascertain their readiness for a mission.

So that no one ever made the same mistakes he had.

After successfully completing a handful of assignments as a young man of under twenty, Nathaniel had developed a brash confidence that had seen him captured and nearly dead for his missteps. Sitting down with two Irish radicals he'd been charged with investigating, he'd drunk deeply of drugged ale they'd procured. *And it cost you far more than your life…*

Lady Victoria Tremaine's heart-shaped visage slid forward.

"Are you always this arrogant, Mr. Archer…?"

That teasing husky-contralto rang in his head as clear now as when that spirited young woman of years ago had breathed them against his lips.

His fingers tightened reflexively upon the page. He slid his gaze over to the misshapen circle upon the top of his hand. Unmoving, Nathaniel stared at the hated mark there.

"If you move, it'll only go worse for you…"

"No. Please… noooooo…" Screams of long ago blended the past with the present.

Fear licked at the edges of his senses, driving back the joyous memories he'd had with Victoria, and leaving darkness in its place. Nathaniel gave his head a firm shake and wrenched his focus away from the marks made by his captors. If he had been less cocksure, he'd never have been captured. He'd have returned and she'd have been there waiting.

His throat worked.

Abandoning Lockhart's file, he sat back and stretched his arms out to his sides. His body protested that sudden movement and he smoothed his features to conceal the agony rolling through him in waves. A well-placed dagger by the ruthless radicals, Fox and Hunter, saw Nathaniel suffering all these years later. Still, his work for the Brethren had long ago drummed into him and all the members the need to conceal any hint of pain or suffering. Weakness could be used against a man. Hadn't he learned that firsthand during his captivity? His palms grew moist. The problem was, the moment he allowed Fox and Hunter to get hold of his thoughts, they held on with a tenacious control.

Do not think of them… do not think of them… you are master of your memories…

Except this time, they'd slipped too far in and could not be so easily silenced. A cold sweat popped up on his brow as his torturers, the two long-dead Irish radicals, fought for control of his thoughts.

"You have anyone you are missing, Archer? Ah, I see you, do." Fox guffawed with laughter. *"A sweetheart, I'm thinking. A pretty English lady. We can find her, Hunter. I wager she'll prove useful to us…"*

"No," Nathaniel rasped, fighting against his bindings. The cords cut into his already bruised and bleeding flesh. *"I'll kill you both. I'll—ahhh… my God, no. Please, nooo."*

His tortured screams of long ago peeling around his mind, Nathaniel curled his nails into the leather arms of his chair, willing those demons gone.

He briefly closed his eyes and concentrated on drawing in steadying breaths—until his past faded, and he was left with the same hollow emptiness that had greeted him upon his return. To the time when he'd learned the only woman he'd loved had married in his absence.

Damn you, Victoria. Damn you for not waiting…

And damn him for not having made peace with her decision.

"Enough," he muttered. Even as he despised the still-present ruefulness and pain of years ago, both served as an eternal reminder of not only what he'd lost, but the need for… "Clarity and focus," he breathed, needing that oath spoken aloud.

Or is that simply a creed you now ingrain into young men and women, the way it was pressed upon you?

Footsteps sounded in the hall and he slackened the death-grip he had on his seat.

Bennett opened the door, admitting Macleod. "Do you require anything else, my lord?"

Lifting a hand in declination, he thanked his assistant. "That will be all."

Even after Bennett backed out of the room, the young agent remained stoically silent at the entrance, his envelope in hand.

"Macleod." Nathaniel came to his feet, grateful for the focus that his work had always demanded. His missions had gotten him through the hell of those two years… and then the pain that had greeted him upon his return to London. "Please join me," he urged, motioning the younger man over.

Tall, not even a hint of a scar marring the sharp planes of his face, with the excitement brimming in his eyes, Fergus Macleod may as well have been a replica of Nathaniel when he'd first been made a member of the Brethren. "My lord," the dark-clad agent dropped a respectful bow and took one of the indicated seats.

Reclaiming his chair, Nathaniel steepled his fingers before him. "I understand your first year has been largely a success." It was a statement, not intended as a question, meant to gauge the other man's confidence.

Macleod gave no outward reaction to that handful of words.

When he'd been of a like age, Nathaniel had thrived on the praise and commendations bestowed upon him. Having been the spare to his brother's heir, he'd always placed pressure upon himself to establish his place in a world ordered by rank and title. Macleod, however, revealed none of that same hunger.

Good.

That lack of approval from others would serve him well. A member of the Brethren didn't work for a man—not even the King—but rather, for the good of England.

"You have received your fourth assignment," he segued to the reason for the younger man's presence.

"I have." Those two, flawlessly delivered syllables spoke of Macleod's affluent origins and family's influence.

Arching an eyebrow, Nathaniel extended a palm. Leaning forward, Macleod handed him that envelope written in Fitzwalter's hand. He paused, his gaze caught upon the sapphire seal: the fierce lions rearing protectively about the Crown remained the same symbol that had been used by the first men who'd formed the Brethren long, long ago. All that had changed was the ink's color, as selected by the man who served as Sovereign. "Well?" he asked, reaching for his glasses.

"A murder investigation, my lord."

"A murder investigation?" he echoed.

Macleod nodded. "The incident in question took place inside the Coaxing Tom."

"Ahh." Through the years the Brethren had their eye on the Coaxing Tom, a den where suspicious activity was frequently carried out.

Their organization was one that had seen members of the Brethren embroiled in precarious missions all over Europe. They'd secured intelligence to help end battles and wars with some of the most ruthless leaders all over the globe. Over the years, the Brethren had also begun to take on investigations into the murders and suicides of kings, princes, or distinguished lords—but only as they connected to plots against the Crown.

Shifting the envelope, Nathaniel shoved his spectacles back on and skimmed the file.

"It involves the murder of a viscount," Macleod explained, his cool tones as casual as one discussing London's weather, and not the ruthless death of a nobleman. "He was discovered with his neck slashed and his belly slit up to his heart."

In his five and forty years, however, Nathaniel had known too many drunken nobles who'd risk life and limb for the forbidden pleasures of those streets. "Is there reason to believe the victim had links to treasonous activity?"

"It is my understanding from Lord Fitzwalter," the younger man explained, "that the gentleman was in quite deep to a number of men; members of the peerage and… dregs from the Dials."

A murder case only, then. It hardly mattered what type of man the nobleman had been while living. The Brethren served Crown and country. As such, it was their responsibility to uncover anyone who would orchestrate or conduct the killing of—

He turned the page abruptly and stopped.

Macleod's voice droned on and on, as Nathaniel stared at the ivory vellum.

Chester Barrett, Viscount Waters.

That single name, inked in black and underlined as was done with all victims and suspects, stood out stark at the top of the sheet. Numb, he moved his gaze over the detailed biography of the murdered lord, bypassing the gruesome details, searching, searching… and finding—

Widow
*Lady Victoria Barrett, the Viscountess Waters, age three and forty. Mother
to three: the Duchess of Huntly, the Marchioness of Rutland, and Andrew
Barrett, Viscount Waters. Respected member of the peerage…*

All these years, he'd faced death so many times. But he struggled
on and survived a heartbreak far greater than the blades and bullets
he'd taken. He'd believed himself immune to the pain of seeing
her name.

Nay… her name, linked with another man's.

Another man's when it should have been me.

But then, he'd given up that right with every mission that had
taken him away from her. He'd known that every time he'd slipped
out of her room and life that was the risk he'd faced. That logical
understanding had never made the agony of it any less.

"There are suspicions the murderer was, in fact, the man's son,
Andrew Barrett, now Viscount Waters…" Macleod was saying.
That perfunctory statement brought Nathaniel whirring back to
the moment.

"What?" he asked on a quiet whisper. Victoria's son was the
leading suspect? His gut clenched. *Bloody, bloody hell.*

"A case of patricide, Your Grace," Macleod needlessly clarified,
misinterpreting the reason for Nathaniel's horror.

"The murder took place…" He scanned the document. "Two
months ago." And only now had an investigation been undertaken?

The other man cleared his throat. "Safest way to flesh out a
criminal. It is—"

"—through a sense of false calm," he cut in, impatiently. Having
born, bled, and lived the Brethren for six and twenty years, he
well-knew the oldest of the credos that served as the foundation of
the organization. "I believe I'm acquainted enough with the rules
of organization," he added, infusing a false drollness into his retort,
when inside his world was ratcheting down about him.

I'll have to see her again.

Victoria, the only woman he'd ever loved. He'd given his heart
to her and, in his absence, she'd found another. And now that
gentleman lay dead with Nathaniel's agents responsible for the
investigation into the murder.

Macleod's cheeks fired red. "Forgive me."

Waving off the apology, Nathan urged the investigator on. "The

Barrett case." He dragged forth a lifetime of experience in subterfuge to deliver those three words so calmly.

"Yes, of course. Fighting was heard between the two on the gaming floors. The witnesses who were interviewed claim it was over a whore, but recent research into the murder revealed the younger Barrett's outrage over the family's finances." His earlier ease and confidence restored, Macleod flipped through the notebook in his hand. As he searched his papers and provided details about his case, Nathaniel sought to focus his thoughts.

This is just another case. He'd encountered enough gruesome murders and violent attacks and underhanded schemes, where this was just another. Or it should be. His heart thudded a peculiar beat and he stared on at the man, casually turning the pages of that book.

By God, I am the Sovereign; leader of the Brethren, required to be nothing but calm and level-headed.

But then, he never had been logical where Victoria Cadence Tremaine had been concerned. Her hold, all these years later, was as strong as in their youth.

"Waters' throat was slashed and he was gutted." Another man would have been chilled by the horrific recounting. He'd witnessed far more horrific sights than the one being described before him now. Instead, Macleod's telling snapped Nathaniel back to his familiar role of superior.

"A robbery?" he asked, hopefully. When one visited the dregs of London, those were, after all, the risks one took.

"Not a single scrap or purse was even lifted from the room," Macleod explained.

Bloody, bloody hell. He'd not ascended to the rank of Sovereign by accepting the most obvious clues. "Most noblemen's sons hate their fathers and find themselves in debt." Hadn't his late, noble sire left his family in the very same straits? "Why should the Waters heir be any different?"

Macleod pointed to his forehead. "The markings carved on his face and body, Your Grace."

Frowning, Nathaniel dropped his gaze and flipped through the file.

"Left him so there couldn't even be a formal viewing of the body."

Nathaniel skimmed the report. This remote, emotionless discourse about case details may have been any other official exchange. Only, this was not any other nobleman or noblewoman's child. This was Victoria's son. A son who belonged to another man... who now lay dead.

"The assailant carved 'adulterer', 'whoremonger', 'drunk', and 'reprobate' on different parts of him."

Spectacles slipping, Nathaniel pushed them back into place and found those details. Yes, no whore or simple street thug would waste their time and risk discovery by desecrating a fancy lord's dead body. Nor would they leave a purse—he paused—regardless of how few coins were in it. As Macleod's voice droned on, Nathaniel lingered his gaze upon the accounting of Waters' body.

Whoremonger... drunk... adulterer... reprobate...

They were just words. Yet, they were words that described the man Victoria had wed. His stomach muscles contracted painfully. For all the time resenting that she'd married another, he'd only ever wanted her happy. *You deserved so much more than this fool who'd met his end in the arms of a whore.* Not that Nathaniel had ever been worthy of her, either. But she'd certainly belonged with a man who loved, honored, and cherished her.

"The boy's a pup," Macleod went on. "I expect with little effort I'll have a confession from him."

"A pup who, if your suspicions are accurate, and the evidence gathered thus indicates, is capable of murder," he pointed out. A flush mottled the other man's cheeks. Such a statement on Macleod's part spoke to his ability to falter. *As I myself did.* Back when the Fox and Hunter, Irish radicals, had captured him and attempted to torture the secrets from him. Gone too many months, life had carried on without him a part of it, and the one person he'd loved, forever lost to him.

"You are correct, my lord. I'll not underestimate Waters' capabilities."

The boy already had. Setting aside the file, he held Macleod's gaze. "Where is the late viscount's wife living?"

Befuddlement flashed in Macleod's eyes. "The viscountess?" He scratched his brow. "Hadn't considered her as a suspect. I will add her to my queries."

Rage burned through him and he modulated his tone. "Do not

presume a question that wasn't asked from my lips," he said on a steely whisper.

The color bled from Macleod's cheeks. "Aye. Of course." He yanked at his cravat, rumpling the silk. "My apologies, my lord. Viscountess Waters is currently residing in her Grosvenor Square townhouse with her son."

Something foreign, something unpleasant, something he'd not felt since the day he'd escaped the Fox and Hunter's clutches, stirred deep inside—fear. Victoria now lived with a man suspected of murder. Her son, and yet also a gentleman, who, by the early reports, was responsible for killing his own father.

"With your ability to sneak about, Nathaniel, I expect when we have babes of our own, they'll have little hope of securing any successful hiding places…"

He absently rubbed that place a bullet had pierced his chest. She'd been within her rights to marry Waters. The moment Nathaniel had been captured, days turned over to weeks, and weeks into months, and months into years, and he'd still held out hope that she would be there—waiting. That hope had sustained him when the blissful ease of death had beckoned. Through every lash and blow he'd suffered at his captor's brutal hands, and the agony of being starved and deprived of drink, she had been the dream he'd clung to. His mouth twisted into a macabre rendition of a smile.

Only to return and find her gone to him—wed to another, mother to one.

Since his return, he'd lost himself in his work and forced all memories of Victoria Tremaine into the distant, far corners of his brain; a place never to be accessed.

Macleod cleared his throat. "Are you all—?"

Nathaniel subdued that query with a hard, narrow-eyed stare. A mottled flush marred the other man's cheeks and he swiftly lowered his gaze. One didn't question the Sovereign on the state of his wellness. Not without casting aspersions upon his character and worth. Then, neither would the Sovereign sit here lamenting what had once been and all he'd lost. "You're dismissed, Macleod."

Revealing the second crack in his control, Macleod jumped up with alacrity. "My lord," he murmured, dropping a deferential bow. He waited, his gaze trained on the pages still clasped within Nathaniel's hand.

Nathaniel followed his stare, and made to hand the assignment back over. To turn over Victoria and her family... "You are dismissed from this case," he clarified.

The younger agent turned ashen.

Of course, to be removed from a mission could only ever be interpreted as a failing on one's part. "I will see you placed on another case, instead. You'll receive the details tomorrow morn." He made a silent point to speak first thing to Fitzwalter regarding a new post. "This matter, however," he lifted the envelope, "belongs to another," he said, offering Macleod more explanation than he'd have given most others.

Guilt knocked around inside. *You, who've prided yourself on conducting each mission with the utmost integrity, should think nothing of your history with the suspect's mother...*

Questions reflected in the other man's eyes. However, he quickly shuttered them. "Thank you, my lord."

"You are excused," he said briskly, eager to be rid of the agent.

Offering another bow, his most recent spy took his leave.

As soon as he'd closed the door behind him, Nathaniel returned his focus to Viscount Waters' murder. "Bennett," he called.

His assistant instantly appeared in the doorway. "My lord?" The young man had an uncanny ability to anticipate when his presence was required.

Nathaniel held up the folder he'd lifted from Macleod. "The Waters murder. Why is this the first I'm learning of it?" He'd trust his life and England in the other man's hands. However, not even he knew of Victoria Tremaine. No one had.

Bennett furrowed his brow. "I trust that is a question reserved for Lord Fitzwalter."

Of course it was. He cursed his muddled mind.

"I want Macleod reassigned," he finally said.

Removing a small notepad and pencil from his jacket, Bennett scratched several notes onto that page. "I'll provide him with another assignment." He continued writing. "Do you have someone in mind for the Waters case?"

Nathaniel nodded tightly. "I do."

Bennett paused and glanced up, expectantly.

"Me," he said grimly.

CHAPTER 2

Conduct careful surveillance of one's suspect…
and those closest to him or her.
Article II: The Brethren of the Lords

London, England
Later that Night

AT LAST IT WAS QUIET.

After too many weeks of interviews with constables and the burial services for her late husband, Lady Victoria Barrett, Viscountess Waters, embraced the blessed silence this night brought to her Mayfair residence.

A candle in hand, she drifted through the hallways. The faint crimson glow sent shadows flickering and dancing upon the faded wallpaper. The gold frames that had once hung now gone after her faithless, drunken husband had sold off anything and everything of value to fund his vices. Her mouth tightened as she continued past the handful of portraits that still remained: her portly, fleshy-faced husband as he'd been memorialized at various points in his life.

She stopped beside one, the sole portrait done of their entire family. Victoria lifted her candleholder closer to the painting and, with her opposite hand, trailed her fingertips over the three children, and the protective mother at their side. If one took a pair of shearing scissors and snipped out that padded lord captured at their side, one would see nothing more than a tableau of a bucolic family. The artist had expertly captured the happiness of two little girls with fingers entwined and the blond-haired boy, with a mischievous half-grin on his face.

She moved her gaze over to herself as a smiling, young lady. Her shoulder angled, and her body bent toward her children— Phoebe, Justina, and Andrew—revealed the cold distance that had existed between Victoria and her late husband. But then, theirs had never been a happy union. It had been nothing more than a formal arrangement made between the late viscount and her now dead father, desperate to hide the scandal his daughter would have brought crashing down upon their family.

A tug pulled at her heart as she touched her mouth in that portrait. Had anyone who'd gazed upon her visage ever noted the sadness there? Or had they seen the image she'd so desperately hoped to craft for her children's sake? She moved her fingers over to the artful chignon memorialized on canvas. Those auburn strands were the same, and though there were a handful of creases at the corners of her eyes, her cream white skin remained, for now, unmarred by the passage of time.

"And yet how much has changed," she whispered into the silence, letting her arm fall back to her side. Needing those words spoken aloud. Needing to breathe them into existence, in an acknowledgement of all she'd sacrificed… and lost.

A tall, powerful form of long ago flickered forward. And she swiftly battled back thoughts of… him. Not allowing herself to think of the man who'd stolen her heart and, with his absence and ultimate death, had promptly shattered it.

Her skin pricked with the feel of eyes upon her and, cheeks warming, she stole a glance up at her deceased husband's likeness. Peering down his bulbous nose with the same disapproval he'd worn in the living, it was as though even in death he chided her for her disloyalty to him and now his memory.

After all, Polite Society expected a widow, regardless of age, should don a bereaved look. At the very least, one should move about with slouched shoulders. In death, it didn't matter how miserable a marriage had been or how many times a nobleman had been unfaithful to his wife. And there could be no doubting that Victoria's marriage had been a cold, empty, ruthless one forged by a desperate young woman with a babe in her belly and a wastrel viscount, equally in want. Only the material need of a fortune had compelled him.

Yes, even as most societal marriages were made to secure fortunes and improve rank and status, expectations continued even in death. A widow must, of course, appear distraught. It only mattered the façade put on by a woman. All the while, many of those ladies freed from the chains of matrimony carried on for the first time, for their own pleasures. Victoria had neither the interest nor inclination to become one of those wicked widows.

For Victoria, who'd adhered to societal expectations for her entire adult life, the task of fulfilling them should be an easy one. Only with her callous husband's passing she couldn't even muster a single modicum of feigned grief. Nor, having suffered through more than two decades of marriage to a heartless, ruthless, whoremonger, should she be *expected* to.

Nonetheless, there was her family to consider… and worse, the scandal.

Victoria curled her fingers so tight that her nails left half-moons upon the soft flesh of her palms.

Her husband had been found murdered inside a scandalous gaming hell, his body beside a drunken, unconscious prostitute. And there were whispers of her son's hand in that act swirling about. Everyone stared even more… and searched for indications of glee from her.

The townhouse quiet, Victoria drifted through the hallways, grateful for the silence. In the dead of night, the world slept. And passersby didn't come to gawk at the front of her home and servants didn't whisper and steal furtive glances. Ones that suggested they searched for hints of the crimes that Society talked freely about.

Having sacrificed herself in marriage to the fat, witless man that had been her husband, she should be permitted those freedoms afforded most any other widows: scandalous affairs—of which she'd not a jot of an interest in—a freedom of movement, Victoria could not, nor would ever be one of those immodest sorts. She'd tasted the thrill of passion and love… and lost it all in an instant.

Dancing on the edge of propriety was not a path she'd care to travel again. No, as a woman of three and forty, others mattered far more than her own wants.

There had first been her children. She would have bartered her soul for them. And for her eldest daughter, Phoebe had, in fact, done so. And now there were her grandchildren. Reputations mattered and rumors followed lords and ladies through time. The latest scandal surrounding her husband's gruesome death, however, was not one that would be easily forgotten. Most particularly, not when questions and rumors swirled about a fight between the insensate Viscount Waters and his son, Andrew.

As such, she would sooner lob off her right hand than bring any hint of shame or suffering to those young babes. Between their father and her son-in-law, the Marquess of Rutland, being one of London's most notorious lords, talk enough was already linked to their family. Of course, society could not see that love had changed that man in ways that greed had destroyed her own husband. It was enough for Victoria to know that she needed to look after hers.

That specific thought in mind, Victoria stole a peek around the darkened parlor. A chill hung in the room, dulled somewhat by the fire that crackled in the hearth. Those dancing, orange flames sent shadows flickering over the walls in a macabre rendering.

She edged over to the floor-length, gold mirror. Her taffeta skirts swished noisily and with her breath held, she paused. A log shifted in the fireplace and unleashed a noisy spray of sparks and embers. Reassured by the silence of her solitary presence, she set her candle in the Italian gilded torcher, and inched ever closer to the mirror draped with bombazine fabric.

She stopped.

Peeling back the silk, she revealed her visage.

Victoria grimaced. Her not at all sad grimace.

Muster a blasted tear. A trembling lip. *Something. You were married to the man. He gave you two of his children...* and by all the world's expectations—had given her three of them. It was a secret that had driven her into that miserable marriage to save her reputation, and had given her eldest daughter a name and respectability. Her heart pulled, as an old ache wrenched with a pain she'd believed long buried, if not at least forgotten.

"I fear one day you'll leave and never return, Nathaniel Archer..."

Nathaniel paused in his dressing. Abandoning his shirt on her bedchamber floor, he stalked over silently with the stealthy steps only a spy could master. He crawled back into the enormous, four-poster bed and gathered her close. "Do you have so little faith in my abilities, love?" A breathy laugh spilled past her lips as he lifted her hair and kissed her nape.

She swatted at his hands. "Nay, rather, you have too much faith in your abilities against other people's evil…"

Nathaniel Archer's face flickered forward and she briefly closed her eyes. She'd not thought of him in more years than she could remember. Nay, she had not allowed herself to think of him. Whenever memories of him slipped in, she pushed them back. For thinking of her youthful self and the dashing, daring stranger she'd met in the alcove of Lord Hazlewhite's townhouse, had the power to gut her still.

Tears filled her eyes and blurred her vision. There they were. The requisite tears. Just for another man and for a dream that wasn't to have been.

"Mother…"

A gasp exploded from Victoria's lips. The fabric slipped from her fingertips as she wheeled about.

Her eldest daughter, Phoebe, stood in the doorway. Her most recently born babe cradled in her arms, it was a beautiful tableau of maternal devotion. It was something Victoria could so very readily identify with.

"Phoebe," she said, dusting her cheeks of those useless drops. "You should be abed." She shouldn't even be here for that matter. Married with a family of her own, she should be in her own townhouse. However, despite Victoria's protestations, since the viscount's death, Phoebe and her family had set up a temporary residence here in a show of solidarity to combat the ugliest of rumors.

"I could not sleep," Phoebe confessed, drifting over. With every step that brought her closer, Garrick's cooing grew louder; the little boy wide awake and alert when most of the world slept on. "Nor could you." It was an observation more than anything.

Victoria stretched her arms out and Phoebe instantly relinquished the precious bundle. Holding him close, Victoria rocked him back and forth in a gentle movement.

"Young Molly who lived at the foot of the hill,

Whose fame every virgin with envy doth fill,
Of beauty is blessed with and so ample a share
They call her the lass with the delicate air.
With the delicate air,
Men call her the lass with the delicate air…"

Garrick's eyes weighed closed and then he slumbered.

"That song always calmed me," Phoebe said softly, bringing her head up. As it once filled Victoria with an easy contentment… "It always soothed all of us."

Nathaniel Archer's discordant baritone whispered around her mind, blending with the remembered sounds of her muffled laughter. *Hush… someone will hear us…* "Yes," she murmured. Even with the threat of scandal brought with his every visit, there had never been a real fear of discovery. She'd simply thrilled at having him close… of being in his arms… of hearing him sing only to her.

"You always sang that one," Phoebe continued. A wistful expression stole over her. "You were there for every hurt knee and sibling quarrel. And yet, for all the memories I have of you, I don't have a single one of the man who sired me."

Victoria stiffened. *The man who'd sired her.* That one great lie born of necessity that had shaped her entire future, after Nathaniel's disappearance. "That wasn't the manner of father he was," she said quietly, carefully omitting the name of the miserable man she'd bound herself to. Rather, Viscount Waters had been cold, cruel, and self-serving. Be it Phoebe, the daughter sired by another man, or those born of his own loins, none had mattered to him. Feeling her daughter's stare upon her, Victoria glanced over.

"Surely he wasn't always that way." There was a faint pleading there that begged to hear a warmth from Victoria—that she was incapable of.

It was not the first time her daughter had put that very question to her. Did she hope for a lie from Victoria's lips? Once, she would have given Phoebe and all her children those assurances. Along the way, she'd not kept the truth of what the now late viscount was from them. Phoebe, Justina, and Andrew had always been keen-minded. They'd seen their father for the reprobate he was. And Victoria had tired of living the lie that he was anything but evil.

Sighing, she claimed a spot on the cream, upholstered sofa. With her chin, she urged her daughter to sit.

Phoebe instantly sank into the tattered folds.

"He was," she said solemnly. "Always that way." She'd not make lies for him in death.

Her daughter drew her legs up and rested her chin atop her knees. "Did you ever love him?" she asked quietly.

No. He'd been the means to a proverbial end. A figure who'd not cared that she had a babe in her belly. As such, she should feel some modicum of gratitude to the man who'd met such a gruesome end. It was surely a mark of her own dark soul that she couldn't muster a hint of sadness for his *loss*. "I love my children," she offered, instead. "And for that, I have no regrets." Had there never been marriage to the Viscount Waters, there would have never been Justina or Andrew. For her three children, Victoria would have made any and every sacrifice—including her own happiness.

"You deserved so much more," Phoebe murmured.

And I wanted so much more. Emotion wadded in Victoria's throat and she ducked her head into the crown of Garrick's small tuft of dark curls. His slight weight and scent, calming; a balm in the two months since her husband had been discovered. "Why are you awake, Phoebe?" she asked quietly, steering the conversation away from tales of broken hearts to safer matters that had guided her existence—her children.

"He did not do it," Phoebe said firmly.

Victoria froze. "No," she said quietly, not pretending to misunderstand. Her son's perceived guilt is all anyone in Polite Society was speaking of.

Phoebe glanced about, lingering her stare briefly on the doorway. When she spoke, her voice came on a hushed whisper. "I saw your face after the constables questioned him. There was a flash of doubt."

She gave thanks for the darkness that concealed her flush. Her daughter had mistaken her initial response. It hadn't been so much doubt, as guilt. After all, the questions put to Andrew had pertained to whether or not he'd ever put his hands upon his father in violence… and he had, and recently, too—because of her.

"Look at me, Phoebe," she said with the same firm resolve she'd used when answering away her then eight-year-old daughter's questions about why her father didn't love her. From over Garrick's slumbering frame, they held gazes. "Your father," how very wrong it was that Chester Barrett should have received the honor of being known as Phoebe, Justina, and Andrew's father, "was cold, heartless, and unkind." *You whore. You're lucky you have a husband…* Chester's vile taunting reverberated around her mind. Garrick squirmed and she forced herself to lighten her hold. "To all," she forced herself to finish. "I know how Andrew felt about him… it is the way so many did. And yet, I know in my heart that my son is not guilty of…" Her mind reeled away from the horrific actions carried out. "Of what he's been accused." Dropping a soft kiss atop her grandson's head, she turned the precious bundle over to her daughter. "You need to return home, Phoebe. You, Edmund, and your three children. You living here," *in this hated townhouse,* "will not result in answers to questions the constables have or even bring peace. Only time will do that."

Grief raged in Phoebe's blue eyes and then tears filled them. "I should feel something." Victoria went still, and then tenderly brushed back the silent, crystal drops streaking down her daughter's cheeks. "He is the man who gave me life and he met a horrible, painful end, and yet…" Her voice dissolved to a barely-there whisper. "I can feel nothing for him."

I cannot, either. And he was the man who'd given Victoria two of her children. As such, what did that say about *her* character? She'd not have Phoebe bear this guilt. "Oh, Phoebe," she cupped her daughter's cheek. "There is nothing wrong in that. He was incapable of loving anyone or anything." Except his vices. "Blood does not a family make," she said with a quiet insistence. "It is the depth of love in one's heart and one's willingness to place another's happiness before even one's own." She stiffened, as a powerful presence filled the room. Victoria glanced over.

Phoebe followed her stare to where her husband, Edmund Deering, the Marquess of Rutland, stood framed in the doorway. Stocky, dark, and slightly menacing, most of London feared him. Victoria, however, had witnessed in so many of his exchanges with Phoebe a tenderness and regard that belied the rumors. Coming to her feet, she smiled at her son-in-law.

"Forgive me," he said in his graveled tones. As he came forward, his attention was on his wife. "I awoke and found you missing."

And he'd cared enough that he, in his bare feet and garments swiftly pulled into place, had searched his wife out instantly. Edmund held his arms out and accepted his son, holding the babe close.

The dark mark upon her own soul presented itself once more. For in this, Victoria knew envy. *I wanted that. I wanted a husband who'd have eyes for only me, and who loved me with that ferocity.*

...I will battle the Devil himself to have you at my side, Victoria Cadence...

And she'd almost had it. "Go," she urged. "I intend to retire shortly." It was a lie. One that her clever daughter's too-knowing eyes saw.

Phoebe hesitated. With a frown, she looked to the floor-length windows. "Be sure to close the window before you find your rooms," she gently chided in a reversal of roles. "Until they find..." *The viscount's murderer.* Her daughter stopped speaking abruptly. However, her worrying lingered in the air as loud as if she'd spoken them.

Furrowing her brow, Victoria followed her daughter's stare. Her heart did a little flip. It was hardly a detail to cause questions or worrying. Probably nothing more than an errant servant who'd been remiss...

Shivers danced along her spine.

And yet, a window cracked two inches had served as a message: a greeting and parting and—

"Mother?" Phoebe prodded, taking a step closer.

"I'll be sure to shut it," she promised, her voice hoarse to her own ears. Shoving aside the nonsensical thoughts, she forced herself to move. Victoria joined her daughter and son-in-law in the doorway and, leaning up, kissed her slightly taller daughter on the cheek. "You needn't worry after me," she assured, brushing Phoebe's hair back. "You should know, we are far stronger than Society credits." The reminder was spoken as much as for herself as for her daughter.

Phoebe gave her a watery smile and returned the kiss. That smile, so very much her father's. "I love you," she said simply.

"I love you, too." Despite the misery they'd all known inside the viscount's life, there had never been a shortage of those words. Victoria had made a vow long ago that her children would always know love. It was a pledge she held to all these years later. She favored Phoebe's husband with a thankful smile. "Thank you, Edmund." Through every interview, visit, and side-eyed stare as she'd embarked from the carriage to her home, Phoebe's husband had set himself up as a sentry of sorts. "For everything." He'd looked after the Barrett family when, until him, no one else but she had.

"There is nothing to thank me for," he said gruffly. The heightened color in his cheeks hinted at his unease, still, with honest sentiments and emotions exchanged.

Garrick stirred and emitted a short wail.

"Go," Victoria urged. "Your son needs to eat and sleep."

Phoebe hesitated a moment. Then with a last parting glance, she started from the room, her husband at her side.

Victoria stared after the departing couple. With their heads bent close and bodies moving in a synchronic harmony, they demonstrated a closeness most women would never know in the whole of their lives.

It was also one that Victoria, for a fleeting time, had known. A melancholy smile pulled at her lips. Her bond, however, had only ever existed as a private secret, that no one had ever known of. And even so, one that would forever remain a private memory. Rubbing her arms, Victoria returned to the room, shrouded in black bombazine. She stopped abruptly and layered her back against the wall.

The black fabric draping over the mirrors and curtains brought her crashing back into the ugly reality that awaited her: one of murder and ugliness and by Society's opinion—intrigue. Victoria closed her eyes. But this was no clever gothic tale. This was her suddenly upended life. And though her existence had largely been a dark one with her husband, there had also been light because of her children. Society didn't care whether Andrew was truly guilty of patricide. For the lords and ladies of London, nothing mattered more than their own morbid fascination with the Barrett family. They didn't care that they were people who knew pain but also love and heartache.

A faint breeze wafted over the parlor. That midnight cold raised gooseflesh along her arms and brought her eyes reluctantly open—and directly in line with that cracked window.

You'll always know the moment I'm here and the moment I leave,

Victoria…

She stared blankly ahead. In the immediacy of Nathaniel's departure, her gaze had been inexplicably drawn to every window of every room she entered. The last time he'd slipped out of her chambers and life, every crystal panel had gotten her through the despair of his absence. And when she'd discovered she was expecting and terror had swamped her senses for what that ignoble fate meant for an unwed lady, every window had been an anchor.

Until she'd forced herself to confront the truth—he was not returning.

It was a thought that had brought her to her knees with the ragged grief of loss in the years following his departure.

With time, all that remained was a dull, empty ache. Far more than she felt for the husband she was even now supposed to be mourning.

Drawing in a shaky breath, Victoria pushed away from the wall and started across the room. Another wind gusted through, whipping the fabric against her purple wrapper and nightshift. Shivering, she gripped the windowsill and stared out, scanning the empty streets.

A lone carriage rumbled across the cobblestones, leaving nothing but silence in its wake.

From beyond her shoulder, a floorboard creaked. Heart thundering, she whipped around. "Wh-who is there?" she called out, desperate to hear even her own voice in the eerie silence. "Phoebe?" She hated the breathless quality to her voice. "Andrew?"

She skimmed her gaze over the shadows dancing upon the walls. What if the Devil had seen her late husband's soul was worthless and had promptly cast him out? *Do not be silly…* She wet her lower lip. "Seeing ghosts at midnight," she whispered to herself. Given the gruesome fate her husband had met at his club, one would surely forgive her for an overactive imagination.

Through the faint crack in the window, the air whistled spookily. Her heart knocking against her ribcage, Victoria wheeled around and promptly closed the window. "Enough." Eager to quit the room, she turned quickly on her heel. A tall, broad-muscled figure stood an arm's length from her.

Terror lapping at her senses, she opened her mouth to scream the household down.

The stranger instantly quelled her cries with his callused palm.

Scrabbling with the fabric of his jacket, she clawed ineffectually at his muscular forearm. Almost a foot taller than her five-foot five-inches, he was larger and broader than most of the small trees she tended in her London gardens. The sheer size of him and his mastery over her sent her fear careening out of control.

Victoria bit down hard on the midnight intruder's hand, but she may as well have been a bothersome gnat that he gave no outward notice of. He adjusted his hold on her; guiding her back against his chest. Flaring her nostrils, attempting to drag breath in, she jammed the heel of her foot against his kneecap.

If anyone comes upon you, Victoria... panic will destroy you. Be calm. Master of your wits. When your assailant loosens his grip, strike. Like this...

Nathaniel's lesson of long ago reverberating in her mind, Victoria made her body go limp. Waiting. Waiting. The stranger, at last, loosened his hold. His hand remained fixed to her mouth. However, he adjusted it, below her nostrils, allowing her to draw proper, steadying breaths. She swiftly brought her elbow back, but he caught it, anticipating that movement. Victoria silently screamed at his anticipatory reflexes.

"Shh," the man demanded against her ear. His breath, a blend of orange and chocolate, penetrated the thick curtain of fear. That sweet smell tangled with a citrusy scent, so very familiar.

Victoria froze, unmoving, as a dull buzzing filled her ears. And her inability to move or think had nothing to do with long-ago lessons of self-defense administered by a spy for the King himself. It had everything to do with that gruff baritone... and scent.

He dropped his arm, freeing her.

Victoria's pulse slowed. She turned and the world stopped.

Nay, with the lesson she'd called forward, she'd merely brought forth his memory. She stared at a figure she'd spent many years first yearning, then mourning for. Numb, she scraped a panicky gaze over his harsh, angular features. White scars marred olive skin that had once been flawless. Faint creases lined the corners of his violet eyes, the only man she'd ever loved. But for those slight wrinkles, he may as well have been a figure carved in time from long ago.

The earth resumed spinning at a frantic pace.

Victoria pressed her eyes closed and drew quick, gasping puffs of air into her lungs. *He is not real. He is not real.* He's nothing more than a ghost, the madness of these past months coupled with fatigue and the horror of her husband's passing. For if he was here before her, then it would mean she'd spent years mourning a man who'd been very much alive… but who'd simply failed to return.

Afraid to move, afraid to so much as even breathe, she searched her gaze over his towering frame before ultimately settling on the gold signet ring upon his finger. The one that marked his place within that nameless organization she'd hated over the years. "Nathaniel?"

"Hello, Victoria," he said quietly, his deep baritone washing over her, very much real.

Oh, my God.

He is alive.

CHAPTER 3

Do not allow oneself to be distracted:
by emotions, feelings, or personal entanglements.
Article III: The Brethren of the Lords

IN NATHANIEL'S TIME SERVING THE Brethren, he'd been shot, imprisoned, tortured, and set free. None of those agonies or suffering, however, could have ever come close to the last time he'd come to Viscount Waters' townhouse.

Upon discovering Victoria had wed another, he'd stood outside this very residence, hoping for a glimpse of her, this woman he'd loved and lost. After that last, final look, he'd retreated... demanding assignments on the Continent, in Africa, the Americas... anywhere but where she was.

As such, he'd never allowed himself the dream of this moment: Victoria Cadence Tremaine before him, a hand's breadth apart, his name falling from her crimson, bow-shaped lips. Now, he drank in the sight of her. Her waist was still trim despite the fact that she'd given birth to three children. Her hips, however, and her breasts were more generous than when he'd last slipped out her window. Yet, even with the passage of time, her heart-shaped face, revealed not even a hint of a wrinkle.

Her impossibly wide eyes met his, stricken. Shock reflected in their expressive crystalline depths.

"Nathaniel," she repeated and stretched a hand out, brushing his chest with her fingertips. She swiftly dropped her arm back to her side. Then she frantically shook her head. "I don't... I don't understand," she whispered. Her gaze flitted away from his and drifted over his shoulder, to the door he'd closed. When Victoria returned it to his face, the panicky glimmer he'd seen in too many faces over the years, hinted at a woman about to take flight. "You aren't real," she said hollowly. "You aren't real," she repeated the refrain over and over.

"I am real," he said quietly. It was said with the same firmness he'd adopted during prisoner negotiations with the French and Spanish.

She took a lurching step back.

Immediately anticipating that movement, Nathaniel slid himself into her path, blocking her escape.

"You are *dead*," she whispered, horror wreathing those three words.

What did a man say to the only woman who'd ever held his heart after all these years? What, when they'd not even had the benefit of a proper parting and closure. "I didn't die," he said gruffly.

She recoiled and retreated, edging further away from him. The backs of her knees knocked into a mahogany table. Victoria shot her hands out to steady herself and then continued her retreat.

Knowing the shock of this meeting on her, he allowed her that necessary distance.

Victoria collided with the wall. "Stop," she rasped, anyway. She held her palms up warding him off. And he, who'd encountered all forms of abuse and torture and thought himself immune to pain, found her delicate hands had the power to wound—without so much as a single strike or touch.

Dealing with her panic the way he had so many skittish others before, he let his arms hang unthreateningly at his side. "I did not die," he repeated into the quiet, in a bid to penetrate the fog that gripped her. He very nearly did die, but the memory of her had sustained him through Fox's torture. Then, when he'd returned and found her married, he'd prayed for a merciful end to spare himself the agony of losing her.

Victoria clenched her eyes tightly, and shook her head back and forth. "No." A keening moan spilled from her and she clamped down at the fuller flesh of her lower lip. "You aren't real."

He moved, positioning himself before her. Nathaniel dropped his palms on either side of her head, framing her between them. *God, how I've missed the feel of her in my arms.* He lowered his brow to hers. "I am, Victoria."

The noisy inhalation and exhalation of her breath filled the quiet of the parlor. Or was that his own ragged breathing?

A tear squeezed past her lashes. He reached between them and caught the drop with the pad of his thumb. His finger shook. "Shh," he whispered useless platitudes and nonsensical words which he'd never been good with.

A strangled sob tore from her throat. With an agonized groan, he drew her into his arms, folding her close. The citrusy-lemon scent that clung to her was unfamiliar and heartbreaking for it. How much had come to pass? How much had changed… in every way between them? And even with that, he buried his face into her auburn curls.

From the time he'd returned to London from that ill-fated mission… to the moment he'd taken offices in England as the Sovereign, he'd never felt home—until now, with her in his arms. *Home.*

And yet, the reunion he'd imagined after escaping—shot, bleeding, and on the cusp of death—had been one of laughter and words of love. Fox and Hunter had robbed both of them of that.

Her slender frame shook with the force of her tears. He anchored her to him, melding with his own agony. He'd no place holding her. With her husband's murder and his investigation of her son, the only reason he'd come was to begin researching his case. *Liar.*

"I d-do not c-cry, Nathaniel Archer… *except when you say goodbye…*"

"*Then I'll simply omit goodbyes, love… and leave you with nothing more than a cracked window…*"

How he'd wished the last time he'd climbed from her window and made for that ill-fated mission that he'd roused her from her slumber, and taken those words from her lips.

He held her while she wept with the seconds dissolving into minutes and time marching on as it had for more than twenty years. Until the evidence of her misery faded into a shuddery hiccough. Nathaniel rubbed his hand in soothing circles over the small of her back. The heat of her skin penetrated the thin fabric of her nightshift and his fingers shook. When he'd last visited this townhouse and witnessed the death of every last dream that had sustained him during his hell, he'd also buried the hope of ever again knowing the feel of Victoria in his arms.

And where the resentment and anger had burned strong then, now there was an aching surrealism to this moment.

Wrestling some space between them, Victoria pressed her palms to his chest and shoved hard. He mourned that distance, for with it came the sting of bitterness—that she'd not waited.

The same spirited glimmer that had first captivated him in that alcove when she'd sneaked off and removed her slippers with him as a silent, wicked witness, glinted in her eyes. "What is this?" she asked in shaky disbelief, swiping frantically at the remnants of tears on her cheeks. "All these years, you were…" her voice fell to a faint whisper, "*alive?*"

At the horror coating those two syllables, he stiffened. *Did you expect she'd greet you with arms wide, a tremulous smile, and words of love?* Such was the fanciful illusion he'd carried in his youth. Time had jaded him, certainly enough to know that when she realized what had brought him back into her life it would quash any fond memories she might still carry. "I was… detained."

She jerked. "Detained?" Victoria shook her head and the braided plait at her neck whipped wildly about her shoulders. "My God. It has been four and twenty years," she rasped. Odd, she should know that detail when she'd married within a handful of months of his being gone. All the old questions he'd forced himself to stop asking, swirled around his mind, once more. "Nathaniel, what are you…? Where—?"

Registering steps in the hall, Nathaniel stalked across the room and lost himself in the shadows.

A moment later, the door opened, quelling all questions Victoria had deserved answers to long, long ago. Even with the dark and distance he'd put between them, he registered the confusion in her eyes. Was that truly all she should feel in this moment? Bewilderment?

And what weakness was it on his part that he wanted it to be more? Wanted to know that even though she'd wed another, she'd held out a secret hope that she and Nathaniel would again one day meet.

The door opened and the figure on the other side walked with unsteady steps across the threshold. Tall, lean, and blond, the gentleman couldn't be much older than twenty years. At having his quarry saunter in, a lifetime of preparedness in the fields brought Nathaniel snapping to alertness. "Mother?" The faint slurring of those two syllables spoke of one who'd imbibed too much.

All the pain and resentment that had come in seeing Victoria again lifted.

He honed his focus on the young man who staggered toward her.

"A-Andrew," she said chidingly, as she smoothed her palms over the front of her wrapper. "What are you doing awake?"

Nathaniel saw everything and missed nothing: from the half-empty bottle of brandy in the new viscount's right hand to Victoria's furtive eye movements as she sought Nathaniel's figure in the shadows.

The recently-minted viscount stopped before his mother, blocking Nathaniel's direct line of view from her. "Who were you talking tooo?" Waters asked, suspicion in his drunken tones.

Victoria brushed off his question. "I was merely talking to myself, as I do."

In all the months he'd known Victoria Cadence Tremaine, she'd never once talked to herself. That was just another slight change; a detail he'd missed with the passing of time. He battled back useless lamentations.

"Because heeee was a bastard and you were better off with only yourselffff for company," Waters said with a caustic laugh.

I should make my escape now while the drunken lad is distracted. Instead, Nathaniel's ears pricked with the palpable rage pulsing in the viscount's words. The damning opinion on the boy's father went to the case Nathaniel had commandeered from one of his field officers. And yet—a vise cinched about his lungs.

Over the years, he'd deliberately avoided stories or details about Victoria or the man she'd married. A man who'd bedded her and given her children because those thoughts had been like a dangerous cancer that had sent him seeking solace in the bottom of a bottle too many times. Now, he'd no choice but to be confronted with the life she'd made for herself—one that he'd never been a part of.

Why… why did you not wait for me?

"Andrew," Victoria scolded. "Give me this." She rescued the precariously dangling bottle from her son's fingers and set it down on a nearby table. "You should be sleeping." Collecting the viscount by the arm, she made to guide him to the doorway.

The young man yanked his arm free and the dagger that had saved Nathaniel's life too many times burned hot from within the confines of his boot. "Can't sleep."

With his gaze, Nathaniel followed his every step. This might be Victoria's son, but the young viscount was also suspected of murder. *And he's sharing a roof with her.* Fighting back a dangerous unease, he edged along the wall while a hushed discourse unfolded across the room. There would be time to piece together details of the late viscount's last night. This moment, however, was not it.

Waters stumbled. Victoria braced her legs and caught her son against her side with a grunt. "You need to stop drinking."

"Cannn't help it. I'mmm verra much his son." He sketched a haphazard bow and promptly pitched forward.

Victoria made a futile grab for him but he landed on his knees. She made another grab for him, but her son ignored that offering.

Making no move to rise, he flicked the bombazine fabric. "Ironic, isn't it? Hanging black for a miserable bastard like *him*." Another empty belly laugh shook his reed-thin frame.

Victoria glanced briefly to the spot Nathaniel had just vacated. With her attention diverted, he slipped from the room.

At any other moment, when presented with her too-often carousing son's drunkenness, all her attentions would be reserved for him.

But this was not just any other moment. Victoria's heart pounded as she sought the last place Nathaniel had stood… before slipping out as he had too many times from her life. Only—

He'd returned.

As though she'd conjured him with her earlier melancholy musings, the only man she'd ever loved had cracked a window and slipped inside: without an answer, an explanation, or anything more than a "hello".

A boulder was weighing on her heart, crushing that organ as

questions screamed around every chamber of her mind.

But she was no longer a girl of eight and ten. She was a mother... nay a *grandmother*... and a widow. As such, she wasn't afforded the same freedom of her unwieldy emotions.

Fighting for calm, she forcibly shoved aside thoughts of Nathaniel and sank down on the floor beside her son. "Andrew, you need to stop this," she said with the same firmness she'd employed when he'd terrorized another tutor out of his post.

He raised his head and stared at her through bloodshot eyes. "Offf course. The gossip."

She flattened her mouth into a hard line, grabbing him by his shirtsleeves. "You know I never gave a jot about gossip," she said tightly.

Having been whispered about because of a faithless, whoreson of a husband, and then her own children having found scandal after scandal, what Society said had always mattered far less than Phoebe, Justina, and Andrew's happiness. With a grunt, she urged Andrew back to his feet, staggering under his weight "What I do care about is your dependency upon a bottle," she said, her breath coming hard from her exertions. It was a vice he'd learned at his late father's knee and, if he weren't careful, would be the ruin of him.

"Just another gift from my dearrrr father," he slurred.

"Blood doesn't define you, Andrew, but rather your actions," she said after she'd gotten him to his feet. By the heavy scent of brandy on his breath, lessons and lectures were better reserved for a later time. Not that she'd ever managed much sway where her son was concerned. He'd too often taken to his father's flairs, vices, and penchant for trouble. Not that Victoria herself had been wholly prone to proper actions in her own youth. Yes, Andrew had received her wild streak, as well. An ache settled in her chest at how greatly she'd failed him.

Muttering incoherently to himself, Andrew made a sloppy grab for his bottle.

Victoria blocked his attempt. "Enough," she ordered, gripping him by the shoulders.

Despite the drunken haze that fogged his eyes, misery spilled from their sapphire depths: a shade darker than her own, belonging to the man who'd given him life. "You were crying," he observed on a jagged whisper.

And this faint glimmer of the boy who'd picked her weeds, handing them over as flowers when he'd seen a sad smile on her lips, revealed himself. Her heart pulled.

"Oh, Andrew," she gathered his palms.

"Over *him*." There was a deadness to that last, slightly emphasized word by which he'd only referred to the late viscount since his murder. It raised gooseflesh on her arms. If she hadn't given Andrew life and knew him the way she did the lines on her palms, she'd have been tempted to believe the whispers. But she'd seen the goodness of his heart; it was a battle he waged with evil and his own self-fulfilling low expectations he had for himself. "How could you cry for him?"

I wasn't. I was crying at the resurrection of the only man I'd ever given my heart to. It was a truth she could not share with him—or anyone. "He was the father of my children," she settled for, offering those words she had given Phoebe a short while ago.

Andrew tossed his head back, laughing uproariously. "And fine children you have to show for it." He sketched another haphazard bow. "A drunken son and two daughters—"

"Not another word," she bit out, commanding him to silence. She'd not have him disparage the only thing she'd done right in her life.

"Forgive me." Her middle-born child hung his head. "Justina and Phoebe never belonged in a category with one such as me."

Again, pain clogged her throat at the lowly image he'd painted of himself and sought to fill every day. Taking his hands, she gave them a firm squeeze. "Don't you do that," she said in gentling tones. "You each hold a portion of my soul." They'd sustained her and given her purpose through not only the misery of her marriage, but the shattered heart that Nathaniel Archer had left her to mend on her own.

Andrew gave no outward show to her words. Instead, he hungrily eyed the bottle behind her. Clenching his hands all the tighter, she forced his gaze back to her. "I understand... what you are feeling," she began.

"Do you?" he countered, in world-weary tones better suited to one two decades older than his one and twenty years.

She bit the inside of her cheek. For the reality was she couldn't empathize with these particular whispers her son faced. Heinous, vile accusations of a child taking his father's life. "No," she quietly conceded. "You are correct. I cannot know precisely how you are feeling but you are stronger than heartless gossip. The investigations have been completed." The constable, who'd spent more nights in their London residence than Victoria's late husband, had been a fixture here, but he'd asked his last question that morn. "We'll all be able to begin a path to healing."

Another broken chuckle left him. "Oh, Mother. Do you truly believe this—" Tugging his hands free, he gestured about the black-draped room. "—can possibly be over? When Society is asking questions and when there are still no answerrrs?"

Her stomach lurched. "The gossips will always talk but—"

"And you simply trust the constables will overlook the gruesome murder of a lord of the realm?"

Victoria troubled her lower lip. In this, Andrew was, indeed, correct. It didn't matter that Society had reviled the late viscount when he'd been living. Those lords, however, ultimately stuck side by side. In death, all Polite Society would care about was that one of their own had been so brutally murdered.

Dangerous warning bells went off at the back of her head. As that realization ushered in Nathaniel's coincidental return from the grave.

A memory flickered to life.

"It is a coincidence meeting you here, Mr. Archer."

"There are no coincidences," Nathaniel whispered against her lips.

Only stark, staggering facts and realities. Victoria dug her fingertips into her temples willing that dark apprehension away.

"You see IIII am riiight," Andrew said with an uncanny supposition. Despite his inebriated state, he so clearly read her fears.

Yes, she did. And yet, she had to let herself believe that there could be peace and new beginnings for her children… particularly Andrew. Victoria firmed her shoulders. "Then we will confront those challenges when they present themselves. There is no point in worrying about what has not yet come to be."

Andrew looked as though he'd say something else on it. But with a sad little shake of his head, he stumbled from the room.

Victoria stared at the doorway after he'd gone. At last alone, she sank into a useless puddle upon the floor. Sucking in a shuddery breath, she covered her face with her hands as the tumult of the past two months, coupled with Nathaniel's reemergence held her paralyzed.

How quickly her world had been upended. When she'd been more girl than woman and found herself with child, alone, without the benefit of marriage, she'd expected life could never be more uncertain and terrifying. How very wrong she'd been.

And yet, she should be thinking solely of her late husband and her broken son. The tears she'd twice been discovered crying this day by her children should have fallen for the state of their family and the gruesome fate Chester had met.

Instead, she remained fixed on the window. A desperate fear enveloped her that she'd merely dreamed Nathaniel's presence here.

She knocked her forehead against her knees. "*You fool. You fool. You fool,*" she whispered the litany into the quiet. And all this time, he'd been alive. She'd mourned him and their last meeting year after year after year. Had tortured herself with horrific possibilities of the fate he'd suffered from his work for the Crown. Because she'd been so very sure nothing could have kept him from her life otherwise.

Her lower lip quivered at the naiveté of that. She'd given him her virtue and heart on nothing more than a promise of more when he returned. For those gifts, he'd left her with a babe in her belly, never to return. Why, he hadn't bothered with so much as a visit or hasty explanation.

A half-sob, half-laugh stuck in her throat. As though an explanation could have ever justified his abandonment. When all a young lady had was her reputation, she'd thrown it all away for him.

You were just as much to blame… you consigned yourself to a hellish marriage with Chester, because of fear and desperation.

She stared vacantly at the opposite wall. If she had been stronger, she would have faced the uncertainty that came in being a mother with a bastard babe in her belly.

"And so, what if you had never married?" she whispered, hugging herself tight. Nathaniel had never returned and she'd thrust herself into a loveless, desperate, abusive union with Chester Barrett because of it. Her marriage may have been a hellish one, wrought with heartache, but it had brought her Justina and Andrew.

Still, that love for her children had never fully killed the wishes she'd carried for more… with Nathaniel.

She had mourned him when she'd believed him dead. Understood his failure to return. But he had not been dead. He had been very much alive… and she knew nothing else of where he'd been or what he'd done.

Or whether he had a family…

Her eyes weighted closed. What if that is why he'd not returned? What if, every time he'd come to her, she'd merely been the secret woman he kept on the side, while being bound to another who had the benefit of his name?

She sank her teeth into her lower lip, hating the agony ripping at her heart. Once she would have scoffed at the idea that Nathaniel Archer had been anything but loyal and loving. Now, everything had proven a lie.

Damning him for reentering her life, and stirring her oldest resentments and broken-heartedness, Victoria laid her head back, taking support from the windowsill.

There remained just one question: why had he returned *now*?

CHAPTER 4

Honor the rank and order of the Brethren.
Article IV: The Brethren of the Lords

"YOU ARE OVERSEEING THE INVESTIGATION of Waters?"

Sipping coffee at his breakfast table, all the morning papers and gossip columns stacked at his side, Nathaniel glanced up to a tall, familiar figure.

"Lord Adam Markham," Nathaniel's butler, Ward, belatedly announced.

"Markham," he greeted. Dropping the current folder he'd been perusing, he came to his feet. Markham, a former member of the Brethren, whose wife Georgina had freed Nathaniel from captivity, stood framed in the doorway. He'd been one of the few friends he'd allowed himself over the years. Having also been captured and tortured by the Fox and Hunter, their bond moved beyond even the close one forged by the Brethren.

"Back to the living, I see," the other man drawled, coming forward, his hand extended.

Nathaniel clasped it in a firm grip, shaking. "Never dead," he reminded his friend, needlessly. After Victoria's marriage, he'd only wanted to disappear and lose himself in the importance and purpose of his work. Those were details, however, he'd shared not even with this man who'd become like a brother to him. "Join me?" He motioned to the sideboard, but waving off that offering,

Markham took a seat near Nathaniel's morning work.

Markham passed a gaze over the stacks of papers. "I see you are as busy as you always are," the other man observed, accepting a glass of coffee from a liveried servant. "But then, that has always been your devotion to the Home Office."

Frowning, Nathaniel reclaimed his chair. "I detect disapproval there." He gave his servants a look and they took their leave.

Is that why Markham had come, to question how he lived his life? Nothing took the retired member of the Brethren away from his wife and family.

His friend spoke candidly, nodding to the papers Nathaniel had been studying. "You work too much." He paused. "You always have."

It is all I have. And it had been enough. *Has it truly, though?* Nathaniel thrust aside that niggling. "It is for the Crown," he said succinctly, neither wanting a lecture, nor needing one on his devotion. If there wasn't his role with the Brethren, what would there be? *Nothing.*

While Victoria has three children and now grandchildren…

Nathaniel stared into the contents of his drink.

"Forgive me," Markham said solemnly. "It was not my intention to come and lecture. Georgina asked that I speak to you. You know how she worries after you."

"I do." Reflexively, Nathaniel rubbed at his chest, the place where a ball had struck him when Georgina had helped him escape all those years earlier. "Please assure her I am fine." He would never resent Georgina or Markham for caring. They'd been closer than even his own family who Nathaniel had but limited dealings with. But then, when one's work called them away, the people who became like kin were those who understood the life one lived.

His friend snorted. "Do you think my wife will be content with your just being 'fine'?"

"No."

They shared a grin.

"She'll not be content until you've set aside your duty to the Brethren and gone into a much-deserved retirement."

A frown chased away Nathaniel's earlier smile. "I cannot do that." Because then what am I without my work? An old, lonely man mourning what he'd lost a lifetime ago?

"Well, then?" Markham encouraged, nodding to the papers. "Tell me about your assignment."

Nathaniel arched an eyebrow. "And I trust this is why you've come."

A glitter danced in the other man's eyes. "I've been too long out of practice if I'm that obvious." Then a hard glint iced over that hint of mirth. "Well?" he demanded, revealing shades of the steely agent he'd once been.

"I hardly think me taking on one of the most notorious cases in England merits a probing line of questioning," he drawled, carefully schooling his features.

"It wouldn't," his friend concurred, reclining in his seat. "*If* you hadn't adamantly avoided any assignments in London." He blew on the contents of his glass. "And then taken on the role of Sovereign. Those are hardly the actions of one who intends to stay out of the public's scrutiny."

He stiffened. When he'd asked to be sent abroad for the Brethren, the few he'd called friends had questioned his motives. He'd been fooled into believing there hadn't been wonderings among his brothers-in-arms. "Did you expect me to decline the opportunity to serve as Sovereign?" he asked instead, sidestepping Markham's observation.

"No," the other gentleman acknowledged. "It's no secret among any of us that you've devoted your entire existence to the Brethren."

Again, the other man's words came more as a chastisement than anything. But then, Markham had spent more than the past two decades married to a woman he loved, and had sired two sons and two daughters. It was no secret that, following his retirement from the organization, he'd vowed a renewed purpose in life through his family.

It is what you once dreamed of, too… the very life Adam and Georgina have. Through your capture, and then your escape and recovery… right up until the moment you entered Victoria's chambers to find her bed untouched and her armoire empty… you wanted those gifts with Victoria…

His heart spasmed.

And now he had his duty and responsibility to the Brethren.

Why did that leave him oddly hollow inside?

Setting down his cup, Markham leaned over and thumped him

on the shoulder. "Regardless of what has brought you back pub-
licly, I am grateful for it." He gave Nathaniel's shoulder a slight
squeeze. "We are happy to have you back as more than a ghost."

Nathaniel offered the now graying former member a smile. "It
is… good to be back."

Nathaniel… where have you been…?

Victoria's husky whisper echoed around the chambers of his
mind. As unsettling as it was to reassert himself amongst the living,
secretly he'd yearned to see her again. To hear his name fall from
her lips… and to give her the apology she was deserving of, while
getting answers about her hasty marriage. Only—his gaze fell to
the documents pertaining to her son's case. Fate was a cruel mistress who'd not even allow him a reunion devoid of anything but
turmoil and certain fury.

Why had he even gone there last evening? It had not been solely
about learning the lay of the proverbial land. Visiting with her
accomplished nothing and advanced his case not at all.

Markham picked up his coffee and took a sip. "My wife will
never allow me to return with that as a sufficient answer as to why
this assignment should merit the efforts of the Sovereign."

This camaraderie and friendship hadn't always existed between
them. Nathaniel had once despised the other man for having been
ungrateful to the woman who'd sprung him free and nearly cost
Georgina her life. Nathaniel's friendship with the Lady Markham,
however, had eventually grown to include her hot-tempered husband—a man who, through his imprisonment, Nathaniel could
feel a kindred with more than anyone else. And yet, it wasn't loyalty that made Nathaniel want to reply, but rather a need to share
the deepest secrets he'd revealed to none other.

Absently, he picked up the latest copy of *The Times*. "I once…"
his gaze automatically found Victoria's name at the center of that
sheet, "knew the lady," he finished quietly, shoving the page over.

Markham alternated his gaze between Nathaniel's face and that
sheet. "Waters' wife?" He raised his eyebrows.

"When we were younger. Before she was married." Back when
he'd entertained the dream of a life together with her. There would
have been babes with her smile and spirit and… he briefly closed
his eyes. All of her. He'd wanted their children to only have parts
of her soul and spirit.

Neither he nor Markham had been ones to fill voids of silence. It was surely the interminable months of solitude forced upon them. This moment was no exception. "So she is… more to you than a case, then," the other man finally said.

Nathaniel gave a curt nod. "I promised to return and marry her, but…" He shuttered his expression.

"Please, don't… don't… I beg you… let me go…" Nathaniel squeezed his eyes shut. "Victoria. I will come back. I will return…" Her vision danced behind his eyes and he clung to it. She was the last thin thread he grasped of his sanity…

"We will let ye leave," Hunter vowed in his thick Irish brogue. Nathaniel's heart leapt. "After ye tell us the name of those within yer organization." With the tip of his dagger, Hunter nicked away at the flesh of Nathaniel's arm.

"No… God… no. Please…"

His own pleas and screams pealed around his mind. And he'd thought there could be no greater pain than the torture carried out by his captors.

Numb, he glanced up, finding his friend's tortured gaze on him.

"Fox," Markham ventured with a similar emptiness.

He offered another nod. For too many years, he'd condemned Markham's earliest treatment of Georgina. But what must it have been to find that the woman was the daughter of the same vile bastard who'd captured and brutalized him? He marveled at that capacity for love and forgiveness.

Abandoning his coffee, Markham clasped his hands together. "She was the reason you wanted only assignments abroad, then?"

After a lifetime of revealing nothing of his time with Victoria to anyone, there was something healing… cathartic even in sharing his greatest pain. Nathaniel forced himself to meet his friend's concerned and, more, faintly pitying eyes. "I was warned the organization came first. Advised against forming connections or having… a family."

"We all were," Markham murmured, his expression darkening.

"And I was content to follow the advice given me by Aubrey at the time. I'd no intentions of… falling in love." His neck heated at sharing such an intimate detail with even Markham. Then, in their path to healing, they two had revealed the darkest parts of their captivity. As such, discussing Victoria should be easier. So why was the thought of her still so bloody hard? He cleared his throat and forced himself to finish his telling. "I had no intention of committing myself to any woman. I was in the middle of an early mission," he said distantly. That long ago night flitted forward. "Lord Hazlewhite was suspected of secreting funds and support to Boney's forces, and I was attending one of his wife's balls." The nobleman, married to a recent French émigré, had roused the suspicions of the Brethren and Nathaniel had been assigned the mission. He gave his head a bemused shake. How very important that assignment had seemed. "I came upon... her in an alcove." Rather, the young lady had stumbled upon his hiding place. The moment she'd yanked up her skirts, and tossed aside her slippers, however, he'd remained cloaked in shadows, appreciating the forbidden view of her delicate limbs.

"Love at first glance?" Markham ventured.

Nathaniel chuckled. "Outrage at first sight. The lady attempted to plant a facer on me." And after that ineffectual attempt, he'd doled out the single-most erotic lesson on self-defense to Victoria Cadence Tremaine, in nothing more than five feet of cloaked space. His smile fell. "I promised her after I'd completed one more mission, I would marry her."

You said that after your last one, Nathaniel...

The memory of her voice, tinged with regret whispered around his mind.

His throat swelled with sadness. Is that why she had married in his absence? As a young lady recent to London, she'd been spirited and strong, but she'd still had her unyielding parents, relentless in their efforts to see her wed. He'd spent years blaming her for not waiting, but he was as much to blame... nay, more so. Every assignment had been critical, with each one more important than the next. The country had been on the cusp of war and, as a cocksure youth of twenty, he'd believed himself capable of saving the Crown and having a woman's heart... in short—having everything.

What a fool he'd been.

"What happened?" Markham's quiet question pulled him back to the moment.

Nathaniel continued in emotionless tones. "After Georgina freed me and I healed, more than a year had passed. I returned and the lady was married." Reading of the young viscountess, with one child and rumored to be expecting a second, had destroyed him in ways Fox had never been able to. Agony burned in his chest and he resisted the urge to rub the wound that would forever hurt. "Married to Viscount Waters," he forced himself to utter that hated name aloud. Where any and every assignment had long ago ceased to faze him, this one set his mind and spirit into tumult. In taking the case over, he was affording himself a glimpse into Victoria's marriage, family, and life as it had existed without him in it.

"And now you are investigating her son."

Had it been any other member of the Brethren, other than one of the Markhams, there'd likely be recrimination there. One never took the assignment where one's judgment and logic could be compromised by personal dealings. Markham, however, spoke with an understanding Nathaniel appreciated. "Do you know anything of the new viscount?" he asked, instead, needing to direct the discussion back to safer grounds, away from his past with Victoria, and to the case involving her son and the murder of the late viscount.

Markham hesitated and, for a moment, Nathaniel believed his friend wouldn't let the talk and memories of Victoria rest but then the other man sat forward. "He attended Oxford with George." Georgina and Markham's eldest child. "They moved in different circles. My son indicated Waters was boisterous. Arrogant." He paused. "Largely friendless and always in search of approval and attention."

Nathaniel caught his chin between his thumb and forefinger. "Does arrogant and ignorant make for a murderer?" Or was it his own wish that Victoria be spared the suffering of her own child's failing that brought forth that question?

"No," Markham admitted. "But myself having been once guilty of those same flaws where my wife was concerned, it's also a testament to a person's capability of dangerous judgment and weakness."

A knock sounded at the door. "Enter," Nathaniel called, shoving a hand through his hair.

His butler entered. "Your carriage, as requested is waiting, my lord."

Of course, his household staff and the men and women who worked for him at his London offices all knew his devotion to punctuality. "I'll be along shortly," he said and the young servant hurried off. Finishing the remainder of his coffee, Nathaniel gathered up his newspapers and documents on Victoria's son's case. "I—"

"Have your work to see to," Markham finished, climbing to his feet. "I will leave you to your business." He paused. "If you require anything, Georgina and I are, of course, here," he vowed.

Grateful for that offer, Nathaniel inclined his head. Given the impending rage when Victoria discovered what had truly brought him back to London, he required all the offers of friendship he could secure.

He and Markham exited, side by side, in a companionable quiet that only they two were capable of. It was an indelible mark left by their time in captivity. And even as the nightmares still came, still visited him at the most unexpected of times, there was also a peace in knowing he was not alone. That someone understood and knew all too well the hell that he'd survived.

Outside, Markham stretched a hand out.

Adjusting his papers, Nathaniel took the offering and shook.

"If ever you need anything," his friend urged, holding his gaze squarely.

"Thank—"

Markham instantly held a palm up, stopping those words. "Don't insult me, Archer."

He grinned and climbed inside the carriage. As soon as the door was shut behind him and he was left alone, reality intruded as it invariably did. His smile dipping, he returned his focus to the Waters file. He set the leather folios down on the bench beside him. Any other time, the official documents would have commanded all his attention. The gossip would have been nothing more than an afterthought that he had one of the clerks read through and compile notes from.

Not this day.

Nathaniel snapped open the copy of *The Tattler*. His gaze instantly collided with her name… and her son's.

There have been reports from within the Home Office that the new Viscount Waters acted at the behest of his mother… the widowed, Viscountess Waters…

With a snarl, he forced himself to keep reading. Victoria's name was being dragged through every London townhouse and, no doubt, country estate.

And I am the man set to investigate her.

It was an assignment he'd originally undertaken because of his relationship with Victoria. Even with his confidence in every man and woman under his command, he'd still not entrust her or her family's fate to anyone else.

Or is it that you simply want to see her again... that after all these years, you've ached to have her near?

Nathaniel's gaze slid to the gossip sheet in his hand.

Nathaniel Archer, the Earl of Exeter, formerly of the Home Office, has personally undertaken the investigation into the murder of Viscount Waters. Lord Exeter will begin questioning Lady Waters and her family and acquaintances.

There were their names, his and Victoria's twined together... just not in the way he'd ever hoped for as a younger man.

The irony was not lost on him: the moment the Brethren had been tasked with the investigation of the late Viscount Waters, Nathaniel had lost her all over again.

Clenching and unclenching the pages in his hands, he resumed reading. And braced for his eventual meeting with Victoria Barrett.

CHAPTER 5

Do not allow personal or familial connections
to influence any aspect of one's mission.
Article V: The Brethren of the Lords

QUIET WAS A PECULIAR THING.

When one didn't have it, one found oneself longing for the comforting silence of it all. And yet, the moment one had that craved for gift, it ushered in nothing but a lonely emptiness.

Having urged Phoebe to return home where she belonged, Victoria sat alone in the breakfast room. Her daughter, son-in-law, and grandchildren had just departed. She felt far lonelier than she ever had in this stark household. As a once-young mother, there had been, despite the misery of her marriage, laughter and excited chattering from her daughters and son. She'd not allowed herself to think of the day they were wed or off on their own with families. Though Andrew remained unmarried, Victoria's life had become a solitary one.

In an un-viscountess-like manner, she shoved the eggs distractedly about her porcelain plate with the tip of her fork. It mattered not that she'd had a husband or that her son lived here, still. Her husband had been, thankfully, absent more than he was present and her son more interested in his clubs and outrageous pursuits than any real meaningful discourse with her.

Selfishly, she wished she'd not encouraged Phoebe and her family to leave. Wanted them here so that she wasn't alone with her own fears for Andrew's future... and thoughts of Nathaniel. And yet with the uncertainty of all Andrew faced, it was now far safer to think of Nathaniel Archer.

She tapped her fork distractedly on the edge of her dish. Why had he come... *now?* Was it possible he'd waited until she'd found herself a widow? That he'd come to regret not returning to her? As soon as the thought slid in, she pushed it back. Nathaniel had always been a man unapologetic and unrepentant where societal rules were concerned. What was the alternative, then? That he'd simply... carried on a life after her? That he'd shattered her heart, left her with a babe in her belly, and a precarious fate to work her way through, and all the while he was living the adventurous, daring life he'd always lived? Numb, Victoria shoveled a forkful of eggs into her mouth and it sat heavy like dust upon her tongue. She forced herself to choke down the swallow. With a frustrated sigh, she dropped her fork. The silver clattered loudly on the table.

"Ahem."

She gasped. Heart pounding, she glanced up. Manfred, the aged butler who'd served loyally in their household more years than they'd ever deserved, flushed. Previously a butler in her own father's household, Manfred, along with Victoria's then lady's maid and a handful of others had accompanied her to her new household. It was then that she'd grasped just how dire the finances were of the man her late father had sold her off to. "Manfred," she greeted warmly. "Good morning." When her own husband hadn't bothered with so much as a smile for their children, Manfred had allowed them to chase him about the townhouse, and engaged in countless games of hide and seek.

"My lady." Avoiding her eyes, he came forward, a stack of the morning papers in his arms. However, he made no attempt to turn them over.

Victoria gave him a gentle smile. "You may set them over here," she directed, tapping the spot beside her.

It was a task she'd given him which his averted gazes and red cheeks had said he'd hated louder than words. Victoria, however, was not a coward. As cruel as the gossip had been, it was wiser to know what one's enemies were writing and saying. Salacious rumors that had been flying all over the papers and throughout

London for two months now, with no proverbial end in sight. Victoria held her arms out and gave him a pointed look.

This time, however, he retained his grip upon them. He swallowed loudly. "Manfred," she urged gently. "You know I've never been one to bury my head in the sand." Presenting a brave face to the world had been a challenge she'd met the moment she'd taken vows to "love, honor, and cherish" the drunken, crass, Chester Barrett.

"No, my lady," he said faintly and, still, he pulled the gossip columns closer to his chest. He shot a frantic glance over his shoulder. "Might I suggest—?"

Victoria cleared her throat.

Looking like one who'd swallowed a plate of rancid oysters, Manfred bypassed her palms, dropped the stack at the opposite end of the table. With the speed he'd shown two decades earlier during games of British Bulldogs with her children, he bolted.

Sighing, Victoria shoved to her feet. What could be written upon those pages that was worse than anything else to precede it? Her son had been accused of patricide. Her son-in-law, Edmund, had been whispered of *helping* her son commit murder and her daughters accused of praying for their father's death long before. All rot and rubbish. Chester had been ruthless. He'd put his hands upon her in violence and hurled vile words at Phoebe, Justina, and Andrew, but through that evil, they'd been full of love and goodness. Of course, that reality was far less interesting than the one Society wished to present to the world. Reaching the end of the breakfast table, Victoria collected her morning reading and returned to her seat, where she set down her stack.

"What could they possibly have to say *now*?" she muttered under her breath, grabbing the copy resting on top. Unfolding the crisp pages of *The Times*, she quickly read through the main stories printed on the front. The Barretts had been the only members of the *ton* to occupy that hated spot since Chester had been discovered. As such, it saved Victoria from searching... from searching... her gaze slowed over the details written there and then stopped.

She remained with her stare locked on two single sentences above all others.

Nathaniel Archer, the Earl of Exeter, formerly of the Home Office, has come out of retirement in order to oversee the investigation of...

A heavy fog settled around her brain, it dulled her ears and sent pinpricks of light dancing behind her eyes. She, at last, had the answer to why Nathaniel had been here... why he'd come—*now*. Victoria's breath lodged somewhere between her chest and throat, choking her. The paper slid from her fingers and she gripped the edge of the table with sweaty palms.

I'm going to faint. She sucked in great, heaping gasps of air into her lungs. *I, Victoria Barrett, who'd faced pregnancy as a young, unwed woman, then the abuse of a husband, and the murder of that same heartless bounder without faltering, am going to collapse here... now... from this...*

For the question of what had brought Nathaniel back into the folds of the living hadn't been answered by the gentleman himself... but by a scandal sheet. The fresh clutch of betrayal ripped through her. It had been one thing when she'd believed Nathaniel had perished at an enemy's hand. It was an altogether different agony to find he'd not only been living but had only returned for the purpose of investigating her son.

And fool that she was, she'd shivered at his touch as she always had not even eight hours earlier. "Manfred," she shouted, her voice shaking with fury, outrage, and pain. She tamped down that hurt. The anger was far safer than that weakening sentiment.

The servant instantly slipped inside. "My lady?"

So, he'd been waiting. He'd always anticipated each move of the Barretts before they oftentimes did themselves. "My carriage," she said tightly. She yanked her gaze back to the page, searching for one important detail. Not finding it, she hurled it aside and grabbed another. And another... until she located the very information she sought.

She registered the dawdling servant and looked up. Manfred implored her with his rheumy eyes. "But my lady..." he whispered. "The gossip." It was a boldness not another servant in the realm would dare venture. He'd always been more family than member of the household staff. In this, however, she'd not be swayed.

For two months, she'd been properly shut away, in pretend mourning over a callous bastard of a husband. She was going out; all those societal expectations for her as a widow be damned. "I want my carriage readied, now, Manfred," she said on a steely order. "I've an appointment." With a man who'd been nothing more than a ghost who'd roused hurt in her heart.

All that was gone. Vanished and quashed by a story written in *The Times*.

"Yes, my lady," Manfred said in pained tones. He then shuffled off.

Alone, Victoria seethed. This time, she grabbed *Lady Pennywhith's News* and read about the *venerated* Nathaniel Archer and his service to the Home Office.

Lord Exeter has served Crown and country for more than two centuries. Titled twenty years earlier for acts of bravery and heroism in ferreting out Napoleon's battlefield plans—

As she scraped her gaze frantically over the page, taking in every last detail, a hollow ache settled in her chest. This man written about in the papers had been known to so many and hailed as a hero. *And all the while, he'd been nothing more than a ghost I mourned.* He'd remained frozen in time, forever the cocksure, dashing spy who'd stolen her heart, and offered her a fleeting happiness and love in his arms.

"Lies," she whispered. All lies.

She crushed the pages and wrinkled them into an unsatisfyingly sloppy ball. A hero is how the world knew him. A bitter-sounding laugh she barely recognized as her own spilled past her lips and echoed around the quiet breakfast room. Wasn't that precisely how she, too, had seen Nathaniel Archer? As a dashing hero? After all, he'd been the man who'd taught her how to properly defend herself and hadn't hesitated to meet her in the gardens, and entertain her fascination with those plants and buds. Or their stolen interludes at museums and circulating libraries. Her breath coming hard and fast, Victoria pressed her eyes closed, fighting for a semblance of calm.

Lies all of it. Nothing but lies. She repeated that litany in her mind, letting it settle there, so it might take root as fact.

From their first meeting to his disappearance, and now his reemergence. Hating the sheen of tears that blurred her vision, she grabbed the gossip columns, filling her arms with them. Her haphazard burden held close, she stalked over to the hearth where a small fire burned and hurled the sheets inside.

A satisfying hiss and crackle filled the quiet as the orange-red glow licked at the corners of those sheets. Then it exploded into a noisy conflagration.

"I take it you read the news," her son drawled from the doorway.

She gasped and spun about. He stood there, his lips twisted up in a wry grin. But for the faint redness to his eyes, he revealed barely a hint of last night's drunkenness. "Andrew," she said, mustering her usual maternal calm, cursing her crack in composure and damning Nathaniel for being the cause of it. She made a show of filling another plate and returned to the table.

Ever the proper lady and mother... that is how the world saw her. She gritted her teeth, wanting to rail at who she'd become and the uncertainty of her son's future.

Striding over to the sideboard, Andrew filled himself a plate and joined her at the table. He snapped a flawless white cloth and placed it on his lap. "And here you believed after two months of investigations by Bow Street and the constables that the matter would simply be laid to rest."

And for all the burning, seething anger and resentment over Nathaniel's treachery, there was an equal measure for her son's casualness. A façade he presented to the world, or not, he could manage at least a modicum of somberness. But blast and damn it all... what was she to say to him? In this, he was right. She had believed the investigators had seen and accepted the truth—Andrew could never be guilty of murder. "It will be sorted out soon," she said evenly as he sliced up a piece of kidney meat. Despite herself, Victoria followed his movements, movements he'd been charged with using upon his father. She bit the inside of her cheek. *Impossible.* It was—

Her skin pricked with the feel of her son's gaze upon her and she quickly whipped her head up.

Andrew hesitated, with the fork halfway to his mouth. "What exactly does something like... *this* getting 'sorted out' look like?" He shoveled a bite of kidney into his mouth. "I mean..." he spoke, his words muffled around the mouthful of food. "Does that look like time in Newgate? A trip to the gallows? Surely not Marshalsea." He swallowed loudly. "After all, it's one thing to wager away a family's fortune and land oneself in debt. It's an altogether different matter to kill one's—"

"Enough," she shouted, slamming her fist down on the table beside her. The porcelain plate jumped, clattering noisily under the force of that thump. She wanted to clamp her hands over her ears and run screaming from the uncertainty that her life and her family's lives had become. She'd never been one to run, however. Registering her son's slack jaw and unblinking stare, she smoothed her palms along her skirts. "I said, enough," she repeated in the more modulated tones the world expected of her. An agitating muscle ticked at the corner of her mouth. She leaned closer, shrinking the space between her and Andrew. "I've tired of your flippancy, as much as I've tired of your bouts of drunkenness."

Always an open book of emotion, her son now sat with his features a perfect mask that revealed not even a hint of what he was thinking… or feeling. She held a palm up, entreatingly. "I *know* what this is doing to you. You present a show of indifference to the world. You let them see just what they expect to see. But I know that is not you. I know this is destroying you inside."

A vein pulsed at the corner of his right eye. "Perhaps, it makes it easier for you to tell yourself that," he said quietly. "To believe there is more good in me than there, in fact, is. I was no more destroyed by father's death than you were."

She flinched. When had her son come to see so much? Feeling exposed, Victoria was the first to look away.

"How very sad for you," he murmured. Even knowing he merely baited her, she lifted her gaze anyway back to his. "You've always wanted to see more in me and from me than is there." Andrew shoved back his chair and the mahogany scraped noisily along the hardwood. Coming effortlessly to his feet, he tossed down his napkin. He smiled a cold, empty half-grin that gutted her. "You've wanted to forget."

Despite herself, the question came tumbling forward anyway. "Forget what?"

"That I am *his* son. And all his darkness, all his weaknesses are mine."

Her throat constricted. Those were the demons he fought… had always fought. She stared after him as he retreated, starting for the doorway. "Andrew?" she called out.

He paused, his fingertips an inch away from the door handle.

"His weaknesses are only yours if you let them be," she said softly, willing those words to take root and grow. "After your…" she flattened her lips, "heart was broken by that woman… you revealed a great maturity and strength."

Andrew faced her. "Which woman do you mean?" He gave his forehead a mocking tap. "Of course, you must refer to Lady Marianne Carew?" A pang struck her breast. He'd only focus on the former part of what she'd spoken. He'd failed to see the good. "The woman I fell in love with and gave my heart to? Is that the woman you mean? The one who attempted to kill Justina's husband and was committed to Bedlam for it?" Ice glazed his eyes. "That was the manner of woman I was drawn to because that is the manner of person I am," he said coolly and her heart broke all the more. "It was foolish for me to pretend I could ever be someone different." His lips quirked up in another one of those eerily empty smiles. "And I expect when I meet with this Lord Exeter, he will see precisely that which is before him."

Having Nathaniel's name fall from her son's lips stripped her of words and the ability to move. She gave thanks when Andrew quit the room.

As soon as he'd gone, she let her shoulders sag. None had ever known of her liaison with the second-born son of an earl. Victoria and Nathaniel's relationship had existed as nothing more than an intimate secret only they two had shared.

How very easy she'd made it for him to carry on with her as he had and never offer her anything more than those stolen nights of explosive passion.

Fury simmered to the surface, once more; safe, welcoming, calming. And she let it fill her, consuming every corner of her being. It drove back the weakness that had riddled her since Nathaniel's shocking reentry into her life last evening.

Her resolve strengthened, Victoria stood with all the regal grace the world had come to expect of her. Nathaniel Archer, now the Earl of Exeter, had destroyed her existence once before. She squared her jaw. She'd see him in hell on Sunday before she allowed him to do it again.

CHAPTER 6

*Official Crown business is to be discussed with
only other members of the Brethren.
Article VI: The Brethren of the Lords*

NATHANIEL HAD ONCE APPRECIATED THE quiet. As a spy, he'd benefited too many times from the barrenness of empty rooms that he'd been able to freely search. He'd also relished the silence as it allowed him to puzzle through riddles that had to be correctly solved in order to save a person's life—oftentimes, many persons.

All that had changed after his capture.

With the brutality inflicted and the torturing he'd endured at Fox's ruthless hands, Nathaniel had come to abhor the silence. It had marked the countless days and months and then years he'd spent alone, with nothing but the loud hum of quiet in his ears for company for almost the whole of each day.

In this instance, however, that once grating buzz wrought havoc inside his mind, distracting Nathaniel from the list of individuals he'd interview… and the questions he should be crafting to put to them.

Listen… and wait… you'll hear me, Archer… and by God, you'll wish you didn't. The maniacal laugh of his other captor, now dead and hopefully burning in hell for his crimes, echoed around the chambers of his mind.

Palms shaking, he tossed down his pen and pressed his fingertips into his temples, willing the ghosts gone, willing his heart into a normal cadence. He dug hard to drive back the demons of his past. A pained, empty laugh burst from him. And yet, who would have imagined he'd prefer the ominousness of the late Fox and Hunter to a meeting with—he glanced down at the list he'd compiled—six people.

Six people who were members of the peerage; respectable lords and ladies, who'd become embroiled in a darkness they couldn't truly understand.

Absently, Nathaniel traced the names of witnesses he'd set out to interview in the coming days.

Lady Phoebe Deering, the Marchioness of Rutland
Lord Edmund Deering, the Marquess of Rutland
Lady Justina Tallings, the Duchess of Huntly
Lord Dominick Tallings, the Duke of Huntly
Lord Andrew Barrett, Viscount Waters
Lady Victoria Barrett, Viscountess Waters

These were Victoria's family. Two daughters. A son. Two sons-in-law.

He stared so long at the names marked there, the letters blurred together. When he'd returned to find her married with a babe and another on the way, he'd left London and not allowed himself to think of her or those children because of the ache for all he'd lost, for what might have been, had been the greatest, final blow dealt by Fox and Hunter. He'd lost his future with her… and her world had gone on.

And what did he have for his five and forty years on earth? He had the Brethren… and his rank within the esteemed organization.

"It is enough," he said in a bid to break the unnerving quiet. He'd saved countless lives and thwarted attempts on the Crown. Oftentimes, it had been Nathaniel's intelligence alone that had circumvented destruction.

Yes, his own life had been duty driven and devoid of emotional connections, from even the two brothers and their families he'd left behind as he'd carried out his work. But people all over England—his kin included—had been rewarded with the gift of security—because of Nathaniel.

All of that mattered.

It has to.

He grabbed his spectacles and jammed them on his face. Because what was the alternative? That he'd lost Victoria, a life with her, babes of his own, born to her, and had *nothing*? As a young man, that truth had grated and roused hatred in him for the woman who hadn't waited.

With both the passing years and a rational mind, he'd accepted the unfairness in his resentment. What proof had she had that he was even alive? None. She'd had none and built a future that had no room for him in it. And life had continued on for the both of them.

Grabbing his pen, he dipped it into the crystal inkwell and immersed himself in his work. He frantically dashed the interrogating questions for Victoria's two daughters. After he'd compiled the first list for the eldest, he dropped his pen. Cracking his knuckles, he studied the formal query he'd put to her. The same questions would be put to the youngest of Waters' children. Nathaniel slid a sheet under the still damp page, for his clerk to copy and mark later, and then reached for another. There were still the sons-in-law to—

A distant bang from outside his office shattered the quiet.

"You cannot… if you take one more step…"

The agent's shouts drifted in and out of focus, growing increasingly louder and nearer.

Nerves instantly on alert, Nathaniel jumped up. He tossed aside his spectacles. Taking his meetings within the Home Offices did not diminish the threats that faced all who served the Brethren. Retrieving the pistol inside his center desk drawer, he strode to the door.

The frantic beat of footsteps as men went running past followed, punctuated by more frantic calls and orders. "Stand down…"

"By God, where is he? I will take down every bloody door until he meets me."

That familiar voice, once teasing and tempting, now filled with a fiery rage his men would be foolish to ignore. Nathaniel stumbled and then his heart picked up a frantic cadence. He yanked the door open to the commotion at the end of the hall.

From over the tops of the heads of the staff filling the corridor, Nathaniel found her. All the air left him on a swift exhale and his arm fell uselessly to his side. Her auburn hair tumbled down about her shoulders and her cheeks flushed with crimson color. Victoria Barrett was a warrior queen of old.

Macleod grabbed her right arm and wrenched it behind her back with a force that would have sent any other woman into a fit of tears. Victoria merely glowered up at the towering man, the fury snapping in her eyes promised death.

"That is enough," Nathaniel commanded sharply, stalking forward. Not breaking stride, he tucked his pistol away.

Every head swiveled his way. His men littering the corridor parted, allowing him instant passage. "As you were," he barked. Without hesitation, the investigators and clerks vacated the hall.

Macleod remained with his grip upon Victoria. The sight of his fingers digging into her flesh, skin as smooth and cream white as the last time Nathaniel had worshiped it with his lips, sent rage spiraling through him. "Release her, Macleod," he bit out, stopping before the pair.

Where the other men in his employ had instantly acquiesced, the young investigator paused.

"I'll not ask you again," he seethed, leveling Macleod with a single black look.

Gulping loudly, the younger man let Victoria go.

Favoring him with a glare, she whipped her arm close. Then she turned the full force of her outrage and fury on Nathaniel. "You bastard," she whispered. It would seem fury was destined to serve as the foundation for their second meeting and their reunion. "You—"

He glanced pointedly to the man studying their exchange with fascination in his keen gaze. "You are also relieved, Macleod." As soon as the investigator had turned on his heel and stalked off, Nathaniel gestured to the opposite end of the hall. "Unless you care to have your grievances aired before my entire staff, I'd suggest you join me," he urged when Victoria remained motionless.

Her slender figure shook. "Do you believe I give a jot about what the gossips say?" she spat.

No, she never had cared for what the *ton* had to whisper or about whom. It had been just one of the reasons he'd fallen so hopelessly in love with her. "My staff does not gossip," he said at last. "I merely suggested a private meeting to allow you your dignity."

If looks could kill, he'd be a pile of charred ash before her black satin slippers. "My dignity," she repeated on a sharp whisper. "My dignity?" She took a lurching step forward and then stopped abruptly.

Patting her hopelessly disheveled coif, Victoria brought her shoulders back. She spun on her heel and continued down the corridor.

Nathaniel followed along behind, his gaze taking in her retreating figure. Clad in an elegant, black satin cloak, the garment pulled and stretched with her every step, highlighting the lush curve of her hips. Yet for her nipped waist, hers was a woman's figure so very different than the narrow-hipped young lady who'd captivated him from their first meeting.

You are a depraved bastard…

Disgusted with himself, he stepped in front of her. "Here," he murmured, turning the handle.

Victoria swept in ahead of him with the regal elegance of a queen laying claim to this sanctified space.

Nathaniel drew the door closed behind them. "I would ask the reason for your fury, but suspect I—"

Victoria shot a delicate palm out, catching him in the cheek. His head flew back under the force of that blow. The loud crack of flesh meeting flesh resounded in his ears. With a shuddery gasp, she drew her clenched palm close to her chest. Horror spilled from her blue eyes.

I cannot strike you, Nathaniel… not even as some form of lesson…

The sight of her, stricken and silent, knifed at him. He'd believed himself incapable of knowing any further hurt where Victoria was concerned, only to be so coldly dismissed by the lady and find he was still capable of an even greater agony. He briefly closed his eyes tight. Preferring her as she'd been, brimming with rage, Nathaniel flexed his mouth. "Your technique has vastly improved since our last meeting," he drawled, rubbing at his jaw with his spare hand. He moved behind his desk and returned his gun back to its proper place.

"Bastard," she hissed, rushing around the broad mahogany piece that had belonged to countless Sovereigns before Nathaniel. "You b-bastard." That slight tremble broke the illusion of her self-control. "How dare you?"

For which crime did she hold him to blame? For having left her all those years ago and never returning as he'd vowed? Or for his case surrounding her son? If he were the true bastard she accused him of being, he'd deride her for her inability to trust in him. To trust he would return for her. "Victoria—"

Victoria's eyebrows shot nearly to her hairline. "You simply come back into my life after all these years and investigate my son for... for..." Her mouth moved but no words came forth.

Of course, you fool. Do you truly believe after all this time, that she'd really thought of you with any remembered fondness? She'd made a life after him. A life with another man. His investigation was the sole reason for her upset. Still, the sight of her suffering wrenched at him. "Victoria," he began softly, gathering her hand in his.

Heat sparked at the press of her skin against his. How he'd longed to again touch her; to feel her fingers twined with his, and—

Recoiling, Victoria wrenched free of his grip and he went cold at the loss of her. "Do not touch me," she spat, her earlier anger again blazed to life. "All these years, you simply disappeared. I believed you were dead, Nathaniel." Her voice shook, a husky quality to her soft, musical voice, wrapped around those three syllables that was his name. Victoria sucked in a shaky breath. "But you weren't dead."

"No," he murmured somberly. "I was not dead." He'd been captured and tortured so much, that there had been times he'd prayed for that fate, and then again, nearly every day after his return when he'd found her married. "I'm alive."

She clutched at her throat. "That is what you'd say? You sneak into my home and crack that bloody window like... like..." He'd once done. That reminder of that secret signal belonging only to them ripped a jagged hole inside his chest, more vicious than the one left by Fox's bullet. "I believed..." She glanced away, but not before he spied an emotion he could not name clouding her eyes.

What? The question pealed around his mind, demanding to be asked. "What did you believe?" Needing an answer. Needing to know why, why she'd married in his absence.

In the end, she gave her head a disgusted shake. Planting her hands on her hips, she glared up at him. "Were you married?"

He opened and closed his mouth several times. "What?" he

blurted.

"Were. You. Married?" she repeated, her voice slightly pitched. "Is that wh–why…" her voice broke, but she resolutely held his gaze, demanding an answer with her eyes.

That query suggested a woman who'd cared. And yet, why should she have when she'd pledged herself to another? "Given the fact that it was you who married in my absence, should it matter?" he replied, unable to keep the bitterness from his tone.

She recoiled, jerking like one who'd been struck in the belly.

The sight of her suffering chased away his useless resentments. He scrubbed a hand over his face. He'd rather sit through another round of torture at Fox and Hunter's hands than bring her any suffering. "Victoria," he began quietly, taking a step toward her. "I've not come to discuss the past." Nothing could ever come in those talks. Nothing but renewed hurts and resentment.

She jerked out of his reach. "No, you have not," she spat. "You've only returned with the purpose of investigating my son for a crime he did not commit."

Her accurate charge brought them back to safer territory. "That is why I've returned," he conceded in grave tones.

Again, Victoria flinched.

In the course of his career, he'd dealt with all manner of incensed individuals: men and women who'd resented questions he'd put to them, many of whom had put on impressive displays of pretend outrage to cover up the crimes they were truly guilty of. As such, he'd become adept at identifying when people put on an expert façade.

Victoria was hurting. Nor was it a lifetime of experience as a member of the Brethren that brought him to that realization, but rather the too-brief time they'd shared. He'd learned every last nuance about this woman. The evidence of her suffering drove back his enmity. She'd always mattered most to him. As such, he still, even with all that had come to pass, would, if he had the power, always make her pain his own.

"Will you sit?" he asked quietly. When she stiffened, he added, "Please."

She hesitated. Then notching her chin up, she moved to claim one of the indicated seats.

"May I take your cloak?" He reached for the garment.

"This is not a social call, my lord."

My lord. When they'd been together, he'd been "my love", "Nathan", "Nate". How much he missed hearing his name fall from her lips. How much he despised the bloody title that had been affixed to his name. "Of course," he said perfunctorily as she slid into her chair.

Reclaiming his, he settled back, resting his palms along the leather arms of his seat.

"He did not do it," she said without preamble, as direct and forthright as she'd always been. "He did not murder my husband."

My husband. Those two words struck like a dull blade to the belly. "There are those who believe he did, Victoria. That he's guilty of the crime of patricide."

White lines formed at the corners of her mouth. "They're wrong."

Had she been any other person who'd come to him with such a defense of a loved one, he'd have scoffed at that empty rebuttal and coolly stated the facts. Then he'd show them the door. Nay, he'd not have even granted the meeting in the first place.

"*If* they're wrong," she went taut at the slight emphasis he placed there. "Then my investigation will reveal as much and your son will be exonerated."

Victoria sprung to her feet with such a rapidity her cloak gaped open. "Bah," she scoffed, slashing the air with a palm. "You'll base your investigation on the words of drunken men and women so desperate for a coin that even their testimony can be bought?"

That valid and rational point was one that men and women of the Brethren would have made. Certainly not a lady of the peerage and not the young, trusting girl she'd once been. But then, life affected them all. How many other ways had Victoria changed in their time apart? "Your husband was murdered, Victoria," he reminded her somberly. God, how he loathed that she'd belonged to another. The mere utterance was like vinegar being tossed upon an open wound every time he imagined her with Waters. "Surely, you'd expect a formal investigation completed that holds the offending person responsible for the crimes."

His wasn't a question. It was a statement made by a man she'd known a lifetime ago, who believed she was still the hopeful innocent he'd left behind. As such, the proper reply would always be a resounding concurrence. That whoever had brutally killed her husband was deserving of punishment and should be brought to justice.

Unable to meet his eyes, Victoria turned, presenting him with her back. She caught her lower lip between her teeth and bit hard to stifle a sob. What would he say about the ruthless woman she'd become that she was content to never know the name of the man or woman who'd taken her husband's life in that brutally heinous way? That after years of being beaten and mocked and called vile names, she was quite content with the knowledge he now writhed and twisted in the eternal flames of hell? That she'd spent nearly every year of her marriage praying she'd be made a young widow to spare her from any more of his abuse?

Strong hands came to rest on her shoulders. Slightly callused, those long fingers were so very different than the short, stubby ones her husband had placed upon her person too many times. Only, this touch was not one of violence or cruelty. Tender and firm all at the same time, even through the fabric of her satin cloak and gown, his touch burned as it always had. Tingles danced temptingly down her back. She bit the inside of her cheek hard between her teeth. Why must his hands upon her affect her so all these years later? Why, even with his betrayals, past and present, should she remember how wonderful it had once been to lay in his arms?

"Victoria?" he asked, his mouth close to her ear, the hint of coffee and citrus, a peculiar blend, and foreign on Nathaniel's lips.

She struggled through the thick fog he'd cast. What had his question been? What had he asked? Then reality intruded: who he was, why he was back in her life… and his plans for Andrew. Victoria stepped out of his arms with a stiff, even control. She'd not show any further weakness before him. She faced him. "The world has already determined his guilt," she said. "I'll not have Andrew—my son—pay for the crimes committed by another." And certainly not for a man who'd never been a true father to Andrew; who'd hurt and abused them all… in different ways.

He dusted a hand over his mouth in a contemplative manner

and, for the sliver of a moment, she believed he'd see the truth of her words and end the official inquiry. "If that is the case, then I'll find it, Victoria." Time should have proven her a fool for hoping, long ago.

My son's fate rests in this man's hands. Shaking, she folded her arms at her middle, hugging herself in a lonely embrace. "I'll ask you one more time, Nathaniel…" His body jerked erect. Was it the sound of his name on her lips? Worry over the favor she'd put to him? "End this. Bow Street, the local constables, they've questioned us all. There is neither guilt nor knowledge of what happened that night."

"Your son was there," he said bluntly.

"And passed out drunk," she rejoined. "In the arms of a prosti-tute in a nearby room. He was accounted for."

"There was an hour and twenty-five minutes when she slept." At the gentleness there, she gritted her teeth. Nathaniel brushed his knuckles over her cheek in a fleeting caress. "An investigation is happening, Victoria. Regardless of whether you wish it or not. If it is not me on the case, it would be someone else. Whether you believe your son's innocence or not. It matters that the world will see him cleared of the charges and accusations."

"Pfft. He's already been found guilty in the eyes of Polite Soci-ety. Even if…" She grimaced. "*When* you find him innocent, the world will still always whisper about him, label him as a murderer." Her son's reputation and honor would be forever questioned and on nothing more than salacious whispers.

She pressed her eyes briefly closed. *Damn you, Andrew. Why must you have gone to those places your father frequented?* On the heel of that, remorse flooded her. Had she been a better mother, had she exerted a greater influence over him, and minimized the impact of his father's wastrel ways, then Andrew's life may have turned out altogether different.

So many damned mistakes.

Nathaniel worked his gaze over her face; those violet eyes with the power to enchant. "This will provide an end to the matter."

An end… "You don't believe me," she breathed. Why should it come as any form of shock that he should doubt the veracity of her claims? *He is a stranger… in every way. And yet, he is also father to my first-born child.* Agony cleaved at her breast and she balled her fingers into sharp claws, leaving crescent marks upon her palms.

Her former lover perched his hip in a damnably casual repose upon the edge of his desk. "I am a man who—"

"Operates under fact," she said tersely.

Facts are not always correct, Nathaniel… "Sometimes they are erroneous and nothing more than incorrectly strewn-together details," she gave him that counter-argument she'd always uttered when he'd throw out that statement.

"Then, they would not be called facts."

Why… he was even more tenacious than he'd been as a young gentleman of twenty. Despite herself and her outrage, a reluctant smile pulled at her lips. "Who'd have imagined it possible?" she muttered.

He quirked a dark eyebrow. "What was that?"

"Nothing," she said quickly, quashing that smidgeon of earlier amusement. "It was nothing." Restive, she glanced about Nathaniel's immaculate office; the floor-length shelving units filled with leather books and folios. The mahogany sideboards and Chippendale tables better suited to a nobleman's townhouse than an agent for the Crown's offices.

How to make him see? Looking back to him, she made one final attempt. "I ask that you not do this," she begged. "I ask you to please let me and my family move on from this." Let them begin to heal and learn to be a family without the oppressive presence of the late viscount.

"I have no choice. Your husband—"

"Do not," she rasped and he fell instantly silent. She flinched. God how she hated her connection to that reprobate and she was destined to be linked forever to him… because of this man. Because he'd left her no choice but to sacrifice herself.

It was your own decision. You yourself walked to that altar and took those vows.

Hating that logic knocking around her mind, she dug her fingertips into her temples, willing that reminder gone. *I wanted Nathaniel to be more. I wanted him to return to me… not for me, and fill our lives with the love and laughter they'd always shared…*

He sighed. "I am sorry."

"Sorry?" Incredulity pulled that single word from her.

"I trust this is difficult for you."

"In ways you can never imagine." She repressed the urge to laugh in his face, fearing if she did he'd mistake her for mad. But then, perhaps that is precisely what the past four and twenty hours were doing—shredding her sanity and leaving her with no path but the one to Bedlam.

Nathaniel's chiseled features may have been carved of granite for as immobile as they were. Ice scraped along her spine, freezing her from the inside. How very cold he was. It only served as a reminder of the fact that he was, and had always been, nothing more than a stranger. "The King has ordered the case be investigated and, as such, it will go forward," he spoke with an air of finality.

He could not be swayed. His one and only love had only ever been to that bloody organization. The same one that had always taken him away from her. She'd just been foolish enough and naïve enough to believe she mattered more. With a sound of disgust, she made to draw her hood on, but he held out a hand, staying her.

"Surely you see, I'm the only person you should want overseeing this case."

A panicky laugh exploded from her and she snapped the fabric of her cloak. "Trust you?" Her voice pitched to the ceiling and she damned the weakness that brought her diatribe tumbling forth. "After I gave you my virtue and you pledged to marry me, you left, never to return." He winced. "You let me believe you were dead, then return all these years later, and just expect I should trust you with my son's fate?" She forced a laugh. "If you believe that, you are either mad, or stupid, or both, Nath—my lord." She'd not allow even a shred of intimacy between them.

His expression grew shuttered. "I had my reasons for not returning, Victoria," he said with more hesitancy than she'd ever heard from him. His voice was gruff.

She scoffed, feigning indifference, even as she wanted to demand answers. She'd not allow him that victory. "I once cared about your *reasons*. Not any longer." He could, at any point, have assured her of his existence. She'd been desperate enough in her love for this man that even that scrap would have sufficed. "The only reason I've come to you now is to appeal to your sense of logic and right." Her gaze snagged on the white-knuckled grip he had upon the edge of his desk. For his calm, he was not as unaffected as this cool façade he presented before her. Finding strength from that, she continued. "Given that…" Her stare collided with a sheet of parchment in the middle of his desk. One name stood out stark and vivid. She shot her fingers out. "What is this?" she hissed, dragging her eyes over that page, already knowing. Knowing without a need for any form of confirmation from him. Victoria lifted her horrified gaze to his. "Nathaniel?"

"They are questions for your daughter."

Our daughter. She was the child born to the two of them that he still didn't know of. A child he'd never met. She choked. That child—Phoebe—had been conceived of love and the reminders of both those gifts had sustained her through the darkness that had been her marriage. He should know… and yet… what was she to say? You left me with a babe in my belly; a daughter, who you now would interrogate? "You intend to question my daughter?" she asked, her voice strangled to her ears. *How am I standing up? How am I speaking clear, coherent sentences when inside I'm splintering into a million shards?*

He dipped his eyebrows. "Victoria, any investigator would speak to the suspect's family and friends to—"

She clamped her hands over her ears to blot out his voice. His deep baritone moved in and out of focus, blending with the ragged breaths she sucked in through her teeth. They would meet at last… father and daughter, both of them knew nothing of one another's existence. Only, it was not to be the teary-eyed reunion she'd held on to hope for when Phoebe was just a babe of two, three, and then even four years old. This was a questioning, where Nathaniel would press his daughter for information that could or would incriminate the new viscount. He'd attempt to use Phoebe's words to see Andrew in gaol… or worse… her mind shied away from the certain fate that awaited a young man accused of patricide. "Enough," she cried out and he instantly fell silent. By God, how she hated seeing his reason, hated knowing he was correct in this. "When is your… appointment with Phoe…" She could never be Phoebe to him. She could never be anything more.

Nathaniel looked at her, a question in his eyes.

"When is your appointment with my daughter?" If he went ahead with this, her already broken family would splinter apart, damaged beyond recovery.

"I've plans to visit tomorrow at fifteen past twelve."

Her stomach pitched. "And my other daughter?" she demanded.

"It is my intention to interview—"

"Interrogate."

"—your entire family," he continued over her interruption. Nathaniel's gaze bore into hers. "Including you."

Including…? Victoria canted her head at a slight angle. Her life had become a farce of which the Great Bard himself could have not plotted and put to page. Nathaniel would put questions to her about her marriage to Chester. Intimate questions that would, no doubt, seek to uncover the details of her union. By the very nature of his work, he ferreted out hidden truths and secrets. *And your sins have come home to roost…* Her palms moistened and she dusted them along the sides of her cloak.

"Given that we'll see one another again and have professional dealings," he started. Professional dealings? Mad, he was utterly mad. "We should speak about the past, Victoria," he said calmly.

"You want to speak of the past? Now?" Disbelief crept into her voice and she gripped the edge of her skirts, scrabbling with them in a bid to keep from falling apart. "I have no interest in hearing what you have to say about the very brief and regretful time we knew one another. In fact, it would be best if not another word was mentioned of it." Shaking her head, Victoria yanked her hood into place, grateful for the protection it provided from his probing stare. On legs that shook, she made her way to the door.

"Victoria?" he called out. She had the round knob in her hand. "It was never my intention to hurt you."

Her throat closed and, swallowing around the painful lump, she forced herself to look at him. "Go to hell, Nathaniel," she said softly.

A sad, empty smile, creased his lips. "I was there long, long ago," he said in hushed tones. "I rather doubt I've ever left."

Not wanting to know what he meant and, worse, not wanting to care what suffering had been his, she swiveled back. Without another glance, she stalked out of his office.

And yet, despite her silent insistence that his desolate pronouncement did not matter, as she left, his haunting words followed.

CHAPTER 7

Go into every and any meeting clear-headed and logical.
Article VII: The Brethren of the Lords

THE FOLLOWING AFTERNOON, NATHANIEL GUIDED his mount through the bustling streets of London with his assistant keeping pace beside him.

After Nathaniel's captivity, closed spaces such as carriages had the potential to send him into a panic, thrusting him back to his time with Fox and Hunter. Over time, in a bid to wrestle back control from those ghosts, he'd forced himself to journey by way of those miserable conveyances and, most times, he was a master over those demons.

Since his meeting with Victoria, however, the memories of those darkest days had been made fresh all over again. He knew better than to go into any appointments or investigations anything less than clear-headed. His work always provided him with a sanctuary of sorts; offering a distraction from the agonizing memories and wishing that weighted enough that a man could drown under their hold.

Today, there was little calm and even less focus. There was no diversion in his upcoming meeting with the Marchioness of Rutland. There was just the cold emptiness of bringing unintended hurt to the only woman who'd ever mattered to him.

I have no interest in hearing what you have to say about the very brief and regretful time we knew one another...

The sting of that profession was as fresh now as when she'd whispered it on her way out of his office. And even as he'd sought to tell himself she merely lashed out because he'd hurt her, because he'd meant something to her, there had been nothing but disdain when she'd looked upon him.

Not two evenings prior. *Two evenings ago, when you sneaked inside her residence, there had been neither shock nor hatred in her expressive eyes.* There had been confusion and the momentary flash of joy.

He scoffed. *You merely saw what you wished to in that instance.* For when she'd stormed his office, there could be no mistaking the vitriol emanating from her person. He clenched his reins, tight.

Nathaniel guided his horse, Tory, down Chesterfield Hill, onward to the Marquess of Rutland's townhouse. For there could be no disputing that Victoria had looked upon him with a palpable hatred pouring from her slender person.

His gut clenched. She had been the one whose memory alone had sustained him. She'd kept him from surrendering to the blissful surcease that only death could bring. And even with all the years that had come to pass, even finding she'd married in his absence and lived a life without him in it, he loved her. He always would. Yet, they'd been two souls whose lives had never been meant to connect. Not fully, and not in all the ways he'd once dreamed of.

That realization robbed him of breath all over again, leaving him the staggered man who'd found out the woman he'd loved had wed another.

There is the Brethren—there would always be the Brethren— and there were years of mistrust and spitefulness with Victoria that could never be overcome. Fueled by the practicality of that reminder, Nathaniel dismounted. He'd an assignment to oversee and a case to resolve. Those facts alone were the only ones that had mattered to him since he'd joined the ranks of the Brethren. They were the only ones that could ever matter. Five years past forty, with two brothers who were more strangers than anything, the Brethren had become the only family he had.

Bennett jumped down, recalling him to the moment.

Nathaniel spoke as the other man hurried to take the reins. "You've copied the questions—?"

"It is done, my lord."

"For the Duchess of Huntly?"

"And the lady's spouse," the dutiful servant offered. He'd always anticipated five steps ahead to what Nathaniel would ask. Pride filled him for the man Bennett's son had proven to be. Was this that sentiment fathers such as Markham and Bennett knew? A pang of longing struck. "The forms are filed away within their folder," Bennett was saying, practical matters of business chasing away an older man's lamentations. "You've everything you require for the appointment."

The appointment. How casually Bennett spoke of it: a conversation they'd had countless times about lords and ladies and men of the gentry and working class who'd earned the attention of the Brethren. Not a single time, however, had he ever thought of those individuals as anything more than a means to an end in the information gathering process. Had Macleod or anyone else undertaken this investigation, Victoria and her family would exist as mere strangers. *She is so much more.* She owned every corner of his heart. *And she despises me...*

"My lord?" Bennett prodded.

Reaching inside the pack attached to his saddle, Nathaniel rescued the Barrett file. "I expect this will not take more than an hour." He'd taken part in enough of these meetings to know the general time spent interviewing a witness.

His folder and notebook held in one arm, Nathaniel strode the remaining length of the pavement to the marquess' front door. He rapped once. While he waited, he surveyed the surrounding townhouses and smartly dressed passersby.

A pair of dandies widely skirted the steps, casting nervous glances up at the marquess' residence. The information he'd gathered on the marquess painted him as a ruthless, callous, cold-hearted scoundrel, feared by Society. Nathaniel managed his first real grin, that wry expression straining the muscles long unaccustomed to smiling. What would those fops and fancy lords think of the ruthless cutthroats Nathaniel had battled in the past two decades he'd served the Brethren? He'd encountered an evil Polite Society only read of in their gothic novels, but couldn't imagine the dark depths of a man's soul. To them, scoundrels such as Lord Rutland would cause them to quake in fear.

His smile dipped. He had come to understand there were different levels of evil where men were concerned. It was a matter of fact and, yet, it was also a matter that affected Victoria's daughter. The darkest scoundrel in London was the man Victoria's eldest child had been bound to. Heavily in debt, had the late viscount forced the girl into a match with the powerful peer? Such a fate was, of course, expected for most ladies in Polite Society. So why did the idea of Victoria's daughter being sold to the highest bidder strike an odd ache inside?

You're getting soft in your old age, you fool. All this melancholy about a woman he didn't even know because of a lady he *had* known for a brief time in his youth, who'd not waited for him.

Adjusting the documents in his arms, Nathaniel lifted the gold knocker and gave it another impatient thump.

The door was instantly opened, revealing a wizened butler with heavy wrinkles and anger in his rheumy eyes.

Nathaniel brandished a card. "I'm here to speak with Her Ladyship, the Marchioness of Rutland."

Collecting the article, the old servant stared at it for a long while. He pursed his mouth in distaste and, for a moment, Nathaniel believed the man intended to turn him out on his arse. But then, smoothing his features, he motioned him forward. "Her Ladyship is expecting you."

A footman came forward. Doffing his black hat, Nathaniel turned it over to the servant. Another young man, clad in a matching crimson livery, came to relieve Nathaniel of his papers. Shrugging out of his cloak, he instead relinquished the garment to the servant's care. With the exception of Bennett, he entrusted his files to no one.

"If you'll follow me," the butler urged in aged tones.

As he fell into step behind the servant, Nathaniel used the opportunity to study the wrinkled butler. One could tell much about a household and how a residence was run by the manner of servants on one's staff. Loose-lipped ones were a sign of disloyal souls only interested in the coin they might earn. Households with primarily young, pretty maids often bespoke a handsy employer and an angry mistress.

The man ambling at a painfully slow pace also revealed much about the marquess and marchioness. When most servants this man's age were enjoying a life of retirement, he remained on. It spoke to his loyalty… for Lord Rutland. It also hinted at a man deserving of that devotion.

"Here we are, my lord," he murmured, bringing them to a stop outside a heavy, oak door.

The details he'd gathered on the marquess' household had served their purpose; grounding him and clearing his head for the upcoming meeting.

The butler opened the door and announced him. "The Earl of Exeter to see Her Ladyship."

Nathaniel stalked forward with purposeful steps and then stopped abruptly. "My…"

Only, it was not the Marchioness of Rutland who greeted him. The air lodged in his chest. *Victoria*.

From where she stood at the heavily-draped window, she whipped about.

Despite his resolve to focus solely on the case and disregard their shared past, Nathaniel drank in the sight of her like a man thirsty for drink with a taste of his first drop. When he'd not been fighting back thoughts of Victoria Barrett and what could have been, he'd embraced the memories of her. Kept them close and—

She narrowed her eyes, swiftly killing his fanciful musings. "My lord," she said tightly.

How did we come to be here?

The butler backed away and Nathaniel ventured forward. He set the small stack in his arms down on a nearby table.

Victoria followed his every movement with a world wariness in her gaze. He mourned the loss of the bright-eyed young lady who'd only had innocence in her smile and heart. He came to a stop behind the high-back white sofa, allowing her distance. It was a strategy employed with skittish men and women under questioning, *and I'm using it now*. On this woman whose life had mattered to him more than his own.

Nathaniel came slowly around, giving her time to retreat. "It is not my intention to hurt you." It never was. He'd have taken twenty years of Fox and Hunter's abuse if it would have spared her even a hint of suffering.

Her throat worked as he stopped a hand's breadth away. He expected her retreat. Instead, she stood breathtakingly strong in her resolve. "If I ever mattered to you, then let this rest," she spoke, her words hushed. "Do not subject my family to this."

Nathaniel worked his gaze over her heart-shaped face and that faint, beloved dusting of freckles upon her nose. "You know I cannot simply set aside my responsibilities."

She yanked her head back so quickly, several auburn curls popped free of her neat chignon. Fire burned in her eyes. "That damned organization always meant more to you than," *me*, "anything or anyone."

That's what she thought. *What other reason did I give her?* He'd let her believe him dead and then reemerged only to investigate her son. He gathered those loose tresses between his fingers. Like satin. The shimmery locks recalling him to all those moments these very curls had formed a curtain around him as she'd lain draped over his naked chest. Her breath caught loudly as he tucked the curls back behind her ears. "Not everyone," he murmured. "*You* mattered more than you ever knew." He'd survived because of her. He only wished that his promise to come back for her and her faith in him had been enough.

Her throat worked. "There is no need for your lies now."

"I never lied to you, Victoria."

A half-sob, half-laugh spilled from her lips.

"I didn't," he defended, her ill-opinion cutting like a knife. She'd been the only person—his own family included—to whom he'd revealed his work with the Brethren. "I understand why you believe I was untruthful to you, but everything between us…" He cupped her cheek and she leaned into his touch, kindling hope.

Her impossibly long, crimson-kissed eyelashes fluttered. His heart swelled at that softening. "*Everything* was real, Victoria Cadence." Nathaniel stroked his thumb over her lower lip, aching to again familiarize himself with that flesh. "Every stolen meeting, every pledge I made you, every word of love were the only real things in my life," he whispered, when his career with the Brethren had made his existence one of lies. "I would have you know that."

He belatedly registered the sound of approaching footsteps. Instantly releasing her, Nathaniel stepped back.

The Marquess of Rutland looked between them and Nathaniel swiftly smoothed his features. "My wife will be along shortly," the marquess said in low, graveled tones. There were no false shows of social niceties; no offer of tea, or a seat, or even a casual discourse about the unfashionably warm weather they'd been enjoying. This was an exchange as he preferred it.

Avoiding his gaze, Victoria slipped out from behind him. She took up a place beside her son-in-law.

A moment later, the marchioness entered. "Is he…" Her words trailed off, as her gaze collided with Nathaniel's.

And he stood frozen, immobile, incapable of so much as a proper introduction. When he'd taken over the investigation and drafted his inquiry for the Barrett children, he'd not allowed himself the thought of what it would be like to come face to face with them. This woman, with her thick auburn hair and flawless white skin, may as well have been a portrait of Victoria upon their first meeting in that alcove. His heart tugged. Had he remained, had they wed, Lady Phoebe Deering was near an age to a child that would have been born to them. *Agony wadded in his throat. I wanted that life with you, Victoria. I wanted to be the man to give you babes and build a life with you…*

"Hello," she said quietly.

Forcing back those melancholic sentiments, Nathaniel dropped a bow. "My lady," he said, his voice hoarsened. "It is a pl…" He grimaced, at that misstep.

Her cheeks blazing red, Victoria moved in a rustle of skirts. She placed herself between Nathaniel and the marchioness, like a tigress protecting her cub. *This is the manner of mother I always knew she would be.* He'd just never imagined that he would be the person from whom she'd be protecting her children. His heart spasmed.

Nathaniel forced his gaze away from Victoria and over to her daughter. "Thank you for allowing me time to speak with you, my lady."

"Did she have a choice?" Victoria snapped.

Her daughter went slack-jawed and she took her mother gently by the arm. "Mother," she said gently.

A silent look passed between mother and daughter, an intimate exchange where words were unnecessary. Even with his experience, Nathaniel was incapable of deciphering the language therein.

Victoria gave a slight, imperceptible nod and reluctantly took a step away from her daughter.

Assessing the cheerful space, Nathaniel motioned to the chairs. "If you'll excuse us while we speak," he said for Victoria and her son-in-law. Reaching inside his jacket, he placed his spectacles on and then gathered his folder. "I expect this should not take more than an hour of your time, my lady." He registered the tension that fell like a thick, London fog across the room.

Victoria and her son-in-law spoke in unison. "I'm not leaving."

Of course they didn't have any intention of doing so. Polite Society feared the marquess but Nathaniel flicked his attention dismissively over the sinister lord. Instead, he fixed on the five-foot five-inch figure of wounded volatile energy at his side. Even with her diminutive size, he honed in on Victoria as the more danger- ous of that pair. Carefully weighing his words, he spoke directly to her. "Certain procedures must be followed during questioning—"

"I don't give a damn about your procedures, Nathaniel. I am not leaving!" Victoria's explosion sucked the energy from the room as with that intimate use of his name, a familiarity between them was cemented... and her astute-eyed son-in-law and daughter, who missed nothing, saw that connection.

"Mother," the marchioness tried again, taking her arm.

"I am not leaving, Phoebe." She held firm this time. "Any ques- tions Lord Exeter intends to ask, he can put to you before Edmund and me."

Her daughter made to speak, but Nathaniel held up a hand. "It is fine," he said quietly. "They can remain." It was an allowance he'd never made to any interviewee before and one he only granted because of his connection to the spirited widow. Unnerved by his lack of self-control, he made a show of gathering the Barrett folder, which contained his questions.

"Please, won't you sit," the young woman murmured, making the first overture of pleasantries as she claimed a spot on the white upholstered sofa. Victoria swept past him, yanking her skirts out of the way to avoid brushing him and joined her daughter. The marchioness gave her mother a faintly chiding look. "Would you care for tea, my lord?" she offered when he'd taken the seat oppo- site her.

"No refreshments are necessary." From the corner of his eye, he detected the marquess sliding into position across the room; his slow, measured steps, a faint limp... and a threat of death in his eyes.

For the ruthless blackguard written of in the gossip pages, one would have to be lackwit to fail and note the gentleman's devotion to his wife. He loved Victoria's daughter. That much was clear in the glint frosting his merciless eyes. He'd the same steely grit to end any who would hurt her that Nathaniel himself had always carried for Victoria.

Only the younger man hadn't floundered his opportunities at love and life the way Nathaniel had.

"As I said," Nathaniel went on, opening his folder. "This should not take—"

"You have forty-five minutes," the marquess spoke in lethal tones. "And not a moment more."

He paused mid-speak and assessed the man who'd set himself up as adversary. The key to supremacy over one's opponent was to establish dominance of wit, before all else. From that, control of the exchange was born. He inclined his head, lingering his gaze on the marquess' right leg. A nobleman without any history in the military invariably only earned those wounds one way. "An old injury, I take it?" he asked conversationally.

Lord Rutland jerked erect.

"A duel over a lady?" he ventured with icy cool precision.

A dull flush marred Lord Rutland's cheeks.

"Get on with your questions," the marquess growled, a muscle ticking an incessant rhythm in the corner of his eye.

Returning to the matter that brought him here, he redirected his attention to the marchioness and the widow beside her. He set down questions already long memorized on the top of the folio. "I was wondering if you could tell me of your relationship with your father?" he began gently, in the calming voice used to ferret out the secrets of the unsuspecting.

Victoria slid her fingers into her daughter's and gave them a slight, supportive squeeze. But then he made the mistake of looking away from his subject and over to her. Grief so potent and palpable poured from her delicate frame, it robbed him of breath. She stared unblinkingly down at the marchioness' hand.

"I didn't have one," Lady Rutland said quietly, her statement devoid of emotion. She spoke as someone who'd come to peace with the existence she'd lived. "None that I can speak of. I was one and twenty before he first really noted my existence."

Nathaniel hesitated, his pencil at the top of the page. He glanced over the wire rims of his spectacles.

The young woman went on almost conversationally. "My father had little use for me outside of the match I might make to save him from financial ruin."

He scratched a note inside his book and looked up. "Did you resent him for being absent from your life?" he asked. It was a question that could have easily been directed to either Barrett woman.

The marchioness distractedly plucked at the fabric of her gown. "As a child, I did," she readily confessed. "As a girl, I wanted to know why he could not love me more, why he could not be like some of the fathers I'd seen in the park while with my mother who would be picking flowers with their daughters or fishing. Or simply being together."

What had begun as a line of questioning meant to probe Andrew Barrett's connection to a murder, shifted. For the first time since Macleod had turned over the file, Nathaniel viewed it not as a way of garnering facts for a case... but rather a glimpse into Victoria's life after all these years. God help him. He'd never considered himself a coward... until now. Now, he struggled to bring forth the inquiry that would reveal just what life had been like for Victoria and her children.

He concentrated on breathing. *Focus on the damned facts. Focus on the details that will lead you to answers about Waters' innocence or guilt... who Victoria had been and how she'd lived with her children in your absence is none of your affair. You lost all right to her...*

Except...

This woman had painted a tableau of Victoria as a young mother, not soon after he'd left her life for good, and how they'd spent their days. Nathaniel discreetly rubbed at the sharp ache in his chest... to no avail. "And as a young woman?" he forced himself to resume his line of questioning.

The marchioness quirked her lips in a wry smile. "As a young woman, I was grateful that I'd been invisible to him. I came to appreciate that he was vile, hurtful, and cruel..." She paused, and glanced to her mother. "...to all.

Nathaniel's fingers curled reflexively around his pencil and, this time, he forced his grip open to keep from snapping the thin wood. Had the late viscount physically laid hands upon her and her children? His heart knocked hard against his ribcage as that question screamed around his mind. In a bid to regain control, he frantically dashed a series of random, unrelated details upon his page.

"Is that all?" Rutland called over in a menacing whisper that would have sent a younger man into fits of terror.

Ignoring that impatient demand, Nathaniel directed another question at Lady Rutland. "What of the Duchess of Huntly? Did your father have a similar relationship with your sister?"

Lady Rutland shook her head. "I'd not tolerate someone speaking for me. As such, I'll not speak for my sister."

Admiration swirled in his breast for the proud and clever woman that Victoria's daughter had become. From her spirit to the rich hue of her auburn tresses, Lady Rutland was very much Victoria's child. He made to close his book, but hesitated, lingering his focus on the gold flecks in the marchioness' eyes. His frown deepened. There was something so very familiar in that stare: a touch of steel and strength and—

"My lord?" Victoria urged.

"I am nearly done." As he spoke, he carefully scrutinized Lady Rutland. Deliberately erasing the earlier gentleness in his voice, he spoke in clipped, perfunctory tones meant to unnerve. "What of your brother? What was his relationship with the late viscount?"

To the lady's credit, she merely lifted one shoulder in a negligent shrug. "As a child, my mother kept me, Andrew, and Justina close. My father had as little use for a male child as he did for a female. That did not change when Andrew grew older."

While the marchioness provided her accounting, Nathaniel's mind tripped upon an old memory.

Burrowed against his side, Victoria tilted her head back to meet his gaze. "Do you suppose we shall have troublesome, intelligent, and daring boys like their father?"

"I want only daughters… brave, bold, and clever daughters like their mother…"

From the corner of his eye, he looked to Victoria. Why had she bound herself to such a man? Had she and Waters ever loved one another? Or had loneliness compelled her into Waters' arms? That hated vision he'd not allowed himself… one he'd wrestled back countless times during his life, slipped in: Victoria spread wide, arms lifted, as she gave herself to another. Bile burned in his throat and he compelled her with his eyes to explain... needing to understand. *Why? Why, did you wed him, Victoria?*

She lifted her chin in silent mutiny, even as a flash of pain flickered in her eyes.

His heart cracked, broke, and bled all over again. And with his inability to set the past aside and focus solely on his investigation, he proved himself far less than the masterful agent he'd lauded himself to be.

Lady Rutland spoke, dragging his attention away. "Lord Exeter." The marchioness ceased her distracted movements. "My father normalized shameful behaviors." Ice crept into her voice, killing her earlier casualness and. As she spoke, she let him inside Victoria's life after Nathaniel. Each word struck like one of Hunter's lashes to his bare back. "His drinking and whoring and wagering crippled our family's finances and brought struggle to each of us."

The pencil snapped in Nathaniel's fingers and he stared vacantly down at the notes he'd made on his sheet, unseeing. *This is the man Victoria had wed.* Unbidden, he looked over to her. A thousand and one questions sprung to his tongue, begging to be spoken.

She stared past him, to a point beyond his shoulder. He would have traded however remaining years he had on his life to take her in his arms and drive back the suffering he saw there.

"Forgive me," he said quietly. For so much. For everything. Tossing the remaining half of the pencil in his fingers down on the tabletop, he withdrew another. "You were speaking of..." Victoria's husband. "...your father and his vices."

"We may have each resented my father for different reasons." The marchioness lowered her voice. "Hated him even. But *many* people hated my father and, no doubt, wished him ill." In short, there could be any number of enemies to have exacted revenge upon the reprobate. "I doubt there is a single soul who would mourn him." A buzzing filled his ears, muffling each admission she made.

"No one will miss you or mourn you... no one cares... not even the agents you protect. So, give us the information we want. Give us their names..."

Nathaniel battled back the mocking taunts hurled at him by his captors. *Do not let them in. Focus on the case. Focus on Victoria and her daughter and her accounting...*

"Beyond that, there's nothing more I can share about my father because, simply put, I didn't know him." Lady Rutland spoke with an air of finality; of one who'd said all she would about the painful life she and her family had known, and intended to say not a word more. But only one sought to inherit...

That reminder he would have given to any other person being interviewed. In this, with Victoria sitting silently on unable to meet his eyes, while her daughter and son-in-law stared on, Nathaniel couldn't bring himself to state that reminder.

Removing his spectacles, Nathaniel tucked them back inside his jacket. "I believe that is all I require, at this time," he said quietly, tucking the papers back in his folder. He gathered the broken pieces of pencil and stuffed them inside his jacket. "Thank you for taking time to speak with me," he said, as he came to his feet.

Lady Rutland smiled sadly. "Dante wrote of there being seven deadly sins. And my father possessed them all. As such, any man or woman capable of that immorality can only have one fate awaiting them... as my father did."

The floorboards groaned under the ungainly footfall of her husband and, without a trace of the hospitality or warmth demonstrated by his wife, he yanked the door open.

And with his records in hand, Nathaniel left, with information that threatened to shatter him, all over again.

CHAPTER 8

Arrive neither late nor early for a scheduled
appointment or meeting—but always on time.
Article VIII: The Brethren of the Lords

THE RULES THAT GOVERNED POLITE Society were altogether different than the ones that guided the Brethren of the Lords. Where coy lords and ladies arrived late to functions as some manner of statement, Nathaniel and the men and women who served under him adhered to lessons on punctuality.

Arriving earlier or later than the scheduled time had opened many to unnecessary risks and dangers, and seen too many of them suffer the consequences for those missteps. As such, Nathaniel was never late.

Or he never had been.

Until today. Following his meeting with Victoria's daughter, he had poured over the notes and file until his eyes ached and the moon hung high in the evening sky. Through his efforts, he'd searched for some sign: evidence that Victoria's son could be exonerated as she'd said, from nothing more than the details previously gathered on the case and the lone interview conducted with the gentleman's sister.

It was, of course, a foolhardy hope that came from nothing more than the need to spare her any further suffering. He stared blankly at the gold velvet curtains drawn in his carriage. Thinking on the assignment he'd undertaken had been vastly easier than thinking about the details her daughter had shared.

"His drinking and whoring and wagering crippled our family's finances and brought struggle to each of us…"

Nathaniel dug his fingertips hard into his temples, wanting to drive back the memory of that damned confession. Wanting to recreate an altogether different narrative for Victoria's life. But there could be no erasing the darkness or replacing it with make-believe. Just as he'd endured hell in Bristol, she had suffered, too.

"I doubt there is a single soul who would mourn him…"

The marchioness' somber admission blended and blurred with the jeering one of his captors. It had been the greatest power they'd leveraged over him; the one taunt that had nearly broken him—the fear that no one cared… not even Victoria. He'd fought past those demons, surviving, for her. To see her again.

In the end, she'd not waited. Instead, she'd suffered a hell of her own.

"My lord?" His driver rapped hesitantly, bringing Nathaniel snapping back to the moment.

His mind still in tumult, he let himself out.

"Crush of guests, my lord," Wayne made his apologies. "Couldn't bring you any closer."

"This will do," he assured. He'd promised Markham to make an appearance for the sole sake of seeing Georgina and then he'd be off. He'd little desire or interest in rubbing shoulders with the peerage. He never had. "If you'll remain here," he smoothed his palms over his lapels. "I'll not be long."

"Of course, my lord."

As he started across the street, Nathaniel managed his first real grin since he'd been handed the file with Victoria and her family's names inside. New to his employ, the graying driver couldn't know that there'd once been a time when Nathaniel had raced miles through unfamiliar and dangerous lands in the West Indies and Americas, hunting down traitors to the Crown. Walking a short distance was only welcome; a time to focus his thoughts and clear his head. He made his way across the street.

Hurrying up the steps of Lord and Lady Markham's well-lit Grosvenor Square residence, Nathaniel sailed through the door held open. From within the recesses of the townhouse, the muffled din of a crowd and orchestra reached him.

"Nathaniel!"

As he turned over his wool cloak to a dutiful footman, he looked to the woman racing down the corridor. Her brown tresses were beginning to show hints of gray and her figure was slightly more round than their last meeting eight years ago. Lady Georgina Markham still wore the inherent kindness that had driven her to set him free more than twenty years ago. "My lady," he greeted, automatically dropping a bow.

Georgina snorted and gave his arm a firm swat. "Bowing and 'my ladying' me, Nathaniel? Should I now, after all these years, expect a discourse on the weather?"

"It has been unseasonably warm—*oomph.*" She settled a firm elbow into his side, earning a small laugh.

"With nothing more than letters all these years and you think to tease," she muttered. The twinkle in her brown eyes, however, softened any hint of reproach. "Come," she urged, looping her arm through his. "We've much to speak on."

"I daresay that during a ball you're hosting is not the ideal time to do so," he said, as she led him down a wide corridor.

"Well, how is one to trust that, if I let you leave now, you won't simply disappear for another eight years, only sending the occasional letter to Adam and me as proof that you still live?" she asked dryly.

"I deserve that," he conceded. They'd been the only true friends he'd kept close; their bond cemented long ago by the torture they'd all endured at Fox and Hunter's merciless hands. Yet, just like Victoria, he'd left them in the past. It was easier: the coward's way to bury the demons of his darkest days. "However, I'm not avoiding either of you." He felt compelled to add that lie. He had been running from the memory of Victoria Cadence Tremaine. His gut clenched. Nay, not Tremaine… Barrett. She was Barrett now. She'd belonged in name and body to the late Viscount Waters, whose murder Nathaniel had taken himself to investigating. "I've been otherwise occupied with my—"

"Your work for the Crown," she neatly supplied, casting a sideways glance up at him.

There was that familiar touch of impatience, coupled with annoyance in the way she spoke of his role within the Brethren.

"And what should I be doing?" he drawled, striving for nonchalance. As soon as the question left him, however, he silently cursed, wanting to call it back for the dangerous door he'd cracked open.

"Oh," she said, casting him another sideways glance. "Dangling grandbabes on your knee, traveling with a wife. Should I continue?"

His smile stuck on his face; strained and painful. The agony of what she suggested gutted him all the more, now that he'd been forced to confront in Victoria and her family all he'd lost.

The revelries of the ballroom grew increasingly louder. But instead of continuing on to the festivities, Georgina brought them to a stop beside a heavy, oak door. Entering ahead of her, he stepped inside the brightly lit parlor.

She closed the door and folded her arms at her chest. "Well?" she demanded.

He tugged at his cravat. The last thing he cared for was further probing into his solitary existence. "Don't you—?"

"Have a ball to attend? My sons are involved in a game of whist and my daughters have a full dance card. I hardly think my presence will be missed."

"Your husband?" he ventured, hopefully.

Georgina smiled, revealing her slightly crooked teeth. "He, however, will note my absence. Nor does it escape *my* notice that you're seeking to distract me." Her grin fell. "Nathaniel," she said gently. "You are late." Of course such a detail would not have escaped a woman who'd devoted several years of her life to the Brethren.

He briefly lingered his stare on the floral curtains and chintz fabric of the sofas. How very different this room and this home were from the first place he'd met Georgina Markham—then Wilcox. His prison had been sparse with nothing more than a wood chair that he'd been bound to and a torn coverlet to sleep upon—when he was not tied like an animal. His hands shook and he flexed his fingers, willing them to cease trembling. Georgina rested a hand on his sleeve and he jumped. "I was seeing to the details of a case."

She motioned for him to sit.

He hesitated, proving himself ten times a coward. For he didn't want her damned questions.

Georgina narrowed her eyes. "Nathaniel," she warned.

Sighing, he claimed the nearest chair. He'd been summoned for a reason. He was grateful for her and Adam's friendship, but still wholly unnerved by her probing. *Because every time she does, she's unerringly close to the mark. You wanted more than the Brethren...* and somehow, Georgina Markham had come to see that over the years.

"You are the Sovereign," she began, as she settled into the gilded King Louis XIV chair opposite him. "*You* don't take over investigations."

"No," he conceded. That had been the way for decades and decades, and it had been one of the fundamental rules of the order he'd left intact. As Sovereign, he oversaw the organization, ensuring that it operated smoothly. He could not divide his time between a case and those other responsibilities. *Yet, you did just that for the Waters case.*

"Not only did you take on the investigation," Georgina folded her arms. "But you did so with one that had previously been assigned to another."

"How did you...?" At her arched eyebrow, he silently cursed.

A slight twinkle lit her eyes. "And you certainly don't get tripped up."

Nathaniel froze. Bloody hell, Victoria's reemergence in his life had thrown his orderly existence into an upheaval. Yet, it was as Georgina pointed out. It was solely him who'd allowed himself to be affected. "How did you know as much?" he asked gruffly. Or had Markham guessed?

A beleaguered sigh escaped her. "Nathaniel, I'm a former agent. I understand how the organization functions. The Delegator hand-selected that case and it would have, of course, gone to someone." She waggled her eyebrows. "Just not, *you.*"

He carefully measured his words. "This case was... is different."

Georgina placed her palms upon her knees, rustling the satin, as she leaned forward. "I know that, Nathaniel," she whispered. "Hence the reason for my questioning. You've placed yourself at risk, through your investigation..." She paused, giving him a meaningful look. "And you've also risked that investigation with prior knowledge."

His neck burned hot with shame.

"I know that," he gritted out. To visit the seedy ends of London and interview ruthless killers put a proverbial mark on his back. And with one unfortunate accident, his death would leave the

Brethren leaderless.

There would be another to slip into your role…

He froze, as that gut-punch of his own fallibility hit him. He'd made the Brethren his everything. And yet, when he died or retired… another would just… step in.

"Despite possibly compromising your life and the case," she said gently, guiding his attention back, "you still took it on? When you've always respected the guiding principles and rules of the organization."

"I knew *her*," the admission burst from him, echoing around the room. "I knew Waters' widow," he clarified in more modulated tones. A lifetime ago.

Georgina settled back in her chair, her lips parted. "Well," she said weakly.

So, she'd not been expecting that. Restless, Nathaniel jumped up and began to pace. "She was…" He grimaced. How to explain just what Victoria had meant to him?

"She was?" Georgina prodded.

He set his teeth so hard, pain shot up his jaw. "Were you always this damned tenacious?"

A husky laugh left her as she rested her palms on the arms of her chair. "You know the answer to that."

He did. She'd defied her father, Fox, and set Nathaniel free… and then had gathered valuable secrets from that bastard and turned them over to the Brethren. Nathaniel abruptly stopped. With his back to her, he stared emptily at the floral painting in her own hand and marked with her initials in the corner that hung above the hearth. He'd never shared anything about Victoria; not her name, not her existence. He had, instead, silently suffered the loss of her. But now, with Georgina's gentle prodding, he wanted to reveal all. Wanted to share all that he'd lost and have someone make sense of what happened from here.

Nothing. Nothing could happen from here.

Because even if he wished life had moved altogether differently for them, he was being tasked with investigating her son. Then there were also his responsibilities as Sovereign… which he'd already compromised the moment he took on the Waters assignment. He scrubbed a tired hand over his face. "I knew her before I was assigned the Fox and Hunter mission," he said, reluctantly turning back.

Georgina's face leeched of color. The lady's husband had not revealed that secret, then. She sat slowly forward, abandoning her negligent repose. "You… *knew* her?" she asked haltingly.

"We… met by chance." One of the first rules laid out and learned by a member was to never form a connection to someone. That one's devotion belonged to the Brethren. A wistful smile pulled at his lips. "I was assigned to follow a nobleman suspected of treason. She entered the alcove where I'd been hiding." *Only rakes, rogues, and scoundrels hide in alcoves. Well? Which one are you?* He chuckled. "I took a while to announce my presence." Specifically, after she'd doffed her slippers and hiked her skirts up to rub her sore feet. "And she hit me over the head with a slipper for my insolence."

Georgina's lips twitched. "The lady sounds… spirited."

It had been an anomaly he couldn't make sense of. All the ladies who'd attended balls, soirees, and dinner parties by his parents, and then brother, had been meek misses.

By God, where is he? I will take down every bloody door until he meets me…

"She is still spirited," he murmured, to himself. He stared at a point just past Georgina. "We fell in love." He spoke quickly, methodically, eager to have the telling done, so he might purge himself of the memories. "I thought I could have both her and my role." Even when he'd been schooled otherwise by those who'd trained him. "I promised I'd return and we'd marry but—" He stopped himself from completing that, not wanting to bring any more hurt to the friend who'd freed him.

Georgina stood in a soft whir of rustling satin. "Because of my father," she ventured.

He forced himself to nod.

Tears flooded her eyes and she pressed a palm against her mouth. "Oh, Nathaniel."

He waved off the apology there. "Do not do that. It is not your fault. It never was." She'd always taken responsibility and ownership for her late father's crimes. She'd devoted herself to the Brethren, freed Nathaniel and Adam, then nearly lost her life to Fox and Hunter… and she'd still make apologies. He was humbled by the strength of her character. It simply recalled his own pettiness in being unable to move beyond Victoria's marrying the viscount. "Regardless, she is the reason I've taken the case. She married in my absence and her son has been accused of murder."

Georgina let loose a long sigh.

"Precisely," he muttered. "Given my connection to the lady, I could not turn the investigation over to anyone else."

"Of course not." Just that, three words simply spoken, that indicated she both understood and did not judge him. Judge him, when any other member of the Brethren, past or present, would have done just that. As such, she deserved the truth.

"She is more than a case," he conceded on a ragged whisper, shame needling at his gut. "If her son is found guilty, it will shatter her. I wanted access to the interviews and details..." Before anyone.

Georgina ran her gaze over his face, searchingly. "You are human, Nathaniel. There is no shame in that."

"There is only shame in it," he said hoarsely.

She covered his hand with her own. "You have always been most difficult on yourself," she said simply. And in that pronouncement, there was an absolution of sorts.

He drew air slowly into his lungs, letting it fill him. How freeing it was to have friends with whom to share these burdens. It made those short months he'd had with Victoria real when, with the passage of time, they'd taken on a surrealism; moments so removed from his life now, that he must have surely just imagined them.

Georgina motioned him back over to his seat. "Is he guilty?" she asked, tentatively.

"I do not know," he confessed. "Bow Street and the constables were unable to resolve the case."

His friend snorted. "And yet, the King should care so very much about a bounder like the viscount that he'd tie up the Brethren's time."

We may have each resented my father for different reasons... hated him even. But many people hated my father and, no doubt, wished him ill...

Georgina's accurate statement and everything Nathaniel had gleaned about the viscount, gave him pause... and then his mind raced. Surely there was more to Waters' connection? Something to merit the mission being tossed into the lap of the Brethren.

"What does your instinct tell you?" Georgina put to him.

"My instincts have been wrong before," he hedged. He'd made

a faulty misstep in seeking out Hunter for a meeting and the end result had been his capture.

Georgina leaned over and tapped him on the arm. "But they've also been right more times than they've been wrong. You wouldn't have become the Sovereign, otherwise."

He shifted, unnerved by that praise. "Very well. At this point, my instincts tell me anyone might have murdered the viscount. He was in debt, he drank, he wagered, and took doxies as lovers in the streets of the Dials." But again, the one who stood most to profit, at this point, had singularly proven to be his heir, the newly minted Viscount Waters. Nathaniel let his shoulders sag. "And I also want him to be innocent." *For her.* It was a damning admission to make, particularly on the heels of having revealed his closeness to the subject of the investigation.

"He might be," Georgina quietly reminded him. "What then?"

What then? His mind stalled. Having returned and learned Victoria was now a widow, he'd still not allowed himself the thought of anything more with her. Having been personally responsible for bringing countless villains to justice, there would always be a risk of her paying the price for their association. "There's a lifetime of obstacles that couldn't be overcome," he settled for, the pronouncement grounded in truth. He winced. "She quite thoroughly detests me. I disappeared—"

"Captured. You were captured," she corrected.

"And there is the matter of my role in her son's investigation."

Georgina made a sound of protest and again leaned toward him. "Nathaniel, my father imprisoned my husband and attempted to have him killed." Her eyes went soft. "And despite that, he loves me anyway."

He dragged a hand through his hair. "It is not the same, Georgina." Over two decades had come and gone. So much damned time lost. "We're different people now. Strangers."

Georgina moved swiftly over and gathered his hands in hers. "If she is a woman who could resent you for being held captive, then she's undeserving of you." She gave his palms a light squeeze. "As she is the only woman you've ever loved, however, I entirely trust that she will forgive you." She held his gaze squarely. "Anything can be overcome. Adam and I are proof of that. As such, the only obstacle between you—is still the Brethren—if you let it be an impediment."

The sound of footsteps in the hall and the door handle being pressed saved him from having to say anything further.

Adam entered. "I see I've been abandoned to the mercy of the *ton*," he drawled. He closed the door.

"Oh, hush," Georgina scolded, coming to her feet. "It was your idea to host an event this Season." She softened that admonishment with a wink.

When Nathaniel had first met the other man, Lord Adam Markham had been a volatile, jealous man so blinded by his time in captivity that he'd doubted his wife.

Adam came forward with an easy grin in place and his hand outstretched. "With the amount of time my wife's been missing, I trust she has put you through a lengthy interrogation."

Lifting his head, Nathaniel grinned. "Enough of one that I'd offer her a position if I wasn't completely certain she wouldn't say no."

His friend gathered his wife's fingers and lifted them to his mouth for a drawn-out kiss. "I'm hopeful that my wife is quite content precisely where she is and that she'll decline that offer."

"Blissfully content," she murmured. As though recalling Nathaniel's presence, she glanced over to him. "I was glad for the day Adam and I both put aside our work for that organization. We made a life for ourselves, and devoted ourselves to our children."

And while members of the Brethren had regarded their retirement with shock and confusion, Nathaniel, who'd once craved the special gift the couple had known, understood... and supported that decision.

Now, he studied the handsome couple before him. The pair looked at one another. It was a tender moment that he glanced away from, an interloper in that closeness. It was a testament to the trust and love that had grown between the couple that Adam didn't display the suspicion he'd once had where Georgina was concerned.

Surely love, if strong enough, was enough to conquer the greatest of divides...

"I will leave you both to your festivities," Nathaniel said, coughing into his fist. "I have an early morning." Having already gathered answers to his questions from Lady Rutland, now came surveilling the lady's movements and monitoring her exchanges.

"You're certain you don't care to remain and—?"

"Quite certain," he interrupted Georgina's offer. Nathaniel quietly let himself out of the room, leaving husband and wife alone. His leather soles fell silent along the hardwood floors of the Grosvenor Square mansion.

"Nathaniel?"

He turned back.

Georgina sprinted down the hall and stopped breathless before him. "It is all right to be human," she said, a gravity in her brown eyes. "The Brethren disabuse the men and women who do their work of the idea that there is a life outside the organization." She caught his shoulder, lightly squeezing. "But there *is* a life, Nathaniel, and it is a very good one."

Uneasy by the power of emotion in her gaze, he nodded awkwardly. "Thank you."

She snorted. "You aren't truly hearing me, Nathaniel. You see that you've been made Sovereign and think the men and women whom you feel responsible for matter most. But you matter just as much."

A short while later, seated once more inside his carriage with Georgina's words ringing in his head, Nathaniel stared out at the passing London streets.

How easily she had spoken of a possible new beginning with Victoria. Hers was an optimism born of the love she'd shared for these many years with her husband.

While his friends had lost the jaded edge that kept one prepared in an uncertain world, Nathaniel had only grown more hardened. He knew the gifts of love and forgiveness and new beginnings were reserved for some fortunate souls… he, however, had never been one of those lucky ones. All he'd lost at Fox and Hunter's hands and Victoria's subsequent marriage to another was proof of that. And he'd since dedicated himself to seeing that no person lost the way he himself did.

What Georgina suggested… what she spoke of… him walking away from his responsibilities—the men and women who looked to him, those he kept from the same rotten fate he'd suffered— how did he just turn his back on that? Who was he then? What did he have?

He'd do well to focus his efforts where they belonged—on the Waters case and not on some wistful fancy fed by Georgina this night.

CHAPTER 9

*When investigating a suspect, observe them in their every setting:
who they call friends and where they spend their days and nights.
Article IX: The Brethren of the Lords*

VICTORIA HAD LEARNED LONG AGO to be suspicious of other
people's plotting. As a young woman, her late parents had been
singularly focused on wedding her off to the most prestigious peer.
Her husband had, by his very nature, been a schemer.

She, however, had never thought she would face such scheming
from her daughters—the pair of them stood in the doorway of
the morning parlor with innocent expressions belied by matching
glints of determination in their eyes.

Pulling her needle through the embroidery frame in her fingers,
she completed her stitch. "To what do I owe the pleasure of this
early visit?" she asked dryly, going through the rote movements:
pierce, pull, repeat. Pierce, pull, repeat. That monotonous movement as staid as the existence she'd lived.

"Is it early?" Justina ventured innocently.

Not lifting her gaze from the peony taking shape, Victoria
snorted. She glanced up as her daughters joined her at the center of
the room, just in time to note the meaningful glances exchanged.
Narrowing her eyes, Victoria set her work down upon her lap.
The key to wheedling information from a person was to unsettle
them. "What?" she asked bluntly. Always keep them unsettled. She

curled her fingers reflexively. Damn Nathaniel. With the lessons he'd shared long ago, he retained a hold over her thoughts even now. She bit the inside of her cheek, suddenly grateful for the distraction her daughters presented.

Phoebe beamed. "It has been two months—"

"Two months and four days," she said quietly. A woman tended to remember the day her shackles were cut free... and her world fell apart, all at the same time.

Her youngest child gathered her fingers. Did Justina take her as brokenhearted in some way? If so, Victoria had proven a greater actress these years than she'd ever credited herself with. "It has been two months and four days since you've gone out," Justina murmured.

Warning bells instantly clamored in her mind. "No." She swiftly drew her hand back and collected her embroidery frame.

"I didn't say anything yet," Justina protested.

"You didn't need to," Victoria directed her explanation at the scrap of white fabric stretched upon the wooden frame. "I'm not going anywhere. I'm a widow," she said simply. And having prayed the whole of her marriage for the early demise of her then husband, God was surely punishing her for those wicked thoughts with the hell that had come with Chester's murder. "Widows are not expected to attend *ton* functions." Not the proper ones and certainly not so soon after the violent murder of one's spouse. Except for the fortunate few like her daughters, matrimony proved very much a prison to most.

What would her life have been like had she found herself wedded to Nathaniel? The needlepoint sliced through the soft flesh of her thumb. Victoria gasped. The frame tumbled to her lap and bounced to the floor with a quiet *thwack!* She popped the wounded digit in her mouth.

"Mother, you've always done what is expected of you," Phoebe went on in somber tones. As if to punctuate that point, she rescued the embroidery frame and held it up.

Pursing her lips, Victoria, in an un-viscountess-like move, plucked it from Phoebe's fingers. "I enjoy needlepoint," she said defensively. *It is a lie. You only took it up when you were pregnant with Phoebe because you needed a diversion to keep from descending into madness.* "What?" she demanded when her daughters exchanged knowing looks. When had they grown up?

"Being shut away here with An…" *Andrew.* Phoebe sighed. "It is not healthy for you to remain here with only thoughts of… of what happened." *The murder.* The word Phoebe couldn't bring herself to speak was murder.

"We want you to accompany us," Justina pressed.

"There is a Captain Cook Exhibit."

At Phoebe's quiet utterance, Victoria started. "Captain Cook," she whispered, letting her quavering hand fall back to her lap.

"The Royal Museum has on display Captain Cook's maps, recordings, and sketches of the Sandwich Islands and the Australian coastline."

While her eldest daughter spoke, her voice growing distant to Victoria's ears, memories came rushing forward.

"Wanting to travel like Captain Cook, love?" Nathaniel's breath stirred the sensitive flesh at her nape, eliciting a giggle. "I fear in introducing you to his works, I've created a world traveler who'll throw me over for her exploration…"

"Oh, hush, Nathaniel… you know I'll only travel with you at my side…"

Her throat constricted. That dream had been one they two had shared. When Nathaniel had ceased to live on as anything more than a memory, she'd taken care to pass all the stories of the great explorer on to their child.

"Mother?"

"I'm not going to the museum," she rasped, jumping to her feet. She didn't want to go and be confronted with more memories of Nathaniel and all they'd shared. A man who'd valued her mind and encouraged her spirit and dream of traveling when no one ever had; not her father, late brother, or husband. And it recalled all over again just why she'd fallen in love with him, and how broken he'd left her. Her heart raced, pounding loudly in her ears, as her gaze went to the doorway.

Escape. It called, potent and overwhelming.

Phoebe settled her hands on Victoria's shoulders, lightly squeezing. "Oh, Mother. Captain Cook is ours. He always was. You always enjoyed our trips to explore his exhibits."

But before Captain Cook had belonged to mother and daughter, he'd been shared by two young lovers. "I can't," she implored, making the safest appeal. "Our family is under Society's scrutiny. What would the gossip be if I'm seen on a jaunt?"

"I'd hardly consider it a jaunt to visit a museum," Justina added. "Why, it is not as though you're attending the theatre or a ball or dinner party."

Victoria felt herself weakening.

"It is early," Phoebe reminded.

"Most of the *ton* will not arise for another handful of hours."

Victoria covered her eyes with her palm. They'd not relent. If she didn't accompany them now, they'd continue to visit each day until she ventured out into the world. "An hour," she said reluctantly. "No more than an hour."

With the same zeal they'd shown as small girls, Phoebe and Justina grinned.

As such, nearly thirty minutes later, Victoria found herself walking through the silent and very empty museum. And despite her earlier horror, trailing at a small distance behind her daughters with the soft tread of her black leather boots against the floor echoing around the cavernous space, there was a calming peace that came in being here.

The darkened interior and soaring Doric columns had always had that effect. It had been a place where she could steal off and explore a world opened to her by Nathaniel… and then there had been the times he'd return from a mission, find her here, and—her cheeks flamed.

You are a shameful creature, Victoria Cadence… hopelessly, pathetically weak where Nathaniel Archer is concerned.

Only—she stopped alongside a glass display case, running her fingertips absently over the smooth, cool glass—for all her anger, hurt, and outrage at his sudden reappearance and his role in investigating Andrew, she'd spent more years loving him than hating him. She'd mourned him in ways she hadn't her own husband.

She—

Her gaze collided with the portrait beneath her fingertips. A familiar one, she'd previously only viewed as a replica within the pages of a cherished gift Nathaniel had given her.

She pressed her palms against the case, leaning closer, transfixed. As a young woman, she'd been fascinated by the exotic figure, his body contorted in the throes of a tribal dance. Now, she stared, riveted by the landscape captured there… those peculiar trees while the moon glistened upon the foreign waters.

I'd wanted to see the world. I'd wanted to journey with Nathaniel at my side.

But life had taken her upon an altogether different path; a solitary one where she was a wife, woman, and mother, devoid of a partner on that journey. How fast time had passed her by. And with it, the dreams she'd carried of distant travels would forever remain the grand illusions carried by an optimistic, young girl.

She glanced up, finding Phoebe and Justina at the opposite end of the museum, engrossed in a discussion at another portion of the Cook exhibit. Whereas her daughters, with their husbands at their sides, had already spread their wings and flown more than Victoria ever had or would. In Phoebe's case, she'd traveled abroad to the places Victoria had long dreamed of. Justina had established one of the most respected salons in London.

And who am I outside of my children?

Oh, they were her greatest gifts and filled her heart with more love than she'd believed possible. But who was she now that they'd gone? She looked to the crudely beautiful drawing. She'd told herself she'd been wholly content with her existence. She'd had her children and needed nothing more.

But then Nathaniel had reentered her life. Slipped back in as quickly as he'd slipped out, reminding her of the dreams she'd had—ones they'd shared together.

A whisper of longing to know more beyond this world gripped her in its dangerously powerful hold. Victoria studied that distant place captured… and froze. Her heart knocked hard against her ribcage as she settled her stare on the figure reflected in the crystal case. Tall, angular features marked with scars, his frame heavily muscled; there was no other lord in all of London such as him.

I've merely conjured him…

"Hello, Victoria."

Except conjurings didn't speak.

Victoria bit the inside of her cheek. "Are you following my daughters and me now as part of your investigation?" she asked in hushed tones by way of greeting.

And by his silence, she had her answer.

"Damn you, Nathaniel," she whispered, hating herself for having wanted his answer to be different. She turned her focus back to the display, a sour taste in her mouth. It was foolish believing the spy who'd given his soul to that blasted organization would find her here for any reason other than the current mission he'd undertaken. He could never separate himself from the Brethren.

"I did come with the intention of following your daughter," he said softly, at her back.

She stiffened as his low, husky baritone drew nearer. "Did you expect she's part of some nefarious meeting to discuss my husband's murder?"

Nathaniel didn't rise to the bait she tossed out. "I didn't expect you would be here."

And why should he? If she were a proper widow, she'd be closeted away at home in a state of false mourning. "Does it matter that I am?" Victoria blinked. Where in blazes had that query come from?

"It does." Those two words, whispered close to her ear, sent delicious shivers through her and butterflies danced in her belly.

Automatically, her gaze went to where her daughters remained engrossed in the exhibit. Victoria gave thanks for their absorption. One glance across the long auditorium and there would be a sea of questions from Phoebe and Justina which she'd rather not answer. She bit her lip, warring with herself. Justina's bell-like laughter rang around the hall, making the decision for her.

Victoria slipped into the darkened antechamber. She opened and closed her eyes several times in a bid to adjust to the dimly lit space and her heart stuttered. Of all the places for her to slip off and with Nathaniel Archer here…

The large, rectangular space had been converted into a replica of the Sandwich Islands discovered by the great Captain Cook. Why, with the towering palms scattered about and a painted backdrop, replete with gleaming crystalline waters and black sand, she and Nathaniel may as well have stepped upon those islands they'd once spoken of.

She stole a glance up, in a bid to gauge Nathaniel's reaction, to see if he was in any way affected. To see if he recalled all the times after they'd made love, wrapped in one another's arms, plotting and planning to visit Cook's legendary islands.

Doffing his hat, he wandered forward, his footfalls silent. It was a feat that, given his height and muscle, was surely a product of years serving as a spy. "You remembered," he murmured, stopping beside an enormous sea tortoise; that artifact frozen upon the blackened sands. "Captain Cook," he clarified, looking over his shoulder.

"Did you think I should forget?" Every moment with this man had been etched in her mind as some of the happiest times. But that was before life intruded and, with it, fear and duty and societal obligations and pressures. She drifted over to his side. "We were to see the world." Victoria hugged herself in a lonely embrace. "And when you didn't return, I read Cook's journals and every book you ever gifted me, and then I passed that love to… my daughter." Her voice grew threadbare. *Our daughter.*

He touched his gold-flecked gaze upon her face. The heated intensity in his violet eyes cascaded over her in a physical caress.

Unsettled by her inability to conceal her emotions where he was concerned, she cleared her throat. "Do you suppose the sand is so dark?" So many times they'd ducked under the covers and read through those books with the same questions.

Nathaniel squatted. He reached past the flimsy velvet roping, meant to serve as a barrier. With his spare hand, he gathered the sand, sifting it through his fingers. "It is darker."

Forgetting the shock of his return, and the questions and hurt surrounding his betrayal, she knelt beside him. "I think not. It would be impossible for sand to be…" *It is darker.* And then his words registered. There was no guessing, no ventured opinions. He spoke in the same absolutes of one who'd ventured to that place. "You've… been?"

He nodded once.

Without her. He'd gone to those foreign lands and had all the questions they'd wondered together over answered. Melancholy tugged at her. But in concert with that sentiment was curiosity. "What of the waters?" Her hungering to know superseded the resentment she'd carried these past days, which was madness. *I should care solely about his investigation of Andrew. Why, in this, her former love may as well be her enemy.*

Nathaniel worked his haunting violet eyes over her face, the way one who sought to commit a person to memory. It robbed her of breath and held her immobile. "Magnificent." Her heart did a somersault within her breast. In this, she could almost believe he spoke of her. Which was foolishness. She was over twenty years older than the vibrant, narrow-hipped miss who'd happily given her virtue over to him. "The seas glisten and, with the black backdrop of the sand, the waves have the hues of the finest sapphires." Of course. He spoke of those glorious islands she'd never see. "I wanted to take you there. To travel to those places with you."

Her chest constricted. His admission didn't fit with a man who'd left her. Unless there were reasons for him to stay away. And yet, all this time without so much as a note? "I wanted to go with you," she said softly. She looked to him. "I wanted to board a ship as we'd talked about, and take my slippers off and feel those sands." Victoria abruptly stopped. She'd already said too much.

"What of you, Victoria?" Nathaniel beat his hat in an offbeat rhythm against his thigh. "Did you… travel in my absence? Visit any of the places we spoke of?"

"Me?" She touched a hand to her chest. A small, quiet laugh escaped her. "I wedded, gave birth, and cared for three children. There were no travels," she finished, unable to keep the laments from creeping in.

"You might still see all those places we…" She raised stricken eyes to his. "*You* longed to."

There was something so very heartbreaking in the emphasis he placed upon that lonely syllable.

What a peculiar moment. They knelt beside one another; former lovers, putting questions to one another. In this, she could almost forget what had brought him back into her life. But his investigation would always be between them—as would his absence these many years.

"I would have gone with you." And because, in this instant, her pride fled, the question she'd told herself didn't matter slipped out anyway, proving her a liar. "Why didn't you return?" she implored. "Was there another and you simply could not find the courage to tell me that?"

He whipped his gaze back to hers. "Never," he rasped. "My work was all that mattered—until you."

"Even after me, Nathaniel. Even after me."

His entire body jerked like one who'd taken a blade to the middle.

Were these spy tricks? Meant to lull information from her? Victoria shoved slowly to her feet. He leapt up and, taking her arm in a tender hold, helped her. Her late husband, in the course of their entire miserable marriage together, had never once extended that consideration. She jammed her fingertips against her temples. "Why are you doing this? Asking me these questions? Is this part of your investigation?"

"No," he said calmly, setting his hat back on his head. "I should be overseeing my case. I should be following the proper procedures—procedures I established." He palmed her cheek. "But then I saw you here."

And he, too, had remembered the shared connection over their Captain Cook. The truth hung on the air between them, as real as if he'd uttered it into the quiet of the antechamber.

Victoria captured her lower lip between her teeth, troubling the flesh.

Nathaniel's gaze fell to her mouth. Heat flared to life within his eyes, turning those unique violet hues, a shade very nearly black.

Her belly flipped over itself as a wicked hungering filled her. To again know his kiss. To know his arms about her. Only, this man, a broader, more powerful version of the youth he'd been. She closed her eyes, briefly. *You fool. Do you truly believe yourself capable of passion after all these years?* Her husband had killed any and all joy that could come with lovemaking.

A hard, callused palm cupped her cheek, bringing her eyes open. No words passed. None were necessary. They stood in a peculiar silence where time stretched on eternally and the world ceased to spin. Nathaniel stroked his thumb back and forth over her lower lip. He lowered his head slowly, giving her time to pull away.

This is the man investigating your son. The man you loved who left. And yet, there was surely an inherent weakness in her. For as he lowered his mouth, she tilted her head back to receive him. Wanting to know if she was still capable of passion… nay, needing to know if Nathaniel Archer could still stir an eddy of desire within her.

He touched his lips to hers.

Victoria stiffened. She was assaulted by the memories of the handful of sloppy, vile kisses her husband had pressed to her mouth, nearly suffocating her with the stench of garlic and brandy. Only—

The fragrant hint of coffee and the citrusy hint of oranges flooded her senses, pushing back those painful embraces she'd known, so that it was only her and Nathaniel. Desire filled her, a distant, unfamiliar sentiment that she'd come to believe herself incapable of ever again knowing.

With a faint groan, Nathaniel cupped her about the neck, angling her head to better avail himself of her mouth. As he slanted his lips over hers, his kiss rekindled a forgotten heat inside her belly. It raged to life like a primitive spark, burning her from the inside out. Victoria melted against him, twisting her fingers in the lapels of his cloak in a bid to be closer. "I have missed you," he whispered against the corner of her lips. He nipped at her lower lip. Then, he filled his hands with her buttocks, bringing her flush with the vee of his thighs. His shaft sprung hard against her lower belly. She swallowed a low, wanton moan, dropping her head back.

"Nathaniel." His name emerged as a breathy entreaty.

And the same way he'd always known how to stroke the flames within, he devoured her mouth, slipping his tongue inside and finding hers. He kissed her long and deep. His tongue branded hers, marked her as his, and reminded her of what it was to simply *feel*.

She whimpered as he shifted his lips from hers. But he merely continued his quest, pressing a trail of hot kisses from the corner of her mouth down to her neck. He lingered his attentions on the pulse that throbbed wildly.

"How I have missed you," he whispered against her skin once more.

And later, there would come the questions about why he'd gone and never returned for more than twenty years. But for now, there was just this. And this is all she wanted. To open herself to the power of her body's response to him.

"I did not know I could still feel like this," she panted.

He responded by tracing the seam of her lips with his tongue.

Moaning, Victoria's legs buckled. Nathaniel swiftly caught her and anchored her against the pillar. The feel of that solid column at her back conjured all the forbidden acts they'd shared in this very museum a lifetime ago. Tangling her fingers in his thick, silken strands, she guided his mouth back to hers.

He devoured her, mating his lips to hers.

Her heart's beating filled her ears, drowning out all sound but for the muffled blend of his breathing and hers, in a frantic concert. She had believed her husband, with his brutal couplings, had killed all hope of feeling this burn between her legs. How wrong she'd been. How blissfully, wondrously wrong.

Long, powerful fingers gently parted her cloak. The cool of the museum's air slapped at her skin and warred with the spreading conflagration inside.

Victoria bit her lower lip hard as he placed a trail of kisses along her décolletage. Her fingers curled reflexively in his hair as she studied his bent head. He darted his tongue out, tracing the tip of that expert organ over her heated skin. His breath coming hard and fast, Nathaniel freed one of her breasts from the constraints of her gown.

A shuddery hiss burst from between her clenched teeth as he gently suckled at the swollen tip. Her lashes heavy, Victoria closed her eyes. *I forgot what it was to feel… this. This splendor.* The deep ache at her core sharpened. Forcing her eyes open, she stared down at the top of Nathaniel's head, air escaping through her slightly parted lips in rapid puffs. The faintest dusting of silver flecked the errant tips of a few black strands. Those silver streaks, however, only deepened Nathaniel Archer's sophisticated handsomeness.

He moved back to reclaim her mouth.

"Mother?"

Victoria and Nathaniel wrenched apart. Through the haze of desire he'd cast, reality slowly sunk its tentacles back into her clouded mind. She slapped her hands to her burning cheeks as Phoebe's concern-laden voice carried to the antechamber.

Oh, my God. What have I done? She'd always been helpless where Nathaniel was concerned, but to forget his abandonment and his investigation?

"Here," Nathaniel whispered against her ear. He hurriedly set her gown to rights and she cursed her shaking fingers' inability to see to those tasks herself. Then, he gathered the loose strands of her hair that had fallen free, tucking them back into their proper place.

He'd always been masterful at that. More skilled than her lady's maid, she used to tease.

"I-I have to leave," she said frantically, stealing a glance at the doorway "And you shouldn't be here, just as you shouldn't—"

Phoebe called out again from somewhere within the museum. "Mother?"

"—be investigating my son," she finished. Alternating her stare briefly between Nathaniel and the exhibit at his back, she turned on her heel.

"Victoria?"

She paused, angling her head back.

"It is not too late for you to travel," he said solemnly. "To see the places you dreamed of and explore those foreign lands."

Phoebe and Justina's worried discourse drifted closer.

Victoria smiled sadly. "I am three and forty years with three grown children and three grandchildren. Those dreams I carried belonged to a girl, Nathaniel. I'm not that girl any longer." With that, she hurried from the antechamber… and promptly collided with her daughter. Victoria gasped.

"Mother!" Phoebe caught her by the shoulders, steadying her. "There you are. We've been looking for you. Justina is searching the other end of the museum for you." Her daughter's lips turned down at the corner, as she settled her focus on Victoria's disheveled coiffure. "Are you all—?"

"Fine," she said quickly. How perceptive Phoebe had always been. "I was… I was…" Her skin heated under her eldest daughter's study. "Distracted by an exhibit," she said evenly. That confession was, at the very least, built on truth.

Phoebe's frown deepened and she peered beyond Victoria's shoulder. "What was the exhibit?" She took a step forward and Victoria caught her by the shoulder.

"No," she exclaimed. "It was another one. Outside here. In another room." *Blast, be calm, Victoria.* However had Nathaniel managed this whole subterfuge business? While her daughter analyzed her the way she might one of the exhibits in this very hall, Victoria made herself go still, silently praying that her daughter would let the matter rest. If she walked inside that room and discovered the lead investigator of the viscount's death there, questions would follow. And love her children as she did, her past with Nathaniel was not one she cared to discuss with them.

Wordlessly, Phoebe held an elbow out. Linking their arms, Victoria allowed Phoebe to lead her from the room… and away from

Nathaniel.

Only this time, instead of the hatred and resentment that had dogged her these past days, she was left with something else... something even far more dangerous—questions about why a man who'd not returned for her should speak about all the places he'd longed to journey with her.

CHAPTER 10

Be it a mission or any aspect of your life,
do not allow yourself a single misstep.
Article X: The Brethren of the Lords

NATHANIEL ARCHER HAD MADE BUT one misstep in his career. It had been a careless one, only a rash man of twenty, drunk with his own self-confidence and sense of prowess, could make. And that misstep had cost him everything. As such, he'd taken care to follow the guidelines set forth by the Brethren… many rules of which he'd re-written, expecting the men and women who worked for him would follow.

And in one darkened antechamber, with Victoria a handful of steps away, he'd tossed aside every lesson, forgotten his case, and taken her in his arms.

His pulse thumped an erratic beat, just as it had since their embrace yesterday morn. When he'd overtaken the mission from Macleod, he'd done so only with one thought in mind: his past relationship with Victoria Cadence Barrett and seeing that her son's investigation was carried out with the greatest integrity and accuracy.

Not for one instant had he allowed himself to think how the mere sight of her would rekindle a deep-aching hunger to again know her—in every way.

Now, being shown through the Duke of Huntly's corridors, his mind should be fixed on the questions he'd put to the young duchess. *And all I can think of is seeing Victoria...*

Lord Huntly's butler looked back. "Right this way, my lord," he said, stopping beside a doorway. The servant knocked once.

"Enter." The occupant's voice boomed from within.

The butler pressed the handle, letting him in. "The Earl of Exeter to see Her Ladyship," he announced.

Folders in hand, Nathaniel stepped inside. He did a sweep of the room, searching for the duchess, braced for the same visceral loathing he'd encountered two days ago with the Marquess of Rutland... and instead finding a more dignified, composed gentleman, alongside a delicate blonde lady. The same lady who'd been at the museum with her mother and sister. He sketched a bow. "Your Graces."

"Lord Exeter," the duchess greeted in a lyrical voice. "Won't you please sit?" As the young couple sat, she motioned to a nearby Italian rococo giltwood and tapestry chair.

Taking his seat, Nathaniel set his folder down beside a silver tea tray and withdrew his spectacles. "Thank you for—"

"Her Ladyship, Viscountess Waters."

That unexpected announcement slashed across Nathaniel's pleasantries.

He and the young couple rose as one. Nathaniel and Victoria's son-in-law dropped respectful bows.

"Forgive me," Victoria said, her breath slightly winded as one who'd run a short distance. Her color flushed, she rushed to claim a spot on the pale yellow Aubusson sofa closest to her daughter.

While that family exchanged morning greetings, Nathaniel used the opportunity to drink in the sight of her. Whereas he'd instructed her to leave during his last interview, now there was no attempt to do so. Always spirited and in possession of a free mind, she'd grown even more into a woman of admirable strength and resolve.

As if to echo his very thoughts, Victoria met his gaze unapologetically. "My lord," she greeted. The blush, however, deepened on her cheeks.

Had she been riddled with the memory of their embrace yesterday, too? Nathaniel bowed his head. "My lady."

How fickle fate was. But for a cruel trick on her part, they'd be using one another's Christian names as they always had, and the case before them even now would have never come to be. Bereft, he carefully placed his reading spectacles on. "I'll not take long," he repeated the rote script he'd delivered for Lady Rutland's interview. "I expect not more than an hour."

"Of course," the Duchess of Huntly said as her husband took her fingers in his. That slight but telling gesture spoke of a marriage based on love. Nathaniel was surely becoming soft in his five and forty years, for a pang of envy struck deep.

Gathering up his file, he withdrew the small notebook and pencil. "Can you tell me about your relationship with your father?" he asked gently. Over the wire rims of his glasses, he studied the subject of his questioning.

Where Lady Rutland's voice had wavered at those confessions, Lady Justina spoke with an impressive calm. "I was invisible until my father saw I was of an age to make a match." Nathaniel frantically scratched his notes upon the page, recording her words. "At that point, I took care to avoid his presence." Her lips twisted. "He schemed to have me wed to a gentleman who owned a significant number of his vowels."

"And who was the gentleman your father intended for you to marry?" he asked, directing that query to his page.

"The Marquess of Tennyson."

Nathaniel froze mid-write. He picked his head up. "Lord Tennyson, you say?" he asked guardedly.

"Yes." She pursed her lips. "A vile man."

A thousand questions swirled in his mind. Lord Tennyson, a member of the Brethren for twelve years now, with the rakish persona he'd established and the carefully cultivated vile reputation, no one would dare suspect him for anything but an indolent lord. And Macleod, Bennett, nor any other member of Nathaniel's damned members or staff had felt it prudent to mention Tennyson's connection to the viscount? Penning a note to call a bloody meeting with Macleod and Bennett upon his return to his office, he continued. "What of your sister's relationship with the viscount?"

"Given you've already interviewed her, I expect you have all the answers you need there."

Despite himself, his lips tugged at the corner. She and her sister were both very much Victoria's daughters. The manner of clever, feisty, courageous children he'd thought they would have together. Focusing on his questioning that was vastly safer and easier than mourning what had never been, he flipped a page in his notebook.

"What of your brother's relationship with your father?" She opened her mouth to, no doubt, issue a similarly cheeky retort, but Nathaniel spoke over her. "Your Grace, given that my investigation centers around the question of your brother's role in your father's death, I trust you understand I cannot simply defer to Lord Waters' statement of that relationship."

The duchess glanced to her mother and Victoria gave her a slow, encouraging nod. "My brother learned my father's ways," she began, sadness tingeing her admission. "He drank, and wagered, and…" Her cheeks pinkened. "Carried on with doxies. Andrew and my father did not, however, have any kind of relationship."

Victoria's husband had been unfaithful to her. What a bloody fool. "At any time, did your brother ever threaten your father? Put his hands upon the viscount?" Anything to hint at a young man capable of violence and murder.

A heavy silence lingered in the air and at that telling pause, he leveled his probing stare on the duchess. She hesitated and then gave a slight nod. "Just once." Those two words came out so faint, he struggled to hear them… but he did.

Bloody hell. This spoke to the hatred the Bow Street Runners and constables had recorded in their notes. "When?" he prodded, when it became apparent the duchess intended to say nothing further on the incident.

"When I was first married. My husband," the Duchess of Huntly glanced over to her husband. "He did not have honorable intentions toward me when we first met. He intended to bankrupt my family."

The duke's features contorted into a paroxysm of grief.

"He did not, however," Justina said twining her fingers through her husband's. "In the end, he did not financially destroy my father, even as he could have."

Nathaniel paused in his writing. Her defense of her husband did not explain the incident that she clearly danced around. "What were the circumstances surrounding your brother's assault?"

The duchess sat up. "It was not an assault."

"Justina," her mother said warningly.

"No, Mother," she gritted out. "I'll not have this man, a stranger, label it with ugly words. Andrew only sought to—"

"Justina," Victoria said, this time more sharply, effectively ending whatever revelation the duchess intended to make.

"It's a question that needs to be answered," he gently explained, directing his statement to Victoria.

All earlier crimson color gone from her cheeks, her face now stood an ashen shade of gray. *Please*, she silently mouthed. That unspoken one syllable plea gutted him. *I'm sorry.* With his eyes, he willed her to see that and believe it. Her teeth sank into her lower lip and she looked away from him.

"Your Grace?" he prompted.

"Andrew grabbed him about the neck. He shoved him into the wall. Choked him." Tears filled the duchess' eyes and she blinked frantically.

It was damning. They were three sentences that offered definitive proof that the new viscount was capable of violence… and more so… he'd been moved to violence against his father in the past. He silently closed his book, setting it aside. "Are you aware of what led to the outburst from your brother?"

The duchess nodded slowly.

There was an art to questioning. A skilled interrogator was both a master of timing and a chameleon; hard-hearted one instant, kind-eyed and patient the next. As such, Nathaniel waited, allowing the young lady the time she required.

"When my father learned of my husband's intention to call in his markers, he took exception with my marriage." Victoria's breath sucked in a noisy breath. "He went partially mad. Went into a rage. Turned violent."

"Violent?" he echoed cautiously.

The young lady gave another nod; this one disjointed and uneven.

Fear coated his skin with gooseflesh. And he proved for all his years with the Brethren he was nothing more than a coward. Because he didn't want to know whatever statement the duchess might make. Didn't want to know because it would let him inside Victoria's world in a way he feared would drive him to madness where Fox and Hunter had failed.

Nathaniel made the mistake of looking over at Victoria. She held herself taut as a bow that was one pluck away from snapping. Their gazes collided and she swiftly looked away. His heart jolted. Always unrepentant and fearless, she could not meet his eyes.

Why?

His tongue heavy in his mouth, he managed to continue his questioning. "Did he strike your brother?"

The duchess shook her head.

"Did he strike you?"

Another shake of her head followed, this time harder. It dislodged a golden curl.

No. Please, God, no. "Did he put his hands on your mother?" *Please, not Victoria.*

There was an infinitesimal pause that stretched into eternity; that deafening silence punctuated by the tick of the ormolu clock atop the mantel. "They were arguing. He was shouting vile, hateful words about her for encouraging us to believe in love. I heard glass breaking and wanted to leave. Instead, I entered the room. He had her by the wrist. Her cheek was red, though we never spoke on it, I saw it. I knew he'd turned violent." For her earlier strength, the duchess' face crumpled and she angled away.

Her husband folded an arm around her shoulder, his soft murmurings lost to Nathaniel.

Allowing her that moment, he fixed on the latter words Victoria's daughter had spoken. *He'd turned* violent.

In his work with the ruthless men Nathaniel had brought to justice over the years, he'd come to appreciate that no man suddenly turned to violence. Invariably, there was a blackness to their souls. The lords who beat their wives, the murderers who left a trail of dead bodies in their wake, had always carried that intrinsic streak. Bile stung the back of his throat. *I'm going to be ill.* Throat convulsing, he glanced over at Victoria. She remained with her stare on her lap, scrabbling with the black bombazine skirts she wore in honor of her departed husband.

Oh, Victoria.

He wanted to toss his head back and rail like an angry beast. Wanted to drag the bastard she'd called husband from the grave and kill him all over again with his bare hands, exacting a vicious torture upon him. Why had she given herself to Waters? Why?

Nathaniel called forth every skill he'd acquired as a spy to speak, calmly. All the while, a riot of fury, agony, and grief swirled in his chest. "When your brother came upon you, your mother, and father, do you recall what he said?"

The duchess opened and closed her mouth several times. "You don't know my brother," she said hurriedly… defensively. "Andrew is incapable of hurting anyone. He's lighthearted and kind." That description of the gentleman didn't fit with the portrait that had been put together by every investigator who'd worked the viscount's case, thus far.

"What did he say?" Nathaniel asked quietly.

The young lady worried at the flesh of her lower lip. "He said if my father touched either one of us again, he would see him dead."

It was a fate Victoria's husband had been deserving of. And yet— *bloody, bloody hell.* Nathaniel forced his fingers to move, jotting down that damning statement. Tamping down a sigh, he closed his book. "Thank you for your time, Your Grace," he said, tucking the book inside his folio; grateful that he'd not previously scheduled an interview with Victoria's son-in-law for this same day. *I need to leave.* "Those are all the questions I have at this time." He removed his glasses and placed them inside his jacket.

Mother and daughter jumped up.

"My son is not a killer, Nathaniel," Victoria said with a calm evenness to that defense. Most wives, mothers, and sisters offered up copious tears or desperate pleas during such an exchange. Victoria had always been stronger than most men he'd known. "You cannot disregard the totality of his life for one statement he made to protect me."

"Thank you—"

"If you thank me or my family once more for our time, I'm going to wallop you, Nathaniel."

Feeling the young couple's eyes on him and Victoria, he dropped a bow. Something in that spirited glimmer in her cerulean blue eyes, steadied him, and kept him from descending into madness from what her daughter had revealed. He ached to reassure her that he trusted her judgment. To do so, however, went against the lessons he doled out to younger men and women just hired to do the work of the Brethren.

With a final deferential bow for the duke and duchess, Nathaniel took his leave. The dutiful butler jumped to attention as soon as the door opened and, instantly, led him back the same path he'd traveled… twenty minutes ago? Twenty years?

Chester Barrett abused Victoria. That sorry, miserable, pathetic excuse of a man had put his hands upon her; marred her flesh… a thick haze of rage fell over his vision and he tortured himself with imagining her as she'd been; her cries and pleas… or had she been stoically silent through his abuse? A primitive growl started in his chest and worked up his throat.

The duke's butler cast a nervous glance back.

Get a hold of yourself. Focus on your case. Focus on every revelation made by Victoria's daughter… both about Andrew Barrett, Viscount Waters, and the Marquess of Tennyson. Nathaniel concentrated on the details of the case, needing that focus to keep him from thinking of Victoria as she'd been, silent and hurting on that damned sofa. To no avail. He was choking, suffocating.

As soon as he stepped outside, Nathaniel filled his lungs with air. Doing a sweep of the street, he quickly located his carriage and made his way for it.

Bennett, standing at attention beside the black conveyance, greeted him. "Did you—"

"Tennyson and Macleod in my office, now," he gritted out.

His loyal assistant swallowed loudly and rushed in the opposite direction to retrieve his horse from a waiting street urchin.

Nathaniel climbed inside. As soon as he settled onto the bench, he shot a fist up, rapping hard on the ceiling. The carriage sprung into movement, rattling through the noisy streets of London. This time, it was not the constraints of the carriage that swamped his mind with horror. *Focus on your questions for Tennyson and Macleod about the investigation into Waters before his murder. Focus on the testimony just provided by the duchess. Focus…* he cursed, tossing the folder onto the opposite bench.

He dropped his head into his hands, his breath coming in erratic spurts. He'd abused her. Viscount Waters had hurled hateful words at her and put his loathsome hands upon her soft flesh. A tortured moan spilled from his lips and he clawed his fingers into his forehead, welcoming the slight sting of pain, wanting to take the suffering she'd known and make it his.

When he'd returned from captivity, he'd found Victoria lost to him… a young mother with a husband and a new life. The agony of losing her had been so great that he'd fled to the Continent and taken up missions on the opposite side of the world so he could escape her. Hollow inside, Nathaniel lowered his hands and stared at the empty bench opposite him. *I should have remained. I should have seen that she was, at the very least, safe… and if she wasn't, I should have taken her and her daughter.*

After all, his very work for the Crown had made him a master of movement and hiding. They could have lived a life together away from the horror that had been the marriage described by her daughters. Instead, he'd been too weighted down by his own bitterness at finding her married.

So many mistakes. Too many damned mistakes.

He laughed, the jaded sound empty and dark. And here, all these years he'd believed his greatest mistake had been getting himself captured. Only to find that he'd erred in every way where Victoria had been concerned.

The carriage rolled at a slow clip through the bustling streets of London before arriving at the offices of the Brethren.

Before the conveyance even came to a full stop, Nathaniel gathered his folders, shoved the door open, and jumped out. His feet collided jarringly with the ground, as that sudden movement sent pain radiating up to the old wound he'd suffered at Fox's hands.

Ignoring the sharp ache, he stalked ahead. His gaze was trained forward. He shoved open the door and marched past the startled clerks and staff. All the young men instantly stood at attention.

"My lord," they greeted with deferential bows as he passed.

"Bennett?" he thundered. Traveling by horseback, his assistant had no doubt arrived ahead of him.

Bennett came bounding down the hall leading to Nathaniel's offices.

"Copy these, and file them away in my office when you're through," he instructed, turning over the Waters file. "Macleod?"

"In your office, already," Bennett assured, instantly falling into step beside him.

"Tennyson?" The bloody spy no one had thought to mention had connections to Waters.

"Also there. Arrived a handful of minutes ago."

As Bennett fell back, Nathaniel increased his stride, finding his office. Both Macleod and Tennyson instantly straightened, arms clasped behind them, gazes directed forward.

This visit grounded him. Kept him thinking on the case and the Brethren and not on the suffering Victoria had endured. Making his way to his desk, he sat. "Why was nothing said?" he seethed, directing that steely demand to the more recent addition to the Brethren.

Macleod coughed nervously. "Didn't seem worth mentioning, my lord."

Nathaniel slammed his fist down, rattling the folders on his desk. "Didn't seem worth mentioning?" The contrite spy instantly paled. Lowering his voice to a menacing whisper, he went on. "In an investigation, you share all. I don't care if the information was about Waters' last meal or how often he took a damned shite during the day, everything is passed on and every detail matters."

Macleod gave a jerky nod of acquiescence.

Dismissing the neophyte, Nathaniel trained his attention on the hardened lord, looking half-bored and half-put out by the meeting. Hired by the previous Sovereign, Tennyson had expertly crafted an image of an unrepentant rake who cared about nothing beyond whoring, wagering, and drinking. "You were courting Waters' daughter." He paused. How bloody wrong it was to assign parentage to that bastard who'd sired her. "What were the details surrounding that courtship?"

"May I?" Tennyson jerked his chin at the sideboard.

Tightening his mouth, Nathaniel nodded. The problem with becoming what or who the Brethren demanded, was that, ultimately, a man could not divorce those aspects of himself from any of his dealings. One became the character. Tennyson was very much the hardened rake. Grabbing a crystal decanter, the marquess poured a tall brandy. With both drink and bottle in hand, he strolled over to Nathaniel's desk with an infuriating calm.

"Well?" he snapped, impatiently when the marquess plopped himself down in one of the seats across from him. Any other day, Tennyson's insolence would have grated. Now, he welcomed a fiery annoyance... anything other than the empty hole that had been made that day in his heart.

"There were suspicions that Waters was linked to the Cato Street Conspiracy."

The unexpectedness of that revelation, gave Nathaniel pause. The recent attempt to assassinate the British cabinet ministers and prime minister had been thwarted because of the Brethren… and Nathaniel was only just learning now of Waters' potential connection? "Macleod, you are excused."

The spy flattened his lips into a hard line. But with a bow, he took his leave.

Macleod forgotten, Nathaniel shifted his attention over to Tennyson once more. "On what grounds was Waters a suspect?"

The marquess swirled the contents of his drink. "Waters visited the Coaxing Tom on Edgeware Road." Edgeware Road… very near Cato Street and the place of the plotting. "He frequently sat down to cards with Thistlewood."

The mastermind behind the plot to radically reform England had been hanged for his efforts. Such a figure didn't seem like the sort a reprobate such as Waters would keep company with. Nathaniel rubbed his chin. "Are you saying Waters had political interests that aligned with Thistlewood's?"

Tennyson snorted, choking on his swallow. "Waters' only interests were in how many whores he could dally with and how much liquor he could consume. It did not take me long to ascertain as much." *His drinking and whoring and wagering crippled our family's finances and brought struggle to each of us…* Nathaniel's gut tightened. The marquess finished his drink and then set the glass down on the floor beside him. "Furthermore," he continued. "The plot to take over the Cabinet continues even with his death. If he were involved for monetary reasons, there are others among the peerage we suspect who've moved over into his role."

Nathaniel sat forward in his chair. "So it *is* possible that his murder was politically motivated, then?" Wanting it to be the case for Victoria. For then it would mean her son was absolved of guilt and blame.

"Possible?" Tennyson shrugged. "Anything is possible." It was just another motto of the Brethren. "However, it is unlikely," the man went on, quashing Nathaniel's fledgling hope. "Whoever the masterminds behind the attempt are, they are politically driven with plans to expand their power in the Minsters' Cabinet—to carve out a dynasty. Waters' willingness to sell me his daughter to pay for his gambling debts is proof enough that he was uninvolved in the Cato Event." The marquess grimaced. "And I very nearly found myself wed to the chit because of it."

Nathaniel narrowed his eyes. The *chit* Tennyson now spoke of was, in fact, Victoria's youngest child. "That will be all," he said in frosty tones.

Hopping up, Tennyson sketched a haphazard bow and let himself out.

When he'd gone, Nathaniel counted twenty beats of the loudly ticking clock. By the information shared here, only one damned likely suspect remained. Then climbing to his feet, he came 'round and gathered the forgotten bottle and snifter.

Pouring himself a tall glass, Nathaniel downed the drink. Only it wasn't the damned case Nathaniel was worried about resolving… it was everything he'd learned this day about Victoria.

CHAPTER 11

Your fidelity belongs first and foremost to the Brethren.
Article XI: The Brethren of the Lords

THE MOON BATHED THE GARDENS in a pale white glow.

Wielding her pruning shares, Victoria frantically clipped away the overgrown rose bushes. There had been a time her gardens had been her sanctuary.

Clip.

A place where she'd first sneaked off to meet Nathaniel Archer, while the world slept on.

Clip.

And then as a place where she'd hidden herself when he'd disappeared. She'd been a young woman with a babe in her belly and her world was about to crash down around her.

Clip. Clip.

There had been a time when these grounds had been meticulously tended by gardeners and lovingly cared for at her hand.

Clip. Clip.

No more. These overgrown gardens, run amok with weeds and deadened shrubs and choking rose bushes, were now a marked symbol of what her existence had become. The wife of an abusive, violent drunkard who'd gotten himself murdered and left their family in ruins… and because of it had seen Nathaniel return like a ghost come for the haunting.

A sharp thorn pierced her leather glove. She gasped. The shears slipped from her fingers, landing noiselessly in the pile of debris she'd cut that night. Victoria sank back on her haunches and, tugging free her glove, eyed the crimson drop that stood vivid upon her pale flesh.

Everything had changed. "Everything," she whispered. She'd gone from a bright-eyed, hopelessly-in-love miss to a terrified woman with a babe in her belly... to *this*.

Victoria hugged her arms and glanced about the walled-in gardens; touching her gaze on the chipped stone statues and ramshackle grounds. These past few days, with Nathaniel questioning Justina and Phoebe—the daughter he'd never known of—she'd no choice but to confront what her existence, in fact, was. She'd blinked and her life had passed in a blur of tedious *ton* functions and creditors calling to pay for the debts racked up by her husband.

Time had marched on, erasing the blush of youthful splendor. She'd lived solely for her son and daughters. Now, what remained were three grown children; two of whom were married and another who'd little interest in her, or the idea of family. She'd told herself that her children were enough, only to find she could admit the truth—she'd wanted more. And she hated that she was forced to confront all she'd lost and all she'd desperately wanted for her life. She'd wanted a partner at her side; someone who would have loved her and their children, who'd have gardened with her and, in their advancing years, journey to places she'd always longed to go to, but never would have dared to go as long as there had been young children.

She followed the small drop of blood as it expanded and then trickled down the side of her finger. What was worse, while Nathaniel and his life were a great unknown mystery to her, today, he'd gathered a glimpse of the empty marriage she'd suffered through. And with every interview he conducted, he'd only glean more.

He'd gather every last sordid, rotten detail of abuse, and philandering, and heartache, until she was laid bare before him.

Crack.

Victoria sat slowly up as the echo of that snapped twig cut across the midnight still. It was another "calling card" that had belonged to only them. Unspoken signals developed between two secret lovers.

She briefly closed her eyes, wanting to tell him to go to hell with precise instructions on how to get there. Both loving him and hating him all at the same time. Shamefully weak in wanting him near as much as she wanted him gone. If he spoke, if he uttered one wrong word, she would order him from her home and out of her existence, only speaking to him when she was robbed of choice.

He sank down beside her, his cloak whipping noisily against his legs. Wordlessly, he held over the forgotten until now pruning shears. Just as he'd done so many times before this when, years after his disappearance, she'd secretly dreamed he'd come to her. Those stolen interludes in her parents' gardens had kept her heart beating.

"You never bothered with a cloak." *Too cumbersome to scale garden walls.* Victoria took the garden tool, folding her fingers tight around it, finding some comfort in the cool metal pressed against her palm.

"I used the servant's entrance through the kitchens," he said quietly. He quirked his lips in one corner, that half-grin dizzying to her senses, as always. "Not quite as adept at scaling walls and buildings as I once was."

Even more heavily muscled than he had been in his youth, there could be no doubting his physical strength or capabilities. Whereas, she? The corners of her eyes had begun to show the hint of wrinkling. How much kinder age had been to him. "What do you want, Nathaniel?" she asked tiredly, feeling years older. "To question me further about my son?" To give her fingers a steadying task, she snipped an errant weed choking the bush, focusing her attentions on it. Focusing on anything but him and what had brought him here.

"I've not come to speak about the investigation or interrogate you," he acknowledged in a husky voice.

And oddly…she believed him. *Is it just that I so desperately want to believe?* She wanted to trust that this man who'd sired her first-born child had felt… and still did feel… some regard for her.

"Why?"

There was a guttural quality to that one word utterance that gave Victoria pause; her shears hung partially open and she forced herself to complete the next cut. *I do not want to answer that question. Not now. I'm not ready.* "I don't know what—"

Nathaniel stayed her hand, catching it in his own. "You do," he growled. "You would have me say it, then? Have you asked the question aloud?"

She made to speak but her gaze caught on the top of his hand. Those puckered scars forming a misshapen circle killed her retort. Her unease shifted, taking on a new form that had nothing to do with an altogether different kind of fear. How did a person come by such marks? Again the question flickered to life.

Nathaniel followed her stare and then swiftly lowered his arm back to his side. "Why did you marry him?" he asked. His voice was so rough with such pain, it cleaved at her.

This is why he'd come—for answers. At last, they'd speak on it. Her tongue felt heavy in her mouth. "Would it have mattered if I didn't?" she ventured, tentatively. "Either way, you were… gone."

"Yes," he rasped, tossing away the shears. "It would have mattered. You would have been happy."

His words brought her up short. He'd cared about her happiness? She tried to resolve that incongruity with the lover who'd simply absconded with her heart and never returned. "I was happy," she said softly. "My children—"

"With a husband," he cut in, his voice ragged. "Not your daughters or son… but happiness with a man who'd been deserving of you."

Oh, God. She bit her quivering lip. After just a few days back in her life, he'd gleaned the secrets she'd kept from all. He'd pieced together that for the misery her marriage had been, her children had sustained her and been the sole happiness she'd found. "You never returned," she rasped, shoving to her feet. In her haste, she stumbled but he jumped up, righting her. "You promised not even God himself could keep you away." A broken laugh tore from her and she folded her arms against her middle. "It took you more than twenty years to return to me."

Grief darkened his eyes. "You were married not even eighty-six days after I'd gone."

She started. He'd known the precise number of days she'd waited before marrying Chester?

Nathaniel dusted his knuckles over her cheek, his thoughts in harmony with her own. "Of course, I knew that."

Why, why should he know? Unless he'd still cared… unless he'd

THE SPY WHO SEDUCED HER

returned and found her already wed to another. Her heart slowed to a painful, uneven beat. "You… came back?"

"I did." He stopped his distracted movements, his arm falling to his side. "You were already married at that point."

If she'd merely been a conquest for a debonair spy, why had he recorded to memory the precise number of days before she'd wed? And for the first time since he'd sneaked into her home and upended her world all over again, questions whispered forward. Ones that she didn't bury this time. Ones she feared the answers to. She lifted her eyes to his. The glow of the moon bathed his rugged features in a soft light. "Why didn't you come to me?" she implored. *Make me understand.*

He stood beside her, immovable like marble, so long he may as well have been one of the stone statues within the gardens. "I was captured."

The earth ceased spinning on its axis. "Captured?" her voice came as though down a long, empty corridor. The sound of her voice was muffled and distorted to her ears as that one word conjured visions of torment and terror.

Nathaniel gave a brusque nod.

That silent acknowledgement weighted her eyes closed. He, invincible, fearless Nathaniel Archer, had been captured. It had been the darkest fear that would keep her awake every time he left through her window to depart for his next assignment. But it had also been the fragile hope she'd carried for his fate when he'd still not returned to her. "When?" she asked, her voice threadbare, already knowing. Knowing before he spoke, confirming that supposition.

"The last time I left you." He clasped his hands behind him, hiding that marked skin from her focus. Oh, God. Her throat closed off. What agony had he endured?

Through her tumult, Nathaniel rocked on his heels and continued speaking. "I was set to investigate a pair of radical Irish revolutionaries in Bristol."

"You were in Bristol," she breathed.

He gave another shaky nod.

My, God. He'd been just over one hundred miles away. That had been all the distance separating them. And yet, he may as well have been sent to the opposite end of the world. He spoke and she clung to every word that fell from his lips, even as each admission brought her world crashing down about her. "They were two men by the name of Fox and Hunter." His gaze grew distant and she knew the moment he'd ceased to see her and only saw the hell playing out in his own mind. She bit her lower lip hard. "They sought an independent Ireland, completely free of England's influence, and were relentless in their pursuit of that… dream." His lips flattened. "It was my fault. I was careless. Cocksure. Arrogant."

Bold, fearless, and confident. That is what he'd been. They'd been just a handful of the reasons she'd fallen in love with him. She gathered his scarred hand; clinging to it. "It was never your fault," she said with adamancy, squeezing his fingers. "None of it." She paused. "What did they do to you?" *Tell me all, so I can make your monsters mine and battle them for you.*

He stared at their interlocked digits and his throat moved. Time ticked by. Nathaniel remained silent so long she thought he'd not let her in. And then…

"They took me prisoner." She strained to hear him. "They kept me in small room… in a basement, chained." Like a dog. Nay, worse than a dog. Her pulse hummed loudly in her ears, distorting his voice. "They starved me. Withheld water. Beat me." His lips twisted in an ugly rendition of his always beautiful smile.

"Oh, Nathaniel," she said, her voice hoarse to her own ears.

He continued with a matter-of-factness at odds with his tensely held frame. "They played a…" he sneered, "game, forcing me to predict where the next blow would come. Would it be my head? My groin? My kidneys?" He absently reached around, touching his lower back.

A sob escaped her and she caught it with her palm.

"If I guessed the correct body part, I'd be spared from that strike." Nathaniel quickly passed his other palm over his eyes. "They merely toyed with me. I was never spared."

"Monsters," she seethed. And she, who'd long believed herself incapable of inflicting harm upon another, wanted to hunt his captors down and bury a blade inside their black hearts.

He lifted his gaze. The bleakness in his violet eyes robbed her of breath.

"They tortured me," his voice emerged as rough as a graveled road.

She stopped abruptly, releasing him. Her body went hot and then cold, icing her skin with gooseflesh and numbing her heart. "Wh-what?" she repeated, hating the tremor there. Wanting to be strong in the face of his suffering. *He was captured. What do you think those men would have done to him?* And God help her for the coward she'd never believed herself to be, she wanted his telling to end. She slowly inhaled the cool night air, filling her lungs with it. Nathaniel deserved more. He deserved her strength. "Tell me all." Her voice emerged with a strength to it.

His face buckled. "They carved parts of me with a knife," he whispered, his voice tinged with every hell and horror he'd known. *No.* Nathaniel flexed his palm. All the air left her lungs as she followed his subconscious movement. "Each time they cut up my skin, they poured hot wax in it."

A piteous moan filtered about the gardens; a sound better fitting a wounded beast. Did it belong to her? Or Nathaniel? In this instance, Victoria could sort nothing out from her own heart's breaking.

I should have been there when he returned. I should have battled his demons and nightmares at his side...

"Where are they?" she managed to ask.

He spoke, his voice coming out flat. "Dead."

In hell. They were in hell where rotten souls belonged.

It was not enough.

His breath came hard and fast. That crack in his usually unflappable composure hit her like a physical punch to the belly.

Allowing him the time he needed, Victoria just smoothed her fingers back and forth over the ruined flesh on the top of his hand. "You are safe now," she said softly. That reassurance was as much for him as for her. Wrapping her arms about him, she simply held him.

His arms hung limply by his side. Then slowly, he lifted them, folding her close.

They clung tight; both taking and restoring strength to one another.

Victoria pressed her cheek against his chest and closed her eyes at the steady, reassuring beat of his heart. *He is alive.* Through evil and agony and despair, he'd triumphed.

Victoria's heart constricted and her tears squeezed past her lashes, dampening his shirt. This is what had kept him from her. How much easier it had been to hate him these past few days than it had been knowing this truth. How could she resent him? He'd spoken of defeating God himself. Yet, with the work he'd under-taken for the Crown, it was the Devil and his demons that he'd battled. "How long were you held there?" she whispered.

He sucked in a breath through his teeth. "Two years." The haunted glitter in the violet of his irises cut her to the quick. "I, the masterful spy, incapable of being discovered, found myself caught and shut away for two years." He chuckled, tears strangling that sound. "On English soil. In bloody Bristol of all places."

The vise continued squeezing all the more, draining the blood from an organ that had ceased to properly beat since he'd begun talking. Many times while married to Chester, she'd viewed her marriage as a prison. She'd feel as though she were suffocating and, in the dead of the night, she'd grab a cloak and sprint out-side, driven by a hungering to escape. Only staying because of the children who'd slept on in the cold townhouse. What must it have been like for Nathaniel to be a prisoner in the truest sense of the word? Two years in a darkened, windowless cellar. She could only manage a meaningless whisper for him. "I..." *I have no words. Nothing to make it right or take this burden away from you.*

"I'm so very sorry," he said on a jagged exhale.

She whipped her gaze back to his. "You would apologize to *me?*" she rasped. *My God.* The only reason he'd not returned as prom-ised was because he'd been captured.

"I did not come."

"Because you could not," she said brokenly, at last understand-ing. Every last shred of resentment she'd carried melted away. In its place was a stinging agony for what he'd endured. How she wanted to take those nightmares from him and make them her own. But the uncertainty she felt in this even more uncertain world they now existed within, she remained silent.

Instead, she folded her arms about him, laying her cheek against his chest. Upon his reemergence in her life, she'd vowed to take the truth of Phoebe's birth to the grave with her. She had sworn he'd never know that, together, they'd created life. *How can I keep that from him now?* Not only had two years been stolen from him, his daughter had, as well. For she'd no doubt, Nathaniel Archer would have never forsaken his daughter—not even for his work. Tears filled her eyes, blurring her vision. He'd lost so much. *We both did.* She, who'd been unable to shed even a pretend drop for her late husband, now wept in silence.

He held himself stiff. "I came back as soon as I was able," he said against the crown of her head. "I would have you know that. I—"

"I know." For now, she did. Her lower lip trembled.

"The thought of returning to you sustained me," The gold flecks in his eyes glinted under the ferocity of that admission. "Through each lash. Through each..." She angled back, to look at him. Victoria wanted to know all of his suffering so he was not alone in his memories. His Adam's apple moved rhythmically. "Through it all, I would dream of the day I returned to you."

"Why didn't you?" Except, as soon as that entreaty came out, she realized the impossibility she'd made of any future between them with her marriage to the bastard she'd bound herself to.

Nathaniel directed his gaze up at the half-moon overhead. "I did."

"What?" she asked, her voice breathless and weak.

"The evening I returned to London, I entered first your parents' residence." He'd climbed that same windowsill that he had so many times. Only that last time, the room would have been vacant.

"And I was not there when you returned," she said needlessly. He'd come for her and she should have been there, with Phoebe, both of them waiting to begin as a family...

He dusted a hand over his mouth. "And I knew," he said softly to himself, a man lost in the remembrance of that night. "Your bed was untouched. Your armoire was bare and the room was empty. You were gone to me."

Victoria stared at a point beyond his arm. Since he'd reappeared in her life, she'd blamed him for having left her... and all along, she'd been the one who'd wronged him.

She was gone to you the moment you chose the Brethren over her. The hell of that night slapped at Nathaniel in slow waves, forcing him back. The gripping agony and then the numbing deadness that had come in losing her returned.

Through the years, he'd not allowed himself to think on it. He'd devoted all his energies and efforts to the Brethren; it had given him a distraction, and then purpose again, in a lonely world.

And eventually, the pain of losing Victorian Cadence Tremaine had dulled… though it had always been there. An ache, not unlike the scars left him by Fox and Hunter, and other mercenary foes intent on harming the Crown.

Victoria rested her palm upon his sleeve and his muscles automatically bunched under that unexpected touch. "Have you been… happy?"

"Happy," he echoed. He chuckled, the sound empty to his own ears. "What is that precisely, Victoria?" His memories of happiness all involved this woman before him and were so distant that they may as well have been dreams he'd conjured.

She wetted her lips. "Did you ever… marry?"

He held her gaze; her eyes brimmed with uncertainty. How could she not know? "There was only ever you." There would only ever *be* her… in any way. "My work for the Brethren became the only partner in my life." He'd devoted his very existence to every mission handed down. The more daring ones that no sane man would have ever wanted and only those with a wish for death sought to take on.

"She has always been your spouse," she said softly, without recrimination. There was only a quiet acceptance. "Your loyalty has only ever been to that organization."

"You—"

Victoria pressed a silencing finger to his lips and his skin burned under the heat of her touch. "Each time you left, you did so with the knowledge that you might not return." And he hadn't, until it had been too late.

"Why did you choose him?" he asked the question that had dogged him after his interview of Phoebe Deering and compelled him here this night. Taking her by the shoulders, he gripped them in a firm hold. "Why Waters?" Why did he want the answer to that? If it hadn't been the viscount, it would have been another. Her lower lip trembled. "Why?" he repeated. Because he needed to know. Spirited, clever, and with a beauty to rival Aphrodite, there'd been no gentleman she could not have had. Why had she chosen a wastrel, fool enough to leave her bed for a whore in the dangerous ends of London?

"Nathaniel…"Victoria's face crumpled and she swiftly closed her eyes. She slipped out of his arms and, unlike their past exchanges since his return, there was no antipathy there. Rather, she lowered her gaze, avoiding his stare.

His back went up, as every last skill he'd honed in his work for the Crown sharpened. There were different ways to elicit information: through threats, commands, false charm.

In this, however, Nathaniel did not want to employ his strategies as an agent. He wanted her to share with him because that was what she wanted.

Victoria drifted away, with the look of a woman at sea. A cloud drifted over the moon, dousing the gardens in darkness. "I was with child," her voice emerged whisper-thin. And yet, it managed to suck all sound and life from the gardens.

Nathaniel stood motionless, afraid to move. Afraid to so much as breathe. And through the fog of horrified confusion, he tried to make sense of the words she'd spoken.

I was with child…

He shook his head. A child? There had been a babe born of their time together. Shock made his breath shorten. Surely, he'd heard her wrong. Surely, he'd misunderstood. "What?" he managed, his voice strangled to his own ears.

Victoria wheeled slowly back. Her eyes, twin pools of despair, shimmered with tears. "You'd been gone a month. You were never gone that l-long," she said, her voice catching. "I told myself you'd been sent further away. By the second month, I'd realized… I missed my menses." She lifted stricken eyes to his and as she spoke, her words rolled together with a frantic pace that matched the speed of his churning thoughts. *Should you really be surprised? How many times did you make love to her?* He fought through the haze of confusion, hanging on to every revelation. "I believed it was my own crying and worrying after you… but then I fell ill. Every morning. I still did not realize." Victoria folded her arms to her chest, her fingers formed sharp claws in the flesh of her forearms. "My lady's maid, however, noted the… changes and went to my mother. Who went to my father and…" She closed her eyes and shook her head. "I did not know what else to do. I…"

"Victoria," he managed nothing more than her name. Nathaniel's legs weakened under him and he shot a hand out, searching for purchase with which to steady himself—coming up empty. He lowered himself to the ground, crouching there.

She'd been with child.

He sank back over his heels as that agonizing truth rooted around his mind. She had been a scared young woman, carrying his babe…

His chest rose and fell as he struggled to get proper breath into his lungs; imagining her alone, scared. His keening moan echoed around the gardens. It had been all he'd ever wanted: a child with her. He dragged his hands through his hair, tugging the strands. A daughter with her smile and spirit and wit. And how bloody close they'd been to being a family.

All these years he'd longed for her. He'd quietly envied his friends for having a family and love… those very gifts had almost been his.

Almost.

A delicate hand squeezed his shoulder and he wrenched his head up, half-crazed. "What happened to the babe?" he entreated, his voice hoarse.

Victoria blinked slowly. Then a single tear squeezed free and blazed a lonely trail down her cheek. "Oh, Nathaniel," she hugged herself in a lonely embrace. And just like that… the weight of the meaning behind her unspoken confession sunk in his mind.

Nathaniel sucked in a breath through his teeth and staggered unevenly to his feet. His entire existence, everything he knew, trusted, and understood suddenly unclear. He stumbled away from Victoria, tripping over himself. His knees collided with the wrought iron bench and he clutched at the scalloped back, finding a lifeline in the cold metal. His mind raced through the math and the details he'd gathered on Victoria's family. It could not be. It could not… "My, God," he whispered, as understanding hit him in the chest.

"It is Phoebe," she said into the quiet, confirming the truth and offering him a confirmation of the impossible.

Only it wasn't impossible. He'd made love to Victoria and, with the brashness of youth, had never taken care to see that he didn't leave her with child. And he had. Unsteady, Nathaniel collapsed onto the edge of the bench. His breath came in quick, frantic inhalations. All these years, he'd had a child. Nay, *they'd* had a child…

he and Victoria. And the lightness in his chest lifted him from the pit of heartbreak.

The daughter they'd spoken of, with her mother's crimson-kissed, auburn tresses, and spirit, strength, and courage—and—

A chill swept over every joyous thought, leaving him cold inside.

Another man had called her daughter. Viscount Waters had given Phoebe his name and—

He dropped his head into his hands and a sob tore from him.

What terror Victoria would have known as a young woman, without the benefit of marriage, unknowing of where he'd gone? She would have been desperate, alone. And not only had he left Victoria to suffer, but he'd brought misery to his own child. He lifted agonized eyes to her, staring at her through the sheen of tears that blurred his vision. "It was my fault you married him." Every tear she'd surely shed, every hurt she'd suffered at Waters' hands had been because of Nathaniel.

She moved in a soft whir of skirts. "No," she demurred. "Don't you do that," she ordered, squeezing into the spot beside him on the bench. "We were young and we were both responsible."

Rashness did not forgive every error he'd made. "I should have made you my wife before I left." And then life would have been so very different for the both of them.

"Then I would have never had Justina and Andrew," she quietly pointed out.

Her other children, a son and daughter given her by a ruthless drunkard. Jealousy burned through him like a stinging poison that invaded every corner of his being. Nathaniel surged to his feet, a black curse tearing from him. He took one jerky step, and another, and then came to a jolting stop.

All these years, he'd believed Fox and Hunter had exacted the greatest pound of his flesh. And yet, even in death, they still took from him, inflicting the greatest torture… which could never, ever be undone.

He stopped abruptly as the full weight of her revelation slammed into him with all the force of a speeding carriage. *I was a father and never even knew.* "I lost everything," he whispered into the nighttime still. The first steps and words. The outings with suitors Nathaniel would have put to greater questioning than any traitor to the Crown. And instead, *his* child, by reports, had been manipulated into a marriage with a ruthless scoundrel.

The man who'd stood at the marchioness'—he clenched his eyes shut—at Phoebe's side had demonstrated a protectiveness and devotion. But what if he, so focused on his questioning, and Victoria had been wrong and she was in as miserable of a marriage as her mother? His thoughts whirring out of control, Nathaniel raked a hand through his hair. "Does he treat her well?" he rasped.

"He loves her, Nathaniel. Their beginning is not the one I would have wanted for her." A cinch tightened about his lungs. "But since they wed, Edmund has looked after us. Keeping us—" She instantly fell silent. Safe. He'd kept them safe. Madness tugged at the far recesses of his mind and he fought to keep from giving in to it. Victoria lifted her eyes to his and gave him a shuddery smile. "He loves her. He's taken her to the places she always dreamed of," she said softly, her assurances an absolution of sorts, of which he was undeserving. "Edmund encouraged her dreams of journeying to Captain Cook's lands. He's even taken her there." There was a wistfulness in Victoria's voice that hinted at longing.

"She enjoys Cook's work?" he managed to ask. His emotion caused his voice to sound hoarse. He was selfish enough to be proud and overjoyed that his daughter took after him in that regard.

"Very much." Victoria brushed her fingers over his jaw and he leaned into that evanescent caress. "We would read his works together."

We'll go there, Victoria… one day, together…

Only their daughter had seen those dreamed of places. And Victoria had remained more a prisoner in these streets of London than he had ever been.

"It felt, when I shared Cook's work with her, that I was sharing a piece of you."

Oh, God. His chest throbbed. "I'm so sorry," he whispered. For everything. For the happiness he'd cost Victoria and the suffering his own child had endured because he hadn't given Victoria the protection of his name.

Nathaniel dimly registered Victoria slipping her fingers into his and locking their digits, clinging to her for all he was. "All I ever wanted was you and a family together." Her lower lip trembled while her tears fell freely, silent, unchecked. "I wanted her," he said, his voice cracking. "I wanted a daughter just like her mother and all these years, I had her and never—" He sobbed, his body shaking.

Three and twenty years of his daughter's life gone.

Victoria stepped into his arms, holding him close. He held on to her with all he was. Nathaniel lowered his head into the soft crown of her auburn curls, matting them with his tears.

He held her, with time slipping by as it unfailingly did, taking the solace and comfort he was undeserving of. "Does she… take after me in other ways?"

"Oh, Nathaniel. She does. In every way." Maternal pride glowed from within her eyes. "She's full of such love and strength." *Just like you.*

Those words hung there.

An errant breeze stirred the alder trees that lined the high, stone, garden wall, rustling their branches.

Reluctantly, Nathaniel set Victoria from him. They stood there, unspeaking as the wind whipped her hem against his cloak. How were former lovers supposed to be after truths were revealed and past wrongs laid bare, with answers at last given? He ran his gaze achingly over each cherished plane of her delicate, heart-shaped face. The beginning of a wrinkle at the corners of her eyes in no way diminished her vibrant beauty. "I should have married you before I left," he said softly. "I should have done so, the moment you stumbled into that alcove and planted me a facer."

Her breath hitched in a jagged intake. "But you did not."

"I was warned that a member of the organization who wedded jeopardized the safety of his loved ones and I was selfish enough that I wanted it anyway." And he had intended to do right by her. Nathaniel turned to go. He took three steps and then stopped. "I was going to marry you," he said somberly, turning back. His throat worked. "I would have, you know that." Even as it changed nothing. "I'd resolved that the mission I'd been handed would be my last." *And you were to have been my forever.* "But I always knew the risks when I left you and did not want you to be tied to a man who might not return—"

Victoria caught a sob in her fist, muffling that sound of her despair.

Incapable of another word, with anguish swirling inside his chest, Nathaniel left.

CHAPTER 12

*An official opinion on a case cannot be
made until a thorough investigation is completed.
Article XII: The Brethren of the Lords*

HE'D INTENDED TO MARRY HER. Had never wavered in his love. And all along, she'd mourned him as dead, only to find that Nathaniel had been taken captive and suffered at the hands of vile monsters.

Grief ripped a jagged hole in her heart.

Seated in one of the leather winged chairs before her late husband—and now her son's desk—Victoria stared absently about this hated room, unseeing. Braced for Nathaniel's visit… and yet, at the same time, as unsteady in the light of a new day as she'd been since he'd revealed the truth behind his abandonment and she'd shared with him the truth of her first born child's parentage.

Footsteps echoed in the hall. They were noisy, faintly unsteady, and in no way belonging to a skilled spy such as Nathaniel Archer.

Giving her head a shake, she glanced up just as her son strolled in.

"Mother," he drawled. He moved for the sideboard, not even sparing her a glance.

She frowned, studying the day's growth on his face, his tousled, golden curls, and wrinkled garments. Since his father's murder and the subsequent accusations that followed, she'd allowed Andrew to wallow in pity. Enough, was enough. "You look like you've been mucking out the stables, Andrew," she snapped.

"And a fine good morning to you," he boomed with mock cheer that set her teeth on edge. Bottle in one hand, glass in the other, he lifted both in salute. "Early as always I see for our special morning visitor." He paused, glancing about. "He's not arrived, has he? I haven't missed it?"

Jumping to her feet, Victoria swept across the room. "Missed it," she muttered. "Give me that." She yanked the bottle from his hand and jammed it back on the well-stocked sideboard. "Both of them," she said tightly, plucking the stem from his fingertips. Liquid sloshed over the edge. The hated smell that her husband had so frequently stunk of filled her senses. She jammed it down beside the discarded bottle. "You have an interview with Lord Exeter and this is how you arrive?"

"Pfft." He strolled away, knocking into a side table. Victoria hurried to right it. "His mind is already made up."

She sank her teeth into her lower lip. "It is not. The earl is conducting his investigation." There was no fairer man than Nathaniel. With the lack of a positive male influence in Andrew's life, her son, however, had little reason to trust that.

"Bah!" He slashed the air with a hand. "Everyone has made up their minds, Mother. I hated my father." Andrew held a finger aloft. "Which is true. Despised the miserable bugger." He stuck up another digit. "He wagered away a fortune that should, by rights, have been mine."

"There was never a fortune," she mumbled. Her father had merely sold her to a dissolute lord to give Phoebe a *name*. It should have been Nathaniel's. Pain pierced her heart all over again.

Her son tossed back his head and roared with laughter. "Of course, *weee* know that," He gestured between them. "But the *ton* quite believes that I offed the blighter to save myself at least some funds to wager away. Blood lets and all that." He stitched his eyebrows. "Or is it, blood tells? Could never remember. If I'd spent more time on my studies instead of whoring and wagering and drinking—"

"Stop it," she clipped out. "I understand you are hurting. However, you are only hurting yourself. With your carousing, you are only feeding rumors and lending credence to the gossip."

Andrew waggled his eyebrows. "Worried about gossip, are you? Having married a bastard like Father, and me as a son, I never took you as one who much gave a jot for the whispering."

She opened her mouth to rain a stinging diatribe down on his ears. To chastise him for being so flippant when their very existence was one strong gust of wind away from knocking them all down. A glimmer of pain lit her son's bloodshot eyes. The fight went out of her. His was all a show; a presentation for the world... including her, as his mother... of what he thought the world expected of him. "Oh, Andrew." Stretching her hand up, Victoria cupped his cheek; once rounded baby cheeks now sharp and covered with growth. "When you were just three years old, one of the kitchen maids came running to fetch me. She'd found you in the kitchens, stuffing your pockets with the Molasses Pulls that were intended for guests your father and I were to entertain that night." She smiled in wistful remembrance of searching out the always precocious three-year-old boy, who, by the time they'd arrived in the kitchens, had already taken himself off—with the whole platter of Molasses Pulls emptied. "When I found you... do you know what you were doing?"

He didn't so much as move. But his eyes followed her every movement.

"Justina and Phoebe had been abed, ill... and they'd been so very sad that they couldn't sneak down to the ballroom to watch the festivities. You'd brought every last piece of Molasses Pull abovestairs to your sisters so they wouldn't be sad." Tears misted her eyes. "*That* is the manner of boy you were..." And the manner of person he could still be.

He stepped back. Then with lurching steps, he moved behind his desk. "I was a babe," he said bitterly as he sat. "I daresay it hardly says much about me that the last *kind* act I'd ever carried out was almost twenty years ago."

"No, Andrew," she said firmly, holding his gaze. "There have been others. You, however, are so very determined not to see the good in yourself." If he continued along with this feigned diffidence, he would see himself hanged... with Nathaniel being the one to name him guilty of that crime.

Victoria scrabbled with the sides of her skirts, her gaze automatically going to the longcase clock. She squinted across the room, cursing her eyes that no longer could pull those small marks on the clock into clear focus. Five before nine o'clock.

Nathaniel would be here soon. *Again.* How did they proceed after last night, now that all the mysteries had been solved, and one impossible barrier—his investigation of Andrew—remained to any possible friendship? Friendship. *You could never be happy with solely friendship from Nathaniel Archer. But with his devotion to the Brethren, there could never be more, either.*

Her son picked up a pen and tapped it back and forth in a vexing staccato.

She looked again at the clock.

Two more minutes until he arrived. For there could be no doubt Nathaniel Archer, now the Earl of Exeter, had always been punctual.

Not always. There had been one time.

I was going to marry you… I would have you know that…

"Perhaps, he will not show," Andrew said in bored tones, the way one discussing the tepid lemonade at Almack's might. He kicked his feet up on the edge of the mahogany desk. "From what I hear of the gent in the papers, he's a pompous sort. I would wager this tedious investigation is beneath him."

Victoria pursed her mouth. There was nothing pompous about Nathaniel Archer. "Given the discourtesy Society has done our family over the years, you would be wise to not put any stock in their *opinions.*" Annoyed, she leaned over and gave his feet a nudge, shoving them over the edge.

Andrew's feet landed on the floor. "Regardless, I will say I'm honored that such a distinguished official from the Home Office should personally oversee *my* case."

The Brethren. The organization was the Brethren. A distinguished network of men and women who'd made sacrifices for the good of the Crown and country. Although she abhorred the Brethren, and always had for the love and devotion Nathaniel had given it, she respected those who'd given of themselves for the betterment of England. As such, she'd not let her son disparage Nathaniel or anyone else who served within that secret division of the Home Office.

Andrew again lifted his feet to the edge of that immaculate mahogany surface, looping his legs at the ankles.

Approaching footfalls sent her heart into double time. *He is here.* What did one say in the light of a new day? How did they act toward one another? *Nothing's changed. The only reason he returned was to investigate Andrew. The fact that the past came to light did not undo everything to come before.* She gave her son's feet another shove. "Do not do this, Andrew," she said in hushed tones.

With a labored sigh, he stood, just as Manfred opened the door.

"Lord Exeter," he announced and then quit the room, closing the wood panel with a decisive click.

While Nathaniel came forward, Victoria studied him for some hint of what he was thinking or feeling. Alas, he was, as ever, an impeccably cool spy, master of his emotions. *What in the blazes is the matter with you, Victoria Cadence? He may have been the only man you ever gave your heart to but he's here now to question Andrew about your late husband's murder.*

As if to punctuate that reminder, Andrew called out jovially. "Lord Exeter." He tossed his arms open as though greeting an old friend. "A pleasure. An absolute…" Her son's lips peeled in a sneer. "Pleasure."

If Andrew intended to elicit some kind of response from Nathaniel, he was to be disappointed. "My lord." Nathaniel's perfunctory greeting raised a slight scowl from the younger man. Then, he looked to Victoria. He swept his thick lashes down, deftly concealing those violet irises, but not before she registered the spark within their depths. "My lady," he murmured.

"Permission to only call you 'my love', and never 'my lady'…"

"Permission granted, my heart…"

Her pulse quickened. "Lord Exeter." She winced at the breathless quality, stealing a sideways peek at her son to see whether he'd noted that exchange.

Andrew yawned. "If I might see to a drink before we begin, my lord?" he asked, already making for that damned sideboard. Victoria gnashed her teeth. One day, she was going to take the bloody broadsword hanging in the Portrait Room, above the gold frame with the first Viscount Waters memorialized, and break apart that hated piece of furniture.

Nathaniel glanced between her and her son. "Of course, please do not allow my presence to detract from how you might normally conduct yourself."

"You don't drink brandy, Lord Archer? Every gentleman drinks brandy."

"Spirits loosen a man's lips, Victoria. Drinking makes him careless. And... I prefer my lips for kissing only yours..."

Only now, it was her son's loose lips that would be careless. He'd paint a portrait of guilt, even when she was confident there was none there.

"Andrew," she began, but her son interrupted.

"My mother expressed her displeasure with my previous drink selection." He laughed, holding up a half-empty bottle of whiskey. "She did not, however, mention anything about a *different* form of spirits." The clink of crystal touching crystal, followed by the steady stream of liquid filled the quiet. After he'd set the decanter down, Andrew wheeled about, faintly unsteady. He tapped his spare palm against his forehead. "My goodness. Where are my manners? A brandy, my lord? Mother didn't say anything about what you may or may not drink."

"No brandy," Nathaniel demurred, lifting a hand. Her son had needed someone like him in his life. He'd needed the stabilizing influence of a loving father, who'd have shown him the perils of alcohol and encouraged him to use his mind.

She and Nathaniel stood in an awkward silence as Andrew hummed a tavern ditty.

"Won't you sit, my lord," she offered.

With a murmured word of thanks Nathaniel settled into one of the leather winged chairs. Victoria hurried to claim the one at his side. How was it possible to both want him near and gone, all at the same time? Those contradictory sentiments were a product of his investigation.

Glass in hand, Andrew returned to his desk chair. "Now, shall we begin?" he urged convivially.

Nathaniel turned to putting on his spectacles and readying his pencil and notebook. He opened his mouth, but Andrew cut in.

"I might be able to save both of us time. Yes, I hated my father. Yes, he was a cruel bastard. I'm hardly bereft that he's dead, merely surprised he didn't meet his maker long, long ago."

"Andrew," she said tightly, looking frantically to Nathaniel—Nathaniel, whose every ounce of focus remained on the disheveled young man across from him.

Ignoring her, he dropped his voice to a whisper. "But then, what is it they say? Only the good die young, eh? As such, I trust that I'll escape the hangman's noose and live to drink another day." His slender frame shook with laughter.

"That is enough, Andrew," she snapped, curling her toes into the soles of her satin slippers. *Damn him, why is he doing this?* Why? *Why?*

He rolled his eyes. "Come, Mother. I've been through how many interrogations, now? Five? Six? I'm rather proficient in the questioning now, Lord Exeter, and merely sought to spare both of us the time."

His movements measured, Nathaniel closed his book and set it aside, resting the pencil atop it. Steepling his glove-encased fingers together, he drummed the tips; all the while eyeing her son over the top. "Your sister, the Duchess of Huntly, indicated your father turned violent."

Andrew scoffed. "Turned violent."

Victoria gripped the arms of the chair hard, wanting the questioning over now, for altogether different reasons.

Nathaniel ceased the silent tapping. "You disagree with the assessment?"

Her son took a sip of his whiskey. "My father didn't turn violent. He was always violent." *Please do not say anything. Please do not say anything.* Apparently, the fates were otherwise too busy that day to hear her pleadings. Andrew whipped his focus over to her. "Isn't that true, Mother?"

Victoria pleaded with her eyes, meeting his question with silence. Just a few hours ago, Nathaniel had lashed himself with an undeserved guilt for a decision she'd made in wedding Chester. She didn't want the ugliest parts of her life laid bare before Nathaniel. Didn't want him trying to assign himself blame for the misery she'd endured.

His features dark, Nathaniel looked between mother and son.

It was Andrew who broke the impasse. "Surely you did not forget that day, Mother?"

"Tell me of that day." That somber prodding from Nathaniel only set her stomach to churning all the more.

She fought in vain to get a protestation out past her tightened throat.

"I heard screams. Horrible ones." And for Andrew's early show of indifference, his composure slipped. Within his eyes were the haunted memories of a young man who'd carried the nightmares of his past with him, always.

"What was it?" Nathaniel quietly asked, his voice steady. Inside, Victoria was splintering apart.

"Please don't," she beseeched, her voice thin. He'd expose her deepest shame to Nathaniel.

Andrew's throat muscles moved. "He had my mother, with her skirts up—" A keening moan filtered around the office. Was that tortured sound her own? "Was fumbling with the fastenings of his breeches."

Her breath rasped loudly in the quiet parlor.

Oh, God.

"You whore... but you are my whore, Victoria..."

The horrors of that day came crashing back like waves of a tempest, battering her, suffocating. Andrew had been a boy of five... Victoria had already managed to thwart her husband's advances for four years, when he'd returned from his clubs, drunk. Her own pleas and efforts to thwart him were futile. Her fingers twitched and she ached to slap them over her ears.

"Tsk, tsk." Andrew wagged a disapproving finger at a frozen Nathaniel. "Aren't you going to ask me what happened next?"

"Andrew," she begged, his name emerging on a tortured moan.

"What...?" Nathaniel's strangled voice was that of a stranger's; unfamiliar and heavy with fear. It drowned out her own whisper-soft plea.

"I grabbed the fireplace prodder—"

"Don't, Andrew," she urged, her voice hollow, hating that he'd take that great act of salvation... for her, and attempt to seal his fate as a man with it.

"And I jammed it in his arse. Stabbed him good, didn't I, Mother? And just five years old," he said softly, as if he spoke solely for himself. "He screamed like a stuck pig, he did," Andrew added with a hideous chuckle. He turned his gaze squarely on Nathaniel. "That day, I told him the next time he hurt my mother, I'd kill him with it. That I'd put it through his throat."

A single tear streaked down her cheek. It had been the last time her husband had ever attempted to force himself on her... or put his hands upon her in any way—until he'd only just recently lashed out at her, blaming her for Justina's marriage to a man who'd intended to bankrupt them.

"Stitches were required. The doctor patched him up. I prayed he'd die, anyway." His lips twisted into a macabre grin that raised gooseflesh upon her arms. "The day I came upon him after Justina's marriage, with his hands upon my mother, I wanted to kill him all over again. And I'm not sorry for one instant that he's gone from this earth. Hell is the only place he belonged." Casually standing, Andrew finished off his drink and set it down. "Take that information and do with it what you will, Lord Exeter." His mouth firmed into the flat line of a man who'd not be countered—by anyone, not even the fierce former spy before him. "But I'm done answering questions about my *dear* father. From you or the Runners or the constables, or the Devil himself come to collect."

Without a backward glance, Andrew stalked from the room. Silence lingered in his wake.

Victoria curled her fingers on her lap, forming a joined fist, staring blankly down at the blood-drained knuckles. She stiffened as Nathaniel, silent as the grave, sank to a knee beside her chair. "Victoria," he began, his voice catching.

She shook her head tightly. "I don't want to talk about it, Nathaniel."

He layered his hands, over hers. And this time, he didn't say anything, just offered his steadying presence. Victoria held herself stiffly erect, hating that his nearness in this was not enough. The gates of her hell had been opened and the demons let out to torture her all over again.

He took her in his arms and she held herself taut against him. She was afraid that if she faltered, she'd never recover from the agony of those excruciating memories. Only—he simply held her. He didn't seek to offer useless assurances. Didn't seek to murmur platitudes. Didn't offer unnecessary apologies and, for that, she was grateful. For ultimately, she had married Chester. It had been a match maneuvered by her father, but one she could have very well declined and suffered through the consequences thereafter. Nathaniel just held her and, at last, she folded into him, filling her lungs with the sandalwood scent of him.

Victoria didn't know how much time passed while they

remained locked in one another's arms, with Nathaniel smoothing his hands in small circles over her back. It was she who broke that tender embrace. "He didn't do it, Nathaniel," she said solemnly. "I know he told you about…" She faltered. "About what he did to my husband to feed the opinions and the gossips." The way one who sought a death sentence might. A cold stole through her. "He didn't do it," she repeated on a tense whisper.

   "I know."

CHAPTER 13

Rely upon both your skill and gut instinct in the field.
Article XIII: The Brethren of the Lords

HAD ANOTHER INVESTIGATOR RECEIVED THE answers Nathaniel had from a suspect's kin, and then been witness to the ruthless admission made about the death of the murder victim, it would have no doubt sealed the young man's fate. But he had devoted more than twenty years of his life learning the nuances of suspects and those guilty of charges and knew—

Andrew Barrett, Viscount Waters had not killed his father.

Nor had Nathaniel's determination been made out of a wanting to see Waters innocent to spare Victoria from further suffering.

Victoria wetted her lips. "You… know?"

"I do," he confirmed, unfurling to his full height. He'd all the confirmation to suit his own opinions, not enough to yet exonerate the lad. And he should be filled with a palpable relief for it. To send Victoria's son to the gallows or banish him to a penal colony would have brought an altogether new suffering for him… and her.

Yet, there was a gaping, jagged hole ripped through his heart, left by the revelation her son had made a short while ago. Viscount Waters had deserved to die the precise, demoralizing, ruthless end he'd met for every hurt he'd inflicted.

Victoria touched his right shoulder. It urged his thoughts away from the torturous path the young Waters had set them on and over to the mission he'd undertaken.

"Your son feels guilty," he finally said. "He wears it in his indifference and hatred. A man who has committed murder is careful with his statements and how he paints previous exchanges with the victim." They certainly didn't speak with glee and relish of the *victim's* demise. "Your son is not a killer." A man who'd defended his mother at five, and again of late, was not the self-centered, mercenary lord Society portrayed him as.

"Thank you, Nathaniel," she whispered, pressing her shaking palm against her mouth. "Everyone believes… no one has trusted me when I argue he is innocent."

"I know." He firmed his jaw. "But that does not mean my opinion will suffice." The lords of London might judge a man as vile while he lived, but there was a code followed and expected to be followed… and the murder of one, may as well have been the murder of all.

A pall fell.

"What now?" she ventured.

How many women would be so collected? So in command, given all she'd suffered and the scandal that had shaken her family. His appreciation for her swelled all the more. "Now, we find who was responsible for your hus…" Nay. Not her husband. He could not bring himself to finish that thought. "For the late viscount's murder." They would locate and bring to justice the true criminal. It was the only way to clear Andrew Barrett, the current Viscount Waters, of any wrongdoing. Nathaniel gathered his leather folder and flipped it open. Suddenly, Victoria's shock-laden question reached him.

"We?"

He paused. "I trust you would know as well as anyone the enemies your husband might have." Not breaking stride, he crossed the room, and hurriedly turned the lock. Feeling Victoria's gaze on him, he looked back.

"What are you doing?"

"We are beginning our investigation." Filled with a renewed purpose, Nathaniel dropped his hands on his hips and did a turn about the office. "I take it this was your," *I cannot continually call that reprobate her husband. I cannot think of him in that way. It will shred my sanity…* "This was the late viscount's office."

Victoria nodded.

Nathaniel took up position behind the broad desk. Sinking onto the edge of the leather chair, he opened the drawer, and proceeded to sift through the contents. Brimming with parchment, the sloppy space was better suited to a negligent young student away to Cambridge for the first time. *Pens. Papers.* He shoved the drawer shut and shifted his attention to the row down the side of the desk. Reaching inside the bottom one first, he stretched his hand far back and searched around.

Victoria sank to the floor beside him; the floral-fragrant scent permeating his senses, momentarily distracting him. "What are you searching for?" She puzzled her eyebrow.

"A hint of who the viscount kept company with and who he was indebted to."

Rising, Victoria hurried to the other side, pulled out the center drawer, and withdrew a black leather ledger. "This contains all accountings on his finances," she explained. "I've already provided this to the Bow Street Runners and constables. They removed them to record copies, they claimed, and then returned when their notes had been completed." Copies which currently resided inside Nathaniel's file and he'd committed to memory.

Nonetheless, he reached for the book. Their fingers brushed and an electric charge singed him. He accepted the ledger with trembling hands. The thrill of her touch ran through him with the same power it had in their youths. Laying the book open upon the desk, he removed his spectacles from his pocket and popped them on the bridge of his nose. He skimmed the first page. Wetting his finger, he turned the next, and the next—his skin pricked at the feel of her eyes on him.

He paused, mid-turn, staring questioningly back. Victoria wore a wistful smile on her timelessly beautiful face; that faint dimple in her cheek, lending her a youthfulness, all these years later. "What is it?" he asked guardedly.

She trailed her index finger along the wire metal rim that tucked around his ears. "I used to imagine us together, older, our children grown, with their own families. We'd be one of those couples who avoided *ton* events and sat in the countryside, reading." Her smile quivered. "In those imaginings, you wore reading spectacles."

The mark of his age reared itself. He was no longer a young spy of twenty. "I am old," he concurred, mourning all the time he'd lost with this woman and the fleetingness of youth. "I'm—"

"Five and forty," she murmured, gently stroking his cheek. "I know how old you are, Nathaniel Archer. You are no older than me."

"Two years," he pointed out. Nearly three.

A husky laugh spilled past her crimson lips. "I've round hips, wrinkles at my eyes, and you, who are more fit than when you were at twenty, would speak to me of age?"

"You are beautiful," he whispered. Relinquishing Waters' documents, Nathaniel cupped her face. "You are even more beautiful now—" He spoke over her sound of protest. "*Even* more," he repeated, "than when you were a fiery girl."

She sank her teeth into her lower lip. "There are times when I still feel as young as I was when we first met. Then I look in the mirror or confront what my life has been these past years and realize I'm not a girl. I'm just any other woman who has suffered through a loveless marriage with a rotted husband." Her voice cracked. "But who dreamed of love lost."

"Does it have to be?"

They both started. It was unclear in that instant who was most staggered by the urgency in that question.

"What?" she whispered.

His heart skittered inside his chest. What had he said? What was he proposing? After a lifetime of service to the Brethren, he'd received the coveted role of leader of that organization. He had men and women who relied upon him. *And I want Victoria.* "Does love have to be lost?" he asked, his voice more steady and clear. "Our love," he clarified.

She clenched and unclenched the bodice of her gown. "I don't… I didn't…" Then she took a hasty step back, tilting her head to look at him. Victoria straightened her shoulders. "What about the Brethren?"

That was what she'd ask. She'd not even answer his original question: the most important one he'd put to her. She would focus on the organization that had always been between them. It had severed his connection to her and cemented his role within the Brethren. But then, why should she not? She had her right and her reasons to be wary of his involvement with the agency.

At the lengthy silence, Victoria gave her head a sad, little shake and made to move.

"I could put it behind me?" he called out, instantly staying her.

Where had that come from? The Brethren was what had kept him sane when he'd lost her. It had given him purpose when the ghosts of Fox and Hunter had haunted him. Could he exist without it? Having given up on the dream of Victoria, he'd not allowed himself to think of a possibility of *anything* with her. If Victoria were in his life he would not need the Brethren as he had all these years.

Victoria's lips parted. But then, she cocked her head at a slight, sad little angle. "It was a question."

He shook his head. "No." Nathaniel grimaced. Is it a wonder she'd construed it as such? "I was not asking—"

Victoria pressed her fingertips to his lips, staving off the lie he'd give her. "Do not insult me by thinking I didn't hear the question there, Nathaniel," she said, sadness glimmered within her eyes. Clearing her throat, she made a show of digging around the late viscount's desk drawers.

Panic swelled in his chest.

A need to make her understand, built within him. "After my capture." She stopped her distracted efforts. "The only thing that kept me sane was my work. My rashness nearly saw me dead. It cost me—" Emotion wadded in his throat. "You. It cost me you." Pain bled from her eyes. "I was eventually named Delegator—the one who handed out missions—and I devoted my life to ensuring the safety of every young man and woman that came to the Brethren. I swore that no one would lose everything as I did."

"You weren't the only one who lost, Nathaniel." Victoria tapped her palm to her chest. "I did, too. And I'm still losing to your Brethren."

I'm losing her. Offer her everything she deserves. "Victoria—"

"This isn't the time." Letting her hand fall, Victoria set to work stacking the papers into a neat pile, toying with the corners. "We were only speaking of hypotheticals, anyway. We have the case to focus on. My son."

And it was that moment when he knew she was gone to him—all over again. Nathaniel dragged a hand through his hair.

"Victoria—"

She quelled him with a look.

He sighed, more coward than he'd ever credited, because he welcomed the distraction from his riotous thoughts. "Aside from the ledgers, has anything been moved, discarded, or replaced?"

"Everything is precisely as he left it." She touched her eyes around the room, lingering briefly upon the sideboard. "Though the sideboard is slightly less stocked in the two months since Andrew was named viscount." Her mouth pulled in a grimace.

Drunkard. The bloody whoreson bastard. Nathaniel stalked over to the concave, two-door sideboard cabinet and inspected the surface space. Ultimately, what mattered most to a man was how and where he oftentimes buried his secrets. He dropped to a knee and felt around the sides of the piece.

Victoria drifted over. "What are you searching for?"

He paused briefly in his efforts. "I'm looking for any compartments that might be used to conceal information." Lying prone on his stomach, he attempted to angle his head to view under the darkened space. But the five-inch gap made it impossible to see anything. Damning his eyes that had lost their sharpness, he squinted. "Most gentlemen with vices have specific places where they hide valuable documents or personal artifacts," he said under his breath, feeling all along the perimeter of the mahogany piece. Those hidden stashes invariably proved incriminating pieces of evidence that had been used to convict many, many criminals.

"Wouldn't it make far more sense to hide it within the cabinet drawers?" Curiosity piqued in her voice as she opened one of those items in question and inspected inside.

"It would be too obvious to do so," he explained. He felt along the scalloped edges of the legs.

She closed the drawer, ending her quick search. "You're wasting your time. My husband wasn't clever enough to hide anything," she muttered. Nonetheless, she lowered herself to the floor, positioning her body parallel to his. She was so close their foreheads brushed.

Nathaniel paused in his search and lifted his eyes to meet hers.

"We are both part of this now," she said. The defensive edge there hinted at a woman braced for a challenge.

What a fool her husband had been. He'd had as his wife a clever, fearless woman to call partner, in every sense, and he'd thrown away that gift. *Just as I'd done before… and again here, in this very room.*

Victoria stopped, her arm partially concealed under the sideboard. "What is it?" she whispered.

"There is no other woman like you." There never had been and there never would be.

A curl flopped over her eye and she blew it back. "I trust with the women you've no doubt worked alongside who kept the Crown safe that you'd be far less impressed by a widowed lady past her fortieth year, crawling around on her belly." Despite the drollness to her tone, contained within was something else—insecurity and more… jealousy.

Victoria made to reach under the cabinet, but he placed a hand on hers, staying it. She stared questioningly back. "When I said there was no one but you, Victoria," he said solemnly. "I meant there was never anyone after you. In any way." He paused, letting that settle in her mind. Willing her to understand that he'd not given himself to another after he'd returned to find her married.

Her breath caught loudly.

His neck went hot. That flush climbed all the way to his cheeks.

"Oh, Nathaniel," she whispered.

Feeling exposed, he nudged his chin at the cabinet. "Victoria," he said again when she resumed her digging. She stopped, yet again, staring at him questioningly. "You gave birth to three loyal and loving children. You endured hell that no woman ought. Yet, through that, still your daughters retained an innocence and belief in love. Do not," he said with firm insistence, "for one instant, diminish what you yourself have accomplished in life."

"I'm a mother, Nathaniel," she said bluntly. "I'm no different from every other woman who has given birth and put her children first."

He pressed his forehead to hers, willing her to see. "You were left with a babe in your belly." *By me. I left you to face that uncertain fate, alone.* "And you built a life that was secure for you and your…" His throat closed. "*Our* daughter." It was the first time he'd uttered those words aloud since she had revealed the truth of Phoebe's existence.

Victoria shoved herself awkwardly up onto her elbows and sat up with her back to the sideboard. She drew her knees close.

Dropping her chin atop them, she rubbed back and forth. With each slight movement, she was very much the contemplative woman who'd sat there, asking him about the places he'd been and the world he'd seen. Then she spoke, breaking the illusion of the splendor of innocence. "I married a monster. And even as I said I'll forever be grateful for Justina and Andrew, the truth remains that I thrust Phoebe into a precarious fate by forcing an undeserving man upon her as father."

His heart cracking, Nathaniel levered himself up and sat beside her; shoulder to shoulder, thigh to thigh. "You must hate me." From the corner of his eye, he caught her swiftly yanking her gaze up. "You and Phoebe were both placed into that precarious state by me." *And me alone.*

Victoria was already shaking her head. "I knew when you first revealed the truth of your existence the dangers… for both of us. I wasn't a child, Nathaniel," she insisted. "I was also aware of the risk that I might find myself with child."

He turned his head to face her. "How is it you are so capable of forgiving me and painting me as a man of honor when you're unable to do the same for yourself?"

Victoria started. She opened her mouth and closed it. She tried again.

He waggled his eyebrows.

"It is altogether different," she mumbled, knocking her shoulder against his.

"We should both resolve to forgive ourselves." For what good could come of dwelling on the years lost and self-recrimination? Neither would restore the missed time. Nathaniel stretched out his fingers.

Victoria eyed them a moment. Then she slid her palm into his, completing that pact.

He smiled. This was the first true, honest expression of joy he'd managed in all the years since he'd been taken captive. And there was something so wholly cathartic… so very freeing in it. Victoria's lips turned up in a matching expression.

"We were looking for hidden compartments, then," she murmured and, unlike before, this was not stilted dialogue but rather a companionable exchange. An easy one. Just as it had always been with her.

"Precisely." He flipped onto his stomach, once again, and Victoria instantly matched his movements. Before he could resume his search, she rummaged around under the cabinet.

"As I said, Chester didn't have a brain in his head. And he certainly didn't have an arm small enough to fit—" She gasped, her eyes rounding like saucers.

"What is—?"

Victoria shook her head. Scrunching up her brow, she stretched her arm further under the base.

That faint *click* as her fingers connected with a latch, the sound of triumph. Yanking her arm out, she sat up with alacrity brandishing a single faded scrap of parchment. Her eyes sparkled with the thrill that accompanied every young man and woman's first important discovery in an investigation. Then, she glanced down and that enthusiasm dimmed. "It is just a name," she said dejectedly. "A woman," she added, unsurprised and faint disgust there. "He had countless lovers and whores. Why would he keep this name hidden?" she asked, turning the scrap over to him.

There had been a reason for the viscount to go through the efforts to conceal it. Taking it, Nathaniel skimmed the page.

Ella Rosenberg

It was a lady's name but it was also more.

"You recognize it, don't you?"

His lips quirked in a droll grin. "If you're able to tell that, then I'm hardly the skilled spy I was during my younger years."

Coming up on her knees before him, she adjusted his spectacles, tucking the wire rims behind his ears in a loving gesture suited for a happy, old, wedded couple. "It is because I know you," she said simply.

"It's a gaming hell." He respected her too much to not reveal all. "One of the wickedest ones. No polite gentleman goes there. Generally, it is a place where nefarious business meetings are conducted." Nathaniel turned the page back around. "It also has a number contained within the letters."

Victoria squinted. With a quizzical brow, she did a search of the page.

"The two l's have been underlined," he clarified.

She gasped. "It was a meeting time."

He firmed his mouth. "Precisely." It did not, however, contain any other identifiers of when the meeting in question was to have been conducted. "Given he was set to conduct this meeting, there were certainly others to have come before it."

And it was the whores, dealers, and guards in there who'd have an idea of who those meetings had been conducted between. Folding the page, Nathaniel stuffed it inside his jacket.

"I want to go with you."

Bloody hell. He dusted a hand over his forehead.

Victoria tenderly removed his spectacles and folded them closed. "I *am* going with you," she amended, tucking the pair inside his jacket. She patted it. "I need to do this. I need to see the world that my husband belonged to. That… my son still does. I want to be there when you discover whatever it is you discover." There was a faint plea there that begged him to understand. "I've had so little control in every aspect of my life."

Nathaniel waged an internal war with himself. He wanted her nowhere near his world. Particularly not that seedy end of London where men were gutted and thrown into the Thames with none the wiser.

"You always sought to protect me," she said softly.

It was why he'd never married her. It was why he didn't want her to join him now. But she deserved to make this choice and own it. And he would be at her side. "This evening," he murmured.

Surprise and skepticism stirred in her eyes. "You would… take *me?*"

He dropped his brow to hers. "Victoria Cadence, you would go regardless."

They shared a tender smile. But then as quick as it had come, hers faded.

"For the whole of my marriage, I fought for any amount of control I could," she said softly, her gaze distant. "And aside from caring for my children, he allowed me no say in anything; our family's failing finances, business decisions. Nothing."

His gut clenched with equal parts pain and hatred for the miserable marriage she'd endured. And for all the years he'd spent resenting her for not waiting, now he had answers as to why. She'd deserved so much more. "I am so sorry, Victoria," he said hoarsely. For everything: lost time, for having failed to marry her when he'd gone. For all of it.

She made a sound of protest, moving closer. "Don't you do that," she chided. "Don't you pity me or take responsibility for decisions we both made." Gathering his hands, she squeezed them. "You are allowing me the opportunity to help absolve my son of wrongdoing and I'd only focus on that gift."

That gift. When most women sought baubles and fripperies, Victoria had never given a jot for any of the material. God, how he loved her.

Some of the pressure eased from his chest. "You'll need men's garments: breeches… and fabric to bind yourself." He made the mistake of dropping his gaze to her large breasts, straining the fabric of her modest décolletage. Lust bolted through him. "And your hair." Auburn tresses he ached to have spread out upon his pillow. "You'll need to plait your hair." She touched those gleaming strands. He swallowed hard with his hungering to run his hands through them. Nathaniel forced himself to continue. "Tuck it up under a cap."

Victoria nodded excitedly. "When will we go?"

It was a bloody sad day, indeed, when he stood here lusting after her and she'd nothing more than anticipation for their investigation. Disgusted, he gave his head a clearing shake. "A hired hack will be two townhouses down." It was no hired hack but rather an unmarked conveyance used by members of the organization when conducting official business. "I'll be waiting." Gathering his folders, Nathaniel started for the door, his mind refocused on the evening's visit to Ella Rosenberg's.

"Nathaniel," Victoria called out when he'd grabbed the handle.

He looked back.

"Thank you," she said, touching a hand to her chest.

Any other proper lady, widowed as she'd been, and the subject of Society's scorn, would have wilted long ago. How strong she was. How strong she'd always been. His heart filled all over again with love for her.

Nathaniel managed a slight nod. He hesitated. "Victoria," he called into the quiet. "Your husband… the viscount, he deserved murdering." And had someone not seen to it before and he had discovered the fate she'd suffered all these years, he would have gladly done the service for the bastard.

With that, he left.

CHAPTER 14

Men and women, regardless of station, are to be given
consideration for work within the organization.
Article XIV: The Brethren of the Lords

VICTORIA HAD NOT CREPT ABOUT since she'd been a young woman. To be precise, since Nathaniel Archer had left London, off on that fateful mission.

As a young woman just on the Market—and always to her parents' chagrin—she'd been one of the spirited sorts. With her then friends, Lady Adelaide and Lady Lillian, they'd been forever sneaking off... or helping one another to sneak off. To avoid an unwanted suitor. To meet with a beloved gentleman.

But just as her friendship with those two women had changed with time, so too had Victoria. She'd learned firsthand that no good could truly come from those thrilling clandestine meetings. Nothing could have drummed that particular point home more than the babe then growing in her belly.

And so, she'd shaped herself into a proper lady—a respectable woman, a devoted mother—and in a bid to spare her children the cruel lash of Society's tongue that came from her late husband's scandalous pursuits, Victoria had donned a fake smile, stifled her spirit, and made herself a pillar of a Society she had always hated.

Yet, all these years later, the thrill that came in throwing over societal conventions flared to life as fresh now as it had been when she'd made her Come Out.

Adjusting the cap that covered her plaited braid tucked up inside, she crept down the alley that led from her townhouse to the streets of Mayfair. With each step, she reveled in the freedom of her movements; unfettered by cumbersome skirts and yet… the occasional rumble of carriages in the distance lent a peril to her nighttime escapade.

Though Victoria didn't care one bit about her reputation, she did worry for her children and grandchildren's futures. If she were discovered, it would only add another layer of ignominy to their already scandalous family.

Her heart knocked several beats faster as she took care to hover in the shadows, avoiding the moonlit-covered path. It surely spoke to a deficit in her character for her excitement outweighed all worrying over respectability.

So this was the thrill Nathaniel had known over the years. In between pining for him and worrying about his well-being, as a young woman she'd secretly envied the work he'd undertaken on behalf of the Crown. She'd ached to know a taste of what his world had been.

And now I will.

Only, she'd seek out information that would exonerate her son, and free him and their family from the rumors abounding.

Victoria reached the end of the narrow path that led out to the streets and stopped; skimming her gaze about, until she located a hack four townhouses down. A sane woman would feel a modicum of fear at venturing out as she was as well as visiting a seedy hell in the dangerous streets of Seven Dials. She filled her lungs with a slow breath, relishing the cool night air. How very empowering this moment was.

And it was because of Nathaniel.

Her husband had believed her brainless. Her sons-in-law had both seen to dealing with her husband. Oh, they'd done so out of love, and she was eternally grateful to them for having prevented her from suffering further abuse at her husband's hands. But not a single one of those gentlemen would have ever sought to include her in matters of business, such as this. Nay… not *any* business. To them, she'd always been and would always be, Phoebe, Justina, and Andrew's mother, in need of looking after.

Nathaniel had placed an equal share of power into her hands. Her heart filled all over with love for him. She took a step and faltered. *Love. Of course, I love him. I've always loved him. It had, just as he'd said, only and always been him.*

She'd never stopped. Not even when he'd returned from more than twenty years absence, after letting her believe he'd died. She would always love him.

Victoria layered her back to the brick wall, borrowing support from that solid structure, and closed her eyes. It was Nathaniel who had always loved another... the Brethren. Oh, she didn't doubt he'd loved her. Believed he even cared about her still. But the drag in his speech and the flash of fear when she'd spoken of him giving up the Brethren had told her all she'd needed to know about any possible future between them.

There were men and women who relied upon him. People who served, who he felt a sense of responsibility for; to see that they didn't suffer the same fate that he had. And she understood that devotion... respected him and loved him for it.

Victoria sank her teeth into her lower lip and bit down hard enough to draw blood. But blast and hell, how she also hated that deep-seated devotion, too. How she wished that she was enough for him. *Stop.* She opened her eyes and opened her mouth to scream.

Instantly anticipating her response, the cloaked figure covered her mouth, drowning out the sound. Panic blanketing her senses, she brought her knee sharply up, catching the stranger right between the legs.

With a sharp gasp, he released her.

Once you've unsettled your opponent, press your suit... too many make one strike and flee... they'll catch you every time as you retreat...

She brought her fist back.

"Victoria," Nathaniel said, his voice gruff, catching her wrist.

She blinked slowly in the dark. And while her heart resumed its normal cadence, in the proper place in her chest, she squinted. "Nathaniel?" she whispered loudly. Doing an up and down sweep, she took in the black frockcoat and wool trousers. His garments were better suited to a shopkeeper or hackney driver than an earl and leader of the Brethren. "You startled me. Did I hurt you?" she asked before he could speak. "I hurt you." She looked down to

where she'd kneed him and then her cheeks exploded with heat.
"I…"

"Had a good instructor, madam," he whispered, close to her lips.

Victoria swatted. "Hush." He'd always sought to keep her from
worrying. "I don't distract as easily as I once did."

"I've lost a good deal of my charm, then," he said with a dryness
that brought her mouth up in another grin.

"You've never been more charming, Nathaniel Archer."

His eyes glimmered. "Even with my graying hair?"

The moon's glow cast its ray upon his black hair and she caught
one of the silver-tinged strands. "Especially with the handful of
gray you've begun sporting." Worry deepened the small wrinkles
at the corners of his eyes. *He is anxious.* It was why he stood here
even now delaying their departure.

She nodded. "It is time."

Nathaniel glanced down the path she'd just traveled and then out
toward the street. When he returned his focus to her, he offered
her a final opportunity to remain behind. "What you'll see at this
hell," he spoke in hushed tones, "is the kind of evil you can't truly
fathom until you step through the doors." It was the world her late
husband had firmly been entrenched in. She was surely going to
the Devil for, even in death, an equally potent wave of antipathy
slapped at her.

"Nathaniel," she said, stripping inflection from her tone. "I've
seen enough of the Devil at work in my life where nothing can
further jade me."

His face contorted in a paroxysm of grief. "I hate that for you.
I—"Victoria held silencing fingers to his lips, staying those words.
She didn't want his pity.

"I'm beginning again." *And I want you to be part of that new beginning.* That profession hung on the edge of her lips, aching to be
spoken. "I'm not waiting for life to unfold while others have control of my fate, or the fate of my family."

He recoiled. "Is that what you believe?" The hurt in that query
wrenched at her. "That you need to do this because I might somehow fail your son?"

Victoria opened her mouth to disabuse him of that notion but
stopped, looking at him. Truly looking at him. The scar upon his
cheek pulled tightly, revealing the tautness in his entire being. *Oh,*

Nathaniel. "Shortly after I had married," she began quietly. "After Phoebe was born, I immediately knew the folly of my decision."

He froze. Agony wreathing his features, and she smoothed those lines away with her palms. "He berated me. He called me vile names before the servants. He…"Victoria released him and balled her hands into tight fists. "He berated Phoebe when he was near and she was crying."Which, given the time he'd spent at his clubs, had been blessedly few times. "Each and every time, I blamed myself. For surely, the scandal and gossip would have been better to brave than the prison I'd confined myself to. I thought myself undeserving of happiness because of my decision to marry Chester."

"Oh, Victoria," Nathaniel said on a ragged whisper.

She shook her head, needing him to see. "It was one act. The ultimate sacrifice to give Phoebe a name. But do you know what, Nathaniel?"

He gave his head an uneven shake. "It would be so very easy to think of everything that went wrong because of my marriage and my decision to wed. But if I dwelled on that, I'd not focus on everything that came after, which is so much more important."

"Andrew and Justina."

"Love," she said simply. "Not only my children, but I've two sons-in-law and beautiful grandbabes." She held his gaze. "You have forced yourself to pay penance for your capture, Nathaniel, and yet you still do not realize."

His entire body spasmed. She longed to take him in her arms and hold him close so she might drive back the demons that still haunted him. "Realize what?" That question came as though dragged from him.

"That even dedicating yourself to the Brethren will not undo that horrible, horrible time in your life. It will always be there." And how she hated that for him. Wanted to make his nightmares only hers. "And you are deserving of happiness, too." It had taken her years to learn to smile again and to find it was all right *to* smile. Victoria gathered his gloved hand in hers and squeezed. "Now, come."

With that two-word utterance, he was restored to unflappable spy. He proceeded to speak, rapidly firing off instructions for the evening. "You will walk ten paces ahead of me. As soon as you enter the hack, I'll continue in the opposite direction and connect with the carriage on Chesterfield Hill." She hurried to categorize all the details in her mind. "When we arrive at the hell, I'll allow five paces between us until we reach it. Then you're at my side." Nathaniel reached inside his jacket. He pressed something cold against her palm.

She glanced down.

The pistol glinted in the dark.

"Tuck this inside the front of your jacket. Keep a hand on it at all times through the garment. Everyone will know precisely what you have there." He dropped a quick kiss on her lips. "Go."

That was it. No verifying that she'd gathered all that and fully understood everything laid out. He hadn't sought to protect her like a wilting flower but had, instead, let her be part of this. With her lightest step in more than two decades, she sprinted down the alley and for the hack. The driver sat in position, his beaver hat low and his hands poised on the reins. Opening the door, Victoria pulled herself up inside with a little grunt. An instant later, the conveyance sprung into movement. There was no servant waiting to admit her or gentlemen to hand her up. In this, and in his orders, Nathaniel had treated her with the same respect he would have any of the members of his staff.

She stifled a smile. And how wonderful it felt to not be coddled in this.

While the carriage continued along at a brisk clip, Victoria sat back amongst the comfortable squabs; the immaculate, gold velvet at odds with the outside of the ramshackle carriage.

She'd lived in a world of black and white for so long. Either a lady was to be cared for… or she struggled through life arduously, without the support or regard of anyone at her side. She had not believed it possible to have both, to have one who'd look after her to see she was safe and protected, but who also trusted and respected her enough to include her in matters directly affecting her and her family's future. She closed her eyes as a wild fluttering unfurled low in her belly.

The conveyance rocked to a stop. Her eyes popped open, just as the carriage door opened.

Instinctively, Victoria reached for her gun just as Nathaniel's powerful form filled the doorway. He moved his gaze from her hand to her face and smiled. "Brava, my love. Brava."

Closing the door behind them, the driver started onward to the Ella Rosenberg. And hopefully, answers that would pardon her son.

CHAPTER 15

When on a mission, do not let one's guard down.
Article XV: The Brethren of the Lords

NATHANIEL HAD SET FOOT INSIDE so many seedy establish-
ments, dark alleys, and dangerous wharves that they'd long ceased
to so much as raise his pulse.

Until now.

With Victoria at his side, they made their way through the club.
The raucous din of laughter and bawdy discourse was near deafening. And even with their shoulders nearly brushing, Nathaniel
struggled to see her through the heavy cloud of smoke that hung
in the air.

*She will be fine. She will be fine. You are at her side. You schooled her in
the carriage on the need for her silence and the importance of her silently
recording every exchange. Focus on the questions you have and the case.*

Those reassurances and reminders a litany in his head didn't do
anything to ease his worrying. "Here," he said in low tones, stopping at a table in the back corner of the establishment. Yanking
out the chair positioned against the wall, he sat. "Sit." He jerked
his chin at the place opposite his.

As Victoria claimed a seat, he began combing his gaze over the
establishment. He shot two fingers up. A moment later, a buxom
serving woman sashayed over. Her large breasts and hips squeezed
into an aged bone corset that pushed the enormous flesh to strain

the article. She had a hard face, heavily rouged, that did little to hide the hard lines of living her life.

"Ya want a good time, luvy?" she purred in her guttural Cockney, rubbing her breasts against his chest.

Victoria's eyes flashed fire.

Favoring the older woman with an affectionate stroke, he grinned. "Another time, luv," he declined, in a perfect mimic of her tones. "Two ales."

She poured first one glass and then, not even looking, shoved it across the greasy, scarred table toward Victoria. "Ya sure, luv?" she persisted, after she'd filled his tankard. Setting aside her pitcher, she massaged his shoulders and placed her lips close to his ear. "Ya smell real noice. Oi can show ya a good time," she promised on a sultry whisper. Her tongue darted out to caress his lobe, even as she reached around and cupped him between his legs.

A menacing growl slashed across the noise of the hell.

Undeterred, the serving wench grinned a lopsided smile. "'Ere with the boy are ya?" she surmised. Sliding around the table, she crept her hands over Victoria's arms. "No bother. Oi can show both of ya a good time." Even as Victoria angled away from the server's cloying attempts, the woman nuzzled her lips against Victoria's neck. "Ooh, an' this one smells even better."

Victoria shoved at the other woman, knocking her back. "Ain't interested."

There was no way anyone could mistake that husky contralto as belonging to a woman. Yet, the serving wench turned her shoulder dismissively, retraining her efforts on Nathaniel.

"Then it's just to be us, then?" She grinned another gap-toothed smile. "All the better. Me name's Maj."

The ice in Victoria's eyes was cold enough to freeze the serving woman. She rose all the more in his estimation for her control. He held up a staying hand just as the whore moved to continue her advances. "We are actually 'ere for information."

The woman instantly straightened, all business. "Wot koind of information?"

"About a nob who used to visit 'ere."

"Used to?" she asked, suspicions dripping from her voice.

"He's dead."

Her expression shuttered and she took a cautious step back.

"Don't know anything about that."

"We didn't mention a name," Victoria retorted, in an impressively accurate Cockney that may as well have belonged to a small street lad.

Finally glancing away from Nathaniel, Maj scowled in Victoria's direction. "If he's a dead nob, Oi don't know anything about it." To admit knowledge of a lord's death could only bring trouble to the people who called the Dials home.

"'e wasn't a friend," Victoria continued, hatred and disgust deepened her voice, lending it a darker quality that masked her femininity all the more.

Understanding dawned in the old woman's glassy eyes. "'Buggered ya, did 'e?"

Victoria flinched and the woman seemed to take that as an affirmation. She looked to Nathaniel. "Can't 'elp ya or yar brother," she said, mistaking his and Victoria's relationship. She wet her lips like a starving man who'd had a plate held out. "Unless ya 'ave coin. Then Oi moight 'ave information."

Everything and anyone could be bought in these streets. But too many men in search of information quickly offered up coin, shattering the cover they'd taken as a man in the streets. "Oi moight 'ave coin… if the information is roight."

Her fleshy lips pursed like one sucking on a lemon.

Nathaniel waited. Ultimately, greed always won out. Desperation had that effect on any person, regardless of station or circumstances. Sometimes it was a hungering for coin to feed an empty belly. In his case, it had been a reprieve from Fox and Hunter's torturing. Regardless, that time had left him with an invaluable lesson on using a person's weakness to his advantage. "Never moind," he said dismissively, already skimming the hell. "Oi'll foind someone else." He shot a hand up.

"No!" Maj made a quick grab for his arm, forcing it back down to his lap. "No need to be rash, luvy. Oi *moight* be able to 'elp. Wot da ya need?"

"Oi'm looking for information about a nob. 'e was a fancy gent who came 'ere for meetings."

"Could be anyone," the old woman pointed out. She scratched at her stomach. "Lots of lords come 'ere."

From across the table, Victoria's eyebrows shot up so high, they disappeared under the brim of her hat. Of course, though she'd suffered through a marriage to a reprobate like Waters, she couldn't realize the extent of underhanded activities lords and ladies of London took part in. In these very streets, even. No one could truly fathom the depth of evil that simmered under the surface of respectability, until one such as Nathaniel and the Brethren were immersed in that darkness. "This one was a viscount. Viscount Waters. Fat, drank 'eavily, wagered even more."

Recognition flared in her eyes and then was quickly gone. "Oi didn't know 'im."

Nathaniel lifted a hand up again.

"But oi moight know someone who did," she said hurriedly. "For the roight price, Oi can give ya the name of the whores he diddled." The serving wench easily tossed out those details about Victoria's late husband.

Not for the first time since agreeing to bring her here, he railed over the decision. He hated that she now saw this side of evil and also had the ugliness of her husband's sins paraded before her. But she was deserving of the truth. He'd sought to protect her more than twenty years earlier and what good had that done her… or them? Discreetly withdrawing a sovereign, Nathaniel made a show of fondling the upper swells of the woman's enormous breasts. Her eyes brightened at the press of the cold coin against her skin. The older woman caught the gaze of someone across the room.

Almost instantly, a slender, dark-haired serving girl sauntered over. Her brown hair in ringlets and her pale cheeks rouged, there was an air of innocence still to the woman, despite the depravity unfurling about the room.

Maj introduced the waif-like beauty who, with the distance of the room erased, was more child than woman. "Kattie's one of our newer girls. The gents tend to favor 'er." The older server sneered. "Ain't that roight?"

It was a clear trap that, even with her tender years, Kattie had enough sense not to fall into. "What do you want?" she asked Nathaniel instead with shockingly cultured tones.

Maj answered for him. "The fellow 'as questions about a nob. A fat viscount." Maj paused meaningfully. "'E 'as coin."

"Oi'm done with ya." Nathaniel dismissed the older woman. "Get out."

Pouting, she plucked her pitcher from the table and shuffled off to another table.

Nathaniel motioned to the vacant chair. "Oi 'ave some questions."

"Ya a constable?" she countered, making no move to take that seat.

He shook his head.

"A Runner," she shot back, the wariness in her eyes deepening.

"Oi'm a man who wants some answers. Oi 'ave coin that Oi'm willing to pay for the roight information."

The girl still remained as she was, revealing far less of the desperation than her older counterpart had. "Who is this?" she asked, nodding at Victoria.

"Oi'm also a man who wants answers," she responded for herself. How effortlessly she'd adopted that Cockney. Pride swirled in his chest. With her wit and strength, she would have been a great agent. Shock went through him… quickly chased away by shame for having failed to even consider a like future for her. It marked him, in ways, no different than her small-minded husband. "And oi want answers," Victoria growled.

"You aren't much of a man," Kattie observed, and Nathaniel went still. But then her next observation broke some of the tension. "I doubt you even have whiskers to shed."

"And ya aren't much of a woman," Victoria rejoined. "Oi doubt ya've even seen sixteen years."

A sad, bitter smile curled Kattie's lips. "You would be wrong on that score." Jerking out the chair, she sat. "You have five minutes."

Nathaniel dropped his elbows and leaned forward. "There was a nob, the Viscount Waters." Recognition darkened the girl's eyes, turning the blue irises a shade very nearly sapphire. He pounced. "Wot did ya know of 'im?"

"I know the world is better off without men such as him in it," she answered matter-of-factly.

Yes, the girl was correct on that score.

"Were ya one of his lovers?" Victoria put forward.

"Lovers?" Kattie scoffed. "You *are* an innocent pup, if that's how you'd refer to what takes place in these halls." A wretched despair contorted the girl's face and she quickly masked it, glancing about. "Four minutes," she warned. When she glanced back, her features were carefully composed.

"Ya didn't bed 'im," he supposed. "But ya 'ad dealings with 'im. To wot end?" Having wagered, whored, and drank while living, Waters' dealings with this woman couldn't have been innocent.

This time, Kattie edged closer. "How much is it to you?" Hope stirred in her eyes, still fresh like her unblemished tones, despite the hell she knew here. It wouldn't be much longer before all innocence was shattered.

"Oi'm not discussing payment until ya begin speaking." Looking to Victoria, he gave her a signal to stand.

"Wait," Kattie rasped, grabbing his hand. "Just… tell me," she pleaded. "How much is the information worth to you?"

He'd negotiated with countless whores, thieves, and beggars over the years where the sight of that desperation had ceased to affect him. Or that had been the way. Now, for the first time in more years than he could remember, something gave him pause. *I have a daughter, not many years older than the woman before me.* The idea of Phoebe ever reduced to such circumstances cut him open, proving him very much human. "It will be worth yar efforts," he promised. "A sovereign for every bit of information that's useful." Regardless of what she turned over, he'd hand her a fat purse to see her through the coming months.

She nodded slowly. "What do you wish to know?"

"Ya weren't 'is lover. So wot use did 'e 'ave with ya?"

"He came here monthly to meet with a man, a merchant. Waters wanted me on his lap whenever he was here, though." She shuddered. "Never anything more, but that was enough." And Victoria had been forced to endure how many painful couplings with that bastard?

His stomach churned and he fought back the nausea, refocusing on his line of questioning. "Why would 'e do that?" When it didn't fit with everything that had been whispered about the whoremonger?

Kattie lifted her shoulders in a little shrug. "If I had to venture a guess, to confuse the other lords. He wanted them believing he was here to diddle a whore. He fondled me and then after his meeting ended, sent me on my way and took his leave."

It had been a cover, then. To what end? Questions swirled around his mind, all demanding to be asked.

"Who was the man?" Victoria asked quietly.

"Mr. Donaldson."

Mr. Donaldson. Nathaniel briefly searched Victoria for a hint that the name meant something, finding only her quizzical brow. "Is that 'is real name?" Nearly every man who conducted business in these seedy parts withheld the truth of his identity. But for the lords whose lineage and rank went forever with them.

"He's a hat maker in Luton. A popular one. Wealthy." Kattie flattened her lips. "How many questions have proven helpful to you?"

In response, Nathaniel carefully withdrew five sovereigns. Making a show of scratching his leg, he turned over the small fortune with the table concealing his efforts.

The girl's throat worked as she stole a glance about and then pocketed her bounty. "I have more," she confessed, at last revealing the desperation all these people here carried. "You've more coin?"

He nodded once, urging her on.

"He was murdered."

Nathaniel pushed back his seat. "All of London knows about the nob who was nicked."

"Wait," she pleaded. She scrabbled with his leave. "*Before* he was murdered... Waters met another gent here—another lord." Her lips peeled in a sneer. "The nobleman invited himself to sit at Waters' table. At first Waters seemed eager to be rid of him. Looking about, shifty-eyed around the room, mostly focusing on the door."

Nathaniel leaned closer, wanting that name. "Who was it?"

"The Marquess of Tennyson."

At the mention of one of his agents, Nathaniel masked his surprise. The *gentleman* had turned over his file and met with Nathaniel following his taking over of the case. Yet... this young girl's information raised questions about what else Tennyson might know. "That will be all," he murmured. Removing a small purse from inside his boot, he handed the velvet sack over to her.

A sheen of tears filled her eyes. "You aren't a street tough," she rightly predicted, shifting about as she concealed the just received money.

"It doesn't matter who Oi am." As clever as she was, and articulate, he'd be wise to hire one such as her. "Oi'm going to send someone to speak to ya tomorrow. There will be more money," he promised. And an interview by Bennett, and then a post, if Nathaniel's instincts were correct about her.

The girl made to rise.

"Kattie?" he said quietly, halting her.

"'as Donaldson returned since Waters' murder?"

She shook her head. "No."

He nodded, sending her on her way. After she'd drifted off, dissolving into the crowd, Nathaniel shoved aside his tankard and stood. Victoria jumped up.

With Victoria a pace in front of him, they made their way through the crowded hell. He followed the slight sway of her hips that if any of the men present weren't already out of their head with drink and opiates, would have seen at a mere glance that a lady moved among their midst in disguise. Her hand remained tucked inside her jacket in that ominous warning, he'd instructed her to use.

God, she was marvelous. The sheer courage and fearlessness of her was unmatched in most men he knew.

They exited through the double-doors of Ella Rosenberg, past the two brutish guards stationed there. The raucous din followed them long after the doors were closed at their backs, spilling out to the dirtied cobbles. Doing a quick search of the noisy streets, Nathaniel consulted his surroundings, seeking threats from within the shadows. Together, they walked briskly toward the waiting carriage at the end of the street.

"Stay close," he said from the corner of his mouth, matching his stride to her smaller one.

Shivers of apprehension danced down his spine. It was a familiar sensation that had saved him countless times before. The one time he had ignored it had seen him drugged, and thrown into Fox and Hunter's cellar. Only this was different. This wasn't solely himself he had to worry after. This was Victoria, whose existence mattered more to him than his own.

Five paces away, a looming figure stepped out of the alleyway and energy surged through Nathaniel's veins. He stopped abruptly, putting a hand on Victoria's arm.

The moon's glow bathed the stranger's pockmarked face in an eerie light, highlighting the macabre curl of a vicious grin. "You asking questions about Donaldson, I understand?" the man asked, looping his thumbs inside the front waistband of his jacket.

"Nathaniel,"Victoria said from the corner of her mouth.

His gut churned. *Why in the hell did I bring her here?* An exchange that would have once invigorated him, left him numb. *I want her far from this place.* "Hand on your pistol. When I tell you to run, you run. Don't look back."

"I asked you a question," the brute compelled, sauntering forward. His modulated tones spoke to an education, and fit more with the double-breasted sapphire frockcoat and buff breeches.

"Seemed more a question than a statement," he drawled. His lazy tones earned a scowl.

The man frustrated easily. It was a useful advantage he'd have pressed any other time; baiting the man to pull the first weapon or advance. Not now. Now, it was different.

"You have questions?"The man crooked his fingers. "Then you may come with me. I'll answer anything you wish to know. You and… the boy."

Fighting to calm the erratic beat of his heart, he stopped, positioning himself so that Victoria was partially concealed behind him. She moved closer so that her body brushed his. Her calm, strengthened his.

"Donaldson doesn't like men asking questions after him." The man lunged.

Go. "Run," he whispered. Charging forward, he lifted his leg mid-run, catching the assailant in his midsection. The man went down hard.

His breath coming fast from his exertions and adrenaline pumping through him, Nathaniel slammed an elbow into the man's nose. The loud crack of bone shattering was muffled by the ungodly scream that filtered from the man's lips. He followed that blow with another.

With a quiet groan, their assailant pitched forward.

"Nathaniel,"Victoria cried.

He spun, about. The air hissed between his gritted teeth as another attacker slashed a dagger at him, slicing up the front of his jacket. Pain pierced his side, hot like fire, and he cursed. His attacker brought his arm back again.

"Not one more goddamned move,"Victoria shouted. The faint click of her gun penetrated the street battle.

Instantly, the man fell back a step. Lifting his own weapon toward the air as though in supplication, he retreated a step.

Victoria stood, gun brandished, leveled on that assailant. The ginger-haired man, near in age to Nathaniel's five and forty years looked between Victoria's pistol… and him. "Lower it," she growled. "Lower your weapon and walk slowly away, or by God I'll kill you," she whispered. Her hands shook and she quickly steadied them.

As instructed, the stranger tucked the gun back inside his jacket. "Donaldson doesn't like questions," he said with a casualness befitting a parlor discussion. "Let those be the last you ask of him." Then abandoning the prone guard, now unconscious on the street, the nameless man lost himself in the shadows.

Victoria rushed forward. "Nathaniel," she cried softly, wrapping her arm about his waist.

He gritted his teeth. "I am fine," he assured her, his voice hoarse. Bloody hell, no matter how far a blade pierced, the pain always burned like the Devil was at play upon a man's flesh. Quickening his step, he urged her the remaining distance to the carriage. He yanked the door open and tossed her inside.

"You are not fine," she whispered after he'd closed the door.

He banged a staccato beat to six on the door. The carriage started onward. Now with the threat gone, Nathaniel shrugged out of his jacket to inspect the wound.

Victoria scrambled onto the bench beside him.

"It is merely a scratch," he gritted out, tugging his shirt up.

"Here you silly, rash man," she ordered, taking over that task for him. Her breath caught loudly. "My God, there is so much b-blood," she said, her voice breaking. Before he could speak, she did a frantic sweep of the carriage and then yanked a kerchief from inside his jacket. "Here." Victoria applied pressure to the slight gash made by his assailant's blade.

As she tended him, Nathaniel studied her bent head. Warmth filled him, driving back all traces of pain and his earlier fear. He'd been in the field for the majority of his life. Only Victoria had ever truly worried after him. To his family, he'd been the negligent son who cared more about traveling the Continent than the Archer name. To the Brethren and Crown, he'd simply been another man willing to sacrifice his life for the good of the country. "It is fine,

Victoria," he said softly. "Truly."

She paused and lifted eyes shimmering with tears. "It is not fine. You were s-stabbed." Her voice broke and she swiftly dropped her focus back to his side.

He'd not remind her that he'd endured far worse. Fox and Hunter had claimed control of their lives for too long. "Victoria," he said in his commander's tones. "Look at me."

She gave her head an infinitesimal shake, refusing to meet his gaze.

Brushing his knuckles along her jaw, he forced her to meet his eyes. "It will be fine. I'll clean the wound, bandage it, and then will be right to continue with the invest—"

"Is that what you believe?" Fire flared in her eyes. "That I care about the investigation more than you?"

He'd hurt her. It was there in her anguished gaze. Except... how could she not care more for the mission they'd undertaken? It was her son's fate and future, and they'd been so very close to answers from the brutes on the street. He gave his head a slight shake.

"Well, I don't," she bit out, going up onto her knees on the bench. "I care about you, you foolish, foolish man. I love you."

Her admission rang around the carriage walls, holding him immobile. That battered-over-the-years organ in his chest rattled slowly against his ribcage. And then thumped a wild beat. "You love me?" he asked hoarsely. After all he'd done, after the shame and pain he'd left her to face alone, she should love him still?

She framed his face with her palms. "Of course I love you, Nathaniel," And all that emotion spilled from her eyes, healing. "But in this moment, I am very, very angry with you for risking your life and—" He cupped his hand about her nape and dragged her mouth to his. She stilled and then melted against him. He plundered her mouth, wanting to seal the vow she'd made and hold on to it eternally.

The carriage jerked to a stop. Victoria pitched forward as their embrace was jarringly ended.

Nathaniel shot a hand out, catching her before she went sprawling.

Her eyes clouded with desire, she blinked slowly. Drawing the edge of the curtain back, she peeked out the faint crack there. "Where are we?"

They were at a place he'd never brought a single soul not officially sworn in as a member of the Brethren. "We are at one of my offices."

CHAPTER 16

*Official meetings are to be held in the properties
and estates belonging to the Brethren.
Article XVI: The Brethren of the Lords*

HE'D BROUGHT HER TO HIS offices.

And at any other time, she'd have been riveted by the absolute trust that he'd share that piece of the Brethren with her. Now, as Nathaniel moved around the room touching a candle to the unlit sconces, she was besieged with panic.

"Give me that, Nathaniel," she said, hurrying over to take the white taper from his fingers. "I can certainly see to lighting a blasted candle." And he? He who'd been stabbed now casually went about his business.

"It is merely a scratch," he protested for the tenth time since she'd discovered his wound.

Victoria froze, the candle wavering in her hands. She stared at the flame dancing back and forth. "Stabbed, Nathaniel," she said hoarsely. "You were stabbed and stab wounds become infected and infections lead to death and—"

He quickly took the candle from her fingers. Blowing out the flame, he set it down in an empty crystal tray. "I am not going to die." His lips curved up in devastating grin. "I've survived far worse."

Her eyes slid closed. Was that supposed to make her feel any better? Thinking about everything else he'd endured and lived to tell the tale of? Only… she bit her lower lip. He hadn't truly told her. He'd glossed over the details of that horrific time and kept those demons to himself.

A knock sounded at the front of the room, cutting across her thoughts.

"Enter," Nathaniel boomed.

The door opened and a servant admitted a tawny-haired man, near an age to Phoebe. Two pots of steaming water in his hands and strips of white fabric draped over his shoulders, the gentleman hurried to set down the burden. There was a methodical movement to the stranger's actions that hinted at one who'd conducted this same act countless times before and it had merely become part of a normal routine.

This is Nathaniel's normal. Being stabbed on a street and sneaking off to a private residence just outside of London, to heal… before venturing back out, down the same dangerous path. She stood a silent observer as he and the young man spoke.

This was the world he belonged to and the one he always would. Hatred burned low in her belly for that organization that required him to risk his life day after day. After she'd discovered why he'd never returned to her, she'd despised the Brethren all the more. But she'd not allowed herself to truly see and accept that Nathaniel was still fully entrenched in that world. Tonight, as he'd fought off their assailants, the truth had slammed into her. As long as he served the Brethren, there could never, ever be anything more between them. For the time would come when he faltered and it would not be his capture that robbed her of him… but death.

Her throat worked. And that would destroy her all over again.

Nathaniel glanced over the top of the slightly shorter gentleman's head. His eyes darkened. He said something to the man, who nodded and rushed off. "Preston will not say anything of your being here," Nathaniel gave that somber assurance when they found themselves alone. "He is employed because of his silence."

A haze of fury descended over her eyes and she welcomed it; that seething resentment was far safer than the despair clutching at her. "Is that what you believe?" she breathed. "That I give a bloody damn about my blasted reputation?"

His mouth parted, but no words came out.

Victoria swept across the room. "Nathaniel, you could have been killed." She looked to his blood-soaked garments. Her breath came in short, shallow spurts. She'd not found him again only to lose him in the damned streets of England, to ruthless brutes. *He was hurt trying to exonerate your son.*

Her legs went weak.

"Victoria," he said gently, his voice coming as if down a long corridor.

"No," she cried, slapping at his fingers. She didn't want his blasted assurances and false comforts. "You almost died," she repeated, her voice pitching to the ceiling, half-mad with an eternal fear she'd carried for him. Unbidden, her gaze went to that loathed mark left by his captors upon his hand. Twice. He'd nearly been killed, twice. *And those were only the times you know.* What of the other instances where he'd risked all for Crown and country? Victoria dug her fingertips into her temples and rubbed.

"I did not—"

"This was just one more time," she rasped, catching the edge of a table and steadying herself. She curled her fingers into sharp claws around the wood. "But how many times were there before this? Ten? Twenty?" He flinched. "Thirty?"

"Victoria," he tried, pleading in his eyes.

"More?" she wailed. Victoria spun and took several lurching steps away from him. "And if it was not this time when you ulti-mately fell, it will be another."

She stiffened as strong, steady hands settled upon her shoulders. Victoria struggled to dislodge his touch, but he retained his hold; in a grip that was both tender and commanding all at the same time. If he took that damned placating tone with her, made light of the attack that evening, or any of the other attempts he'd faced before, her control would snap.

Instead, he moved his lips close to her ear. His breath stirred those delicious shivers within. He placed a kiss at her temple. That was all he offered; no false assurances or promises of invincibility.

A fat teardrop squeezed past her lashes and wound a path down her cheek. "I hate the Brethren," she whispered, her voice hollow. "I hate the hold they have over you that has kept you from me." And forever would.

"I am not going to die, Victoria."

There it was. The same seven words he'd given her before every mission that had taken him away. Her shoulders sagged and she forced herself to face him. "Oh, Nathaniel. You cannot see… that it is inevitable. You will eventually falter. Someone will ultimately triumph, and you will be…" Her voice broke. *Say it. You need to say the words so you can both hear them together.* "You will be killed." She lifted ravaged eyes to his. "And I cannot bear to lose you all over again."

With a groan, he drew her into his arms, holding her close, allowing her to borrow his strength. Only… she was no longer a girl to be shielded and protected. The heat of the blood-soaked fabric reminded her all the more of Nathaniel's fallibility.

Drawing in a slow, even breath through her lips, she stepped away from him. "Sit down," she instructed. She pointed to a chair.

Silently complying, Nathaniel followed her movements.

She hurried to rinse her dirt-stained hands within the first bowl of water and then joined him. With fingers that faintly trembled, she tugged his shirt free at the back of his breeches. "How many times?" she asked, pausing in her efforts.

He didn't pretend to misunderstand her question. "There would be too many for me to even hazard a guess."

Too many. Victoria tugged the white lawn shirt up and over his head, tossing it to the floor. It landed in a whisper of fabric on a nearby sofa instead. Her breath hitched loudly. "Oh, Nathaniel," she whispered. Her heart broke into a thousand shards. She searched an agonizing gaze, not over the recently suffered wound, but the vicious scars marring his once flawlessly perfect chest.

Still heavy with muscle and covered in a light mat of dark curls, the skin puckered and pulled in places. Victoria sank to her knees and touched a small circle; the flesh a faded white, slightly raised. "Did they do this to you?" Or had there been so many enemies that all the wounds and brushes with death blurred together? Whoever had inflicted this pain, she wanted to take the pistol he'd gifted her and shoot it at the men who'd hurt him.

At his silence, she looked up. White lines formed at the corner of his tightly held mouth. He offered a curt nod. "That was the final," his lip peeled up in a sneer, "gift given me by Fox and Hunter. Fox's daughter helped me escape and, as I fled, shots were fired."

There had been a woman who'd helped free him. It was the first mention he'd ever made of how he'd wrestled free. Gratitude for that nameless woman filled her. Until Victoria drew her last breath, she would be forever grateful.

"The rest," he continued on casually, "with the exception of a few errant blades, were largely the handiwork of my captors. They were determined to mark me forever with the cause they fought for."

And for the first time since his shirt had come off, she moved her gaze away from the scars upon his chest and noted the inked mark upon his arm. Victoria inched closer to study the sword. The hilt began at his shoulder with the blade continuing several inches upon the sinew of his powerful forearm.

"It is a—"

"Tattoo," she finished for him. They'd studied enough of Captain Cook's books on his voyages to the South Pacific for her to recognize the dyes and pigments indelibly marking his skin. "They did this to you?" she whispered, tilting her head back.

He forced an indolent grin. "It was hardly as romantic as we'd thought it when we read about the Raiatean man, Omai, presented to King George."

No. It wouldn't have been. Victoria trailed the tip of her index finger over the broadsword. That modification to Nathaniel's body had been an act, not voluntarily undertaken as it had been by Cook's crew, but something forced upon him. Just another heartless act of treachery that left him forever marked as a reminder of his time in captivity. "What is it?"

"Caladbolg." She furrowed her brow. "It is an old tale about Fergus mac Róich, a king in Irish mythology. The tale tells that he was tricked out of his kingship and partners with an enemy queen to take back that which was stolen." Nathaniel spoke as one who'd been handed that story over and over. "It is hideous." He made a grab for his shirt, but she shot a hand out, capturing his wrist.

Victoria forced it back to his lap. "I don't see it as ugly." Nothing about this brave, fearless, and dedicated man could ever be ugly. She held her eyes squarely with his. "I see it as beautiful." She spoke over his sound of protest. "I hate that the choice to mark your flesh belongs to them, but I see this broadsword as a testament of your strength." Victoria caressed her lips over the tattoo. "And your courage." She followed it with another kiss. "And your ability to survive untold horrors and still retain your goodness."

Nathaniel stopped her before she could again place her mouth there. He caught her to him and dragged her onto his lap, adjusting her so that she remained tucked against his uninjured side. "I'd not have you make me out to be something I am not," he said bluntly. "They broke me, Victoria. They reduced me to a man who pleaded and cried, and who would have sold his soul if the Devil had decided it was worth a trade."

Agony knifed at her. How could he still not see? "They may have broken you, Nathaniel," she said gently, caressing his cheek. "But *you* put yourself back together, afterward. You alone." His Adam's apple bobbed and she placed a gentle kiss upon his throat. *And how I wished that it had been me at his side, helping him find his way, again.* Wishing, however, had never brought about any good. As such, Victoria stood. "Now, come, let me put you together." Hurrying over to the table, she gathered the scraps of fabric and dipped them within the bowl of clean water.

As Victoria tended his injury, she worked in the companionable silence between them. Upon her inspection, their assailant's knife had scraped the flesh and not pierced the skin. Nathaniel remained motionless through her ministrations.

Hopping up, she fetched the bindings Preston had left on the front table. While she wrapped Nathaniel's chest, she began to sing.
"Young Molly who lived at the foot of the hill,
Whose fame every virgin with envy doth fill,
Of beauty is blessed with and so ample a share
They call her the lass with the delicate air.
With the delicate air,
Men call her the lass with the delicate air…"
Plucking the scissors from the floor, she snipped the additional fabric, and tucked and tied it about him. From where she knelt at his feet, she paused to assess her work. Expertly wrapped, the cleaned and cared for flesh should heal easily. "There," she murmured.

Nathaniel cupped her cheek in his hard, callused grip. The feel of him, masculine strength and aching tenderness, blended together. It gripped her in an intoxicating hold. "You still remember that song."

Her lashes fluttered and she leaned into his touch. "Of course I do. I always found peace when I sang it. The melody made me feel closer to you."

"How I have missed you."

Were those whispered words his or her own? She gasped as he suddenly drew her up onto his lap, dragging her by the lapels of her jacket so their chests met.

They remained frozen, their breaths dueling in a rival frantic rhythm, their eyes on one another's mouths.

With a moan, Victoria stretched up and claimed his lips. She shook as he caught her jaw, holding her close so he could avail himself fully of her mouth. There was a desperation to his kiss that matched her own. He guided her legs around him so they hung over the sides of the chair; that slight, seductive angling of her body brought her core against his hard, flat belly. The wantonness of sitting astride him in breeches stirred a growing ache between her legs. Frantically, she moved her hips.

Nathaniel deepened the hot stroke of his tongue. The taste of orange and coffee on him singed her senses. Tangling her fingers in his long strands, she clung to him, boldly mating her mouth with his.

She cried out as he broke the kiss. "I have missed the feel of you in my arms," he said hoarsely. He worked his hands between them and quickly divested her of her jacket. Her shirt followed suit, landing in a growing heap of garments beside his chair. Then freeing the pin that held together her bindings at the back, he slowly unraveled the long, white fabric. With every scrap that fell away, the hungering to feel his hands upon her grew. Soon, she sat upon his lap, naked from the waist up.

His breath rasped about them; ragged and rough, with desire… *for me*. And God help her, she, who'd believed herself incapable of feeling this wickedly wonderful hungering again, burned to know his touch once more. She needed to feel him moving between her legs as she came undone in his arms. Half-afraid the warmth would fade and she'd be reduced to the figure incapable of knowing desire, she stood.

Unapologetically, she shucked her breeches and kicked them aside so she stood naked before him.

His gaze fell to her body, and her confidence instantly faltered. The places where her skin had stretched during pregnancy served as a grotesque mark of her age. Her hips now wider, and her breasts less pert and proud as they once were, she never bemoaned the changes more to her body. She'd been uncaring when her late husband had hurled mocking words about her naked form after she'd given birth to Phoebe. This man, however, was different. She wanted him to remember her as the beautiful woman she'd once been. Victoria folded her arms, in a self-conscious bid to shield herself.

Nathaniel caught her arms. "No," he urged in graveled tones. Bringing his palms up, he cupped her large breasts, bringing the flesh together. Desire pooled between her legs as he tweaked the already pebbled tips. They tightened all the harder under his attentions. "So beautiful." He caught one of those tips between his lips and suckled.

Her head fell back and a blissful moan spilled past her lips. "I am not," she panted, gripping his head to hold him close. "I am old and plump. But when you touch me, I feel that way." Again. It had been so very long since she'd felt like a woman.

"You have never been more beautiful," he growled, as he shifted to her other breast, laving the engorged bud.

Victoria moaned, pumping her hips, searching for his touch.

He instantly obliged, palming her mound. That faint pressure, a mere tease of what she desperately wanted… craved. And then he obliged, giving her precisely what she sought.

A small scream exploded from her, echoing wantonly about the room as he slipped a finger inside her sheath. Biting her lip, she lifted into his touch. At the same time he worked her wet channel, he resumed suckling a nipple until her head lolled back and forth. She was afire; every corner of her being from her soul to the skin he now worshiped was freed from all that had come before. So all she knew and felt was him.

Desperate to feel his flesh hard against her, she wiggled out of his arms. Dropping to her knees, she worked free first one boot. She tossed it across the room. The other aged, black Hessian followed, landing with a thump. Hungry for him, Victoria urged his breeches down. He stood, taking over the task, sliding the fabric low, over his narrow waist, past his oak-hard thighs and firm calves, until he stood before her in all his naked splendor.

Her blood thickened as she automatically stroked a palm up his powerful leg, reacquainting herself with the feel of him. As a young man of twenty, he'd been beautiful. As a man fully grown, his body bearing the marks of battle and life, he was glorious in his masculinity. From amidst a thatch of black curls, his shaft sprung hard and proud against his flat belly. Victoria caught the solid length of him, folding him in her grip.

The air hissed between his teeth and his body jerked.

Reveling in her power over this strong, fierce man, she stroked him in her fists, in the touch he'd shown her. Slowly, and then increasing in speed.

"Victoria," he pleaded, making an attempt to pull her hand away. She resisted his efforts. Leaning down, she flicked her tongue around the plum-tipped crown of his manhood. "I need you now," he gasped and joined her on the floor. In one swift move, he brought her under him, parted her legs, and plunged deep inside her. The walls of her channel closed convulsively about him as he stretched her.

She cried out, her entire body buckling under the exquisiteness of his entry. His was not the tender, gentle joining of when they'd first made love. This was a fierce, unapologetic taking, and she tossed her arms wide reveling in the feel of his hard thrusts. He slammed into her again and again, keening her name as a plea of sorts that only sharpened the aching need threatening to consume her.

Sweat beaded on his forehead and fell unchecked over his eyebrows. She reached up, catching those crystal drops, brushing them back.

"I have missed you," he breathed against her neck, suckling the skin, nipping it. There would be marks and, by God, she could not bring herself to care about anything but simply feeling.

"I have missed you, too," she moaned, lifting into his frantic thrusts, matching each relentless drive of his hips. Each stroke brought her higher and higher to that glorious edge of surcease he'd carried her to so many times before. Only him. It had only ever been him and would forever only be him. Pinpricks of color danced behind her vision. *Close. I am so close.* "Nathaniel," she begged.

He sunk his fingers into her hips, using her body as the leverage he needed. He pounded harder and harder, his breath coming in ragged spurts. "Come for me," he demanded.

His words set her free. Victoria screamed, the sound tearing from her throat, endless, ringing in her ears, and echoing around the room. Desire crashed over her in waves, pulling her under, and she gave herself freely over to the power of it.

A strangled shout of elation burst from Nathaniel's lips. He tossed his head back, howling like a primitive beast. He spurted in an endless stream inside her; his shaft pulsing and throbbing as he emptied himself. Gasping, he sagged, catching himself with his elbows before rolling onto his side. He dragged her against him, holding her close.

As their chests rose and fell together, a contented smile curled Victoria's lips… and she turned herself over to sleep.

CHAPTER 17

Never be distracted: ever.
Article XVII: The Brethren of the Lords

NATHANIEL HAD GOTTEN HIMSELF THROUGH the darkest moments in his life with thoughts of Victoria. When he'd been locked away in a cellar, tied to a chair, his body bruised and bleeding, he'd called forth the memory of her. And she had sustained him. He'd ached to again know Victoria Cadence; to feel her skin against his and swallow her breathless cries.

The moment he'd learned she married in his absence, he'd given up on every last hope of holding her in his arms. And now he had. Yawning, he shifted the slumbering, buxom figure closer, welcoming the heat of her body. A faint snore stirred the whorls of hair upon his chest. She snored.

It was something new; something she'd never done as a girl. And yet, to be in possession of that intimate detail earned a lazy grin. His eyes heavy with exhaustion, he forced them open and then cursed as a shaft of light momentarily blinded him.

Light?

Nathaniel's eyes flew open. He took in the crack in the curtains that revealed the early morn sky.

Oh, bloody, *bloody* hell.

Panic knocking about his chest, Nathaniel carefully disengaged himself from the woman wrapped like a vine about him. Padding across the room, he hurriedly washed off with the now cold water brought by Preston—he squinted, attempting to bring the numbers of the long-case clock into focus—four hours ago. Oh, bloody, bloody hell.

Ten minutes past six, the world would soon be rising and there was the matter of seeing Victoria returned and ensuring that she escaped notice. Hastening his movements, Nathaniel retrieved an alternate pair of garments neatly hanging in the simple, walnut, Louis Philippe armoire and proceeded to dress.

As he adjusted the fabric of his cravat into a simple Maratte knot, he looked at the mirror to where Victoria remained curled on the floor. He winced. *I made love to her on the bloody floor like a common street doxy.*

Of course, as young lovers there had been no place where they hadn't made love: from her bedroom to empty parlors.

He paused, the white silk fold of his cravat incomplete. She'd deserved so much more. In his youth, it had been enough knowing that he'd one day wed her, after… after…

There had always been an after.

Nor had she questioned it. She'd given herself freely to him. Stomach knotted, Nathaniel resumed his efforts. But the guilt remained strong; bitter tasting in his mouth. *She still does deserve more.*

"Never tell me you are intending to slip out the window and leave me with nothing more than a slight crack."

He started, whipping his gaze over to the owner of that sleep-husked contralto. A faint glitter of teasing danced in her eyes and, yet, looking past it, he saw the indecision. The real question there. "I was not leaving you. My days of missions are at an end." They had been since he'd been named Sovereign by the previous holder of that post, Lord Weston.

Victoria slowly sat up, dragging her knees up to her chest. She dropped her chin atop them, looking so bloody innocent, so vulnerable, that his heart ached. "Your missions will never be at an end, Nathaniel."

He opened his mouth to disabuse her of that incorrect supposition.

"If it were not my son's case, it would have been another."

"You are wrong," he said tightly and his resentment swelled.

"You would question my motives? You think I only took over this assignment because I seek the thrill of the hunt?"

Victoria pushed herself to her feet. The sun's early morn rays bathed her nude frame in a splendorous beauty to rival the lush fertility goddess, Aphrodite. She joined him at the mirror, holding his gaze within that bevel panel. "Of course, I do not doubt your reason to look after my family. I do doubt your ability to fully divorce yourself from the Brethren."

"It is all I have known," he said impatiently, swiping a hand through his tousled hair.

"That is not true," she said softly. "You also know me. I, however?" She sighed, her generous breasts moving up and down with that slight exhalation. "I will never be enough, but how I wish that I were."

"You are wrong," he countered sharply, gathering her by the shoulders.

Victoria arched a regal, auburn eyebrow. "Am I?"

Footsteps padded in the hall, diverting him from a reply. *Is it just that I seek a reprieve from thinking about what she suggested… and what it would mean for my future?* The steps, however, moved on, merely serving as a reminder that the world around them continued to awaken. "You have to return home. You cannot be seen with me." Not only would the scandal be harmful to her reputation, it would be ruinous to the credibility of her son's investigation. He opened his mouth to explain as much, but Victoria held a palm up.

"I do understand the implications of the world learning that the lead investigator for my son's case is, in fact, also my lover."

Her lover. It was what they'd always been… lovers. *I want more… with her.* The staggering truth of that slammed into him. He wanted what she'd dangled before him—a relationship out in the open, as a married couple.

His mind spun under the force of that revelation, a future that stood at direct odds to the mantle of responsibility he'd been granted. Grateful that she hurried through her ablutions, he hurried over to his armoire and withdrew a drab wool dress.

As he stalked over, the garment outstretched, Victoria eyed it; upset simmering under the surface. "Garments are kept here for those men and women who need a sudden disguise," he softly explained. "Here," he murmured, gently bringing her back to him.

After he'd helped her into the chemise and then dress, he paused while catching her gaze in the mirror. "I have not lied to you. Nor will I ever. I told you there has never been another." He turned her about and proceeded to notch each button.

"What was her name?"

He stopped.

"The woman who helped free you?"

His heart beat hard and he stared blankly at Victoria's back. With that simple question, the gates of that hell that would always be with him cracked open. Details he'd taken care not to think of or share with anyone... until Victoria. And yet, he wanted to let her in—in every way. Wanted to reveal not only the horrors he already had... but everything, including the name of the woman who'd saved him.

Victoria glanced over her shoulder, concern in her revealing eyes.

His fingers shaking, Nathaniel resumed buttoning the modest dress. "Georgina Wilcox." He owed his very life to her. "Her name was Georgina Wilcox."

"What... happened to her?"

"She married a former member of the Brethren, both whom I call friends." He neatly sidestepped the horrors that Georgina herself had endured.

Both of his friends had the right of it when they'd left the Brethren behind to marry and have a family. Had Victoria been waiting, Nathaniel would have gladly traded it all for those gifts.

"How very strange that you have an entire life with friends I do not even know." There was a trace of sadness to her words.

He wanted her to know them.

Finally dressed, Nathaniel lingered with his hands upon her shoulders. After all these years of wanting her, he'd be forced to let her go—again. And for the first time in a very long time, he found himself resenting every last obligation and duty that belonged to him.

Victoria softly spoke, interrupting his disordered musings. "What happens from here?" Between them? "With the information we discovered last night."

The information. Her late husband and the evidence revealed by the serving girl, Kattie. Of course. She did not refer to a future together. That realization struck like a blow.

Masking his face to hide that disappointment, he fetched his jacket and drew it on. "I'll meet with Lord Tennyson and gather what other information he might be able to share regarding Chester's appointments with Donaldson. I'll also have investigators conduct additional research on the gentleman." In the streets of the Dials and the respectable inner circles of Polite Society and the gentry. Nathaniel smoothed his palms over the lapels of his jacket. "Bennett will see you home." He opened his mouth, wanting to say more. But there would be time enough later. Now, he had a responsibility to unearth the connection between Waters and Donaldson.

After a long carriage ride through the unfamiliar, barren streets where Nathaniel's private office was kept, Victoria finally arrived home.

She grimaced. In an altogether different outfit than what she'd left with. Seated on the carriage bench, she sat patiently, staring out the edge of the curtain waiting for the signal Bennett had indicated he'd give when it was time for her to exit the conveyance. This whole subterfuge business was vastly less thrilling in the light of a new day. Even more so with discovery and ruin all one quick misstep away.

Knock-Knock.

Heart jumping to her throat, Victoria hastily pushed the door open and leaped down. Sprinting along the pavement and up the handful of steps, she gave thanks that Manfred, ever tardy at his post in his old age, had declined her efforts of retirement. And also, that Andrew did not rise past the noon hour, most days. And—

Victoria let herself inside, quietly closing the door behind her.

"Mother?"

Shrieking, Victoria spun about to face the owner of that very familiar and very scandalized voice. Her stomach sinking all the way to the soles of her borrowed slippers, she stared back at Phoebe and Manfred.

The ghost of a smile hovered on the servant's aged face.

How peculiar to find one capable of the same horrified shame at three and forty as twenty. Forcing a smile that threatened to shatter her cheeks, Victoria gave a jaunty wave. "Phoebe!" Her voice emerged as a high squeak. *Bloody, bloody hell. Be breezy. Recall every time you donned a smile and deceived your mama and papa.* "Lovely to see you," she lied through her painful grin.

Manfred shuffled from the foyer, but not before Victoria detected his shoulders shaking with mirth.

She cleared her throat. "Er… yes… well, so very good of you to visit. If you'll excuse me?" She got no further than the base of the stairs.

"So good of me to visit?" Phoebe asked, incredulity seeping from every syllable.

She eyed the path to freedom the staircase represented. Mentally, she contemplated just how much of a lead she would require to put enough distance between Phoebe and herself before—

"Mother," Phoebe snapped.

"Uh… yes… of course it is always good of you to visit," she trilled. "I've never been one of those mothers who… who…"

Her eldest child propped her hands on her hips. "Sneaks about and smells like she's been…" *Mucking out stables. Do not say it. Please, do not say it.* "…mucking out stables." Oh, blast, it was a sorry day, indeed, for a mother when one's child took to using one's own admonishments against her.

Phoebe arced a single eyebrow up. She was so very much Nathaniel's daughter with that slight gesture that Victoria's heart pulled. Only this pull was altogether different. Once upon a week ago, he had existed as a ghost who lived only in her memories. Now, he was very much alive… and knew of Phoebe's existence. *Phoebe also deserves to know.* She was a woman entitled to the truth surrounding her origins. "Mother?"

That prodding sprung Victoria into movement. She started up the stairs. Phoebe instantly fell into step beside her. "I hardly believe this conversation should be had in the middle of the foyer," she muttered under her breath.

"No. But arriving by hired hack, in a dress better suited for a servant than a widow in mourning is perfectly acceptable," Phoebe shot back in hushed tones.

Fair enough. Nonetheless, Victoria remained stubbornly silent until they were closeted away in her rooms.

"Well?" Phoebe demanded.

"I am taking part in the investigation of the viscount's murder," she said without preamble.

Her daughter's mouth fell open and she leaned back against the paneled doorway.

That lesson on always unsettling one's adversary handed down years earlier by Nathaniel, proving just as valuable and accurate, now.

After a long stretch of silence, Phoebe finally responded. "What?" she asked. Then she pushed away from the door.

Victoria presented her back and, immediately anticipating the unspoken request, Phoebe came over and hurriedly unlatched the neat row of buttons Nathaniel had seen to early that morning. Memories of last night came flooding back and a wave of heat slapped at her cheeks. Victoria gave thanks that her back remained toward her daughter.

"Are you blushing?"

All relief was instantly quashed as she glanced to the forgotten mirror across the room. The same bevel panel that revealed her damnably guilty flushed cheeks. Blushing at three and forty. Who would have believed it possible? And before her daughter, no less. She sighed, swiping a hand over her face.

"Mother, what is going on?" Phoebe urged. The worry in those words sharply twisted her maternal guilt.

Victoria shook her head once. She'd resolved to tell Phoebe… all. She'd simply not anticipated that she would need to do so… so… quickly. Hurrying over to the floor-to-ceiling length French Vernis dressing cabinet, Phoebe tugged out a black satin day gown. Black… as was expected… to mourn a man who was better off dead. She sank wearily into the satinwood dressing chair.

Phoebe, who'd oftentimes been more friend than daughter, stepped effortlessly back into that role. She fell to a knee beside Victoria and collected her damp palms. Only this time, she did not press her for answers, but sat in patient wait.

"I knew Lord Archer… Nathaniel…" No, that was no longer how Society knew of him. "Lord Exeter," she amended once again.

"You knew him…?" Phoebe ventured, and that hesitant three-word question came with a woman's wisdom that saw more.

"When I was younger. A girl." Not so young by Society's standards, and expected to wed and begin bearing children. But with the passage of time, Victoria had come to appreciate just how little of the world and life a person knew in those tender years. "I had recently made my Come Out," she said softly, letting the gates open on her memory of that first meeting with Nathaniel. "He came upon me and I was…" Her lips quivered in a watery smile. "…*entranced*." A small laugh bubbled past her lips. "Not at first. At first, I was horribly outraged that he failed to announce himself after I entered a hidden alcove at our host's home."

"You were more than friends," Phoebe put forward hesitantly, the way one did when trying to solve a complicated riddle.

Did she seek confirmation because it was unfathomable to believe Victoria had ever been young and innocent, sneaking about, and captivated by a gentleman? "His work made anything more between us… impossible," she settled for, not yet ready to share all with Phoebe, allowing herself more time. *You had time.* "And this man," *Your father. He is your father… a man I believed dead…* Victoria focused on breathing to keep calm.

"Lord Exeter," Phoebe elucidated, as though there was another gentleman in question. "He invited you to take part in his investigation?"

Despite her frenzied thoughts, Victoria found a droll grin. "Is it so very hard to fathom that your mother of three and forty years might be useful at such an endeavor?"

"No," Phoebe blurted with a damning alacrity. "I simply find it unlikely that an old, seasoned investigator would seek help… from *any* lady, regardless of age or acquaintance."

Victoria frowned. "Nathaniel is not… old. He…" At Phoebe's pointed stare, the heat in her cheeks deepened. Of course, it was a silly, irrelevant point to debate. And yet, distinguished, quick-witted, and stoically calm, he evinced a greater command and vitality than men twenty years his junior. "He did not ask me," she felt compelled to add. "I insisted on being part of it." And he'd allowed her that role. No man: not her late husband, nor son, nor sons-in-law would have ever dared permit her that control.

"He is exposing you to harm," she said bluntly.

Victoria stared at her daughter's tense features. "For one who craved love, adventure, and self-control, Phoebe, that is an unforgivable statement to make," she said gently, without recrimination.

Phoebe winced. "Mother, you are talking of dealing with and about murderers. Men who carried out a heinous act of violence." She again gathered Victoria's hands. "There is altogether a difference in taking ownership of one's life and partaking in actions that could see one killed."

She cocked her head. "Is there, though?"

Her eldest child stared unblinkingly. "Why... yes... of *course* there is a difference." Phoebe surged to her feet.

Victoria sighed. "Oh, Phoebe," she said in gentling tones. "We've always sought to look after one another's happiness. To see that we knew love and were safe. And your desire for both is now blinding you to what I want." She pressed her fingertips to her heart. "For me." Nineteen years younger than she, her daughter, however, could not know what it was to see time march on so quickly, and wonder where one's youth and vitality had gone. Victoria was almost two decades older but she was still capable of unlocking the mystery of her husband's death... and why... even traveling...

It is not too late for you to travel... To see the places you dreamed of and explore those foreign lands...

"You are my mother and I resent this Lord Exeter for involving you... whether you wished to be part of his investigation or not," Phoebe said, her voice sharp.

This Lord Exeter...

Her throat tightened.

"Mother?" Phoebe called as Victoria rose and made her way across the room. "Where are you...?" Her question trailed off as she knelt beside her bed. Finding the loose floorboard, she used her nails to grip it by the edges and work it free.

Victoria reached inside the cleverly carved out space and withdrew a small jewel-encrusted tome.

"What is that?" Phoebe asked breathlessly. All earlier frustration was gone, replaced with the streak of curiosity she'd inherited from her father.

"Look at the title," she encouraged, further whetting her daughter's wanting to know.

All the air left Phoebe on a loud exhalation. "It is *Rubaiyat of Omar Khayyam.*" She trailed her fingers reverently along the spine. "Surely this is not a first edition?"

"A first edition?" She shook her head. "No." Phoebe's shoulders sank with a tangible disappointment. "This is *the* book from Captain Cook's very own recordings." Positioning herself so that her back rested against the bed, she urged Phoebe to sit beside her. "All these years, I had to tuck it away."

Phoebe's face darkened. "Father." Victoria had always hated that her brutish husband had been bestowed the honor of that title from Phoebe… from any of her children. Never more, with Nathaniel returned and again part of her life, did she hate it as she did.

"If he had known I was in possession of this, he'd have likely carved out the stones for sale, unaware of the true value of what he held. So," she said matter-of-factly, "I hid it away, showing it to none." Not even Phoebe, who had shared a like love of Captain Cook. "I did not want to risk us speaking in front of him and him overhearing and…" She shrugged. "This was just easier."

"Yet, how very heartbreaking it was that you had to hide it away all this time," Phoebe said wistfully.

It hadn't been entirely, though. Under her bed, where she rested her head each night, there had been a peace and having that small scrap of Nathaniel, still. It had been another connection she'd retained of him, that made their time together real. "Then, after he died, I could not bring myself to take it out because it had been tucked away so long."

Phoebe fanned the pages, periodically pausing to skim the Farsi passages.

"You never asked me why I loved Captain Cook."

Her daughter started, blinking like an owl startled from her perch.

She patted her hand. "It is all right. Sometimes, as children we just accept the world around us, unquestioningly. It was Nathaniel. He was the first to open my heart to the possibility of exploration. We poured over Captain Cook's works together, dreaming of traveling and, together, seeing the world." Tears clogged her throat and she struggled to speak past the emotion there. "The Sandwich Islands was to be our place." Just as Wales had been Phoebe and Edmund's.

Phoebe set the book aside and came up on her knees. "Oh, Mama," she whispered, her voice catching. "I did not know."

"Why should you have? You wouldn't because I did not tell you… until now."

Her daughter searched her face. "Why did you not marry him? Why?" she implored.

"I believed him dead." There it was. The beginning of every revelation her daughter deserved.

"You did not wait for him?" she asked stricken. Phoebe slammed a fist against her open palm. "You had a man you loved, who shared your interests, and treated you kindly, and encouraged your use of your mind and, instead, you wed *Father?*"

Is that how Nathaniel had felt upon discovering she'd wed? A dratted sheen blurred her vision and she angrily swiped at her eyes. Her tongue felt heavy in her mouth. "I was with child." Just four words and yet powerful enough to suck all life from the room.

Phoebe turned to stone at her side. "What?" she whispered.

Her tears, those useless expressions of pain fell unchecked down Victoria's cheeks. "It was you, Phoebe. You were that babe."

Phoebe shook her head slowly.

Victoria nodded, hugging herself tight.

Her daughter lurched awkwardly to her feet and backed away, knocking into the gilded vanity. It rocked and the lone bottle of perfume tipped onto its side. Phoebe dug her fingertips into her temples. "Where did he go? Why… what manner of man leaves a young woman with a babe in her belly?"

It was a fair question, for which Nathaniel was undeserving of sole guilt. "We made every decision together. I knew the risks when I… when we…" Mother and daughter blushed together. "He was once a spy."

"He worked for the Home Office?"

Even while Phoebe was entitled to truths, there were others that could never… for the good of the Crown be shared. As such, she remained silent, letting her daughter keep to the erroneous conclusion she'd drawn. "He was captured. I did not know," she said quickly. "Until now. Until he returned to investigate your brother," she finished lamely.

The confusion and pain etched in the heart-shaped planes of Phoebe's face gutted her with the same ferocity of picking her up sobbing after her first fall. "And you simply trust that this man who abandoned you is not simply taking advantage of a former connection… as a weakness to seek out more information."

Victoria recoiled. "No." The denial burst from her chest. "He would not do that."

"He has been gone for more than twenty years." There was a panicky edge to her usually collected daughter that ratcheted her own disquiet. *He would not do that. He sought to help.* Thrusting aside that niggling of doubt, she struggled to stand. "I should have told you," she said hoarsely, reaching for Phoebe. "I did not know how… or when to…" She closed her eyes and inhaled through her nose. Phoebe had deserved the truth long before Nathaniel's reemergence in her life.

Her daughter clutched at her throat. "All these years, I've sought to understand how such a hateful man gave me life and it was all a *lie?*"

Victoria turned her palms up, willing her to understand the desperation that had compelled her to sacrifice her heart and future… for the security afforded. "I was young. My father offered a way for my child—you—to have a name and respectability, and I took it, Phoebe. I-I would have you know it was all for you." She sobbed until she thought she might break.

Delicate arms folded around her and Victoria cried all the harder. And in a tender reversal of roles, Phoebe rubbed a hand soothingly over her back. "I always sought to understand why a woman such as you, whose heart was full of such goodness and strength, should have ever bound herself to one such as Father. You had no choice."

Victoria's tears dampened the bodice of her daughter's black taffeta gown. "I had a choice of whether to tell you or not. And I decided to keep your origins a secret."

"Shh," Phoebe murmured, stroking the top of her head. "You did the best you could. You sacrificed all for me." Phoebe's voice broke.

"For us." It had always been the two of them, together.

"I want you to be at peace. I want his intentions to be honorable," Phoebe said.

"They are." They had to be. Because what was the alternative… that *everything* had been a lie? "They *are* honorable," she repeated once more for herself. She knew Nathaniel the way she knew her own soul.

And, at last, as mother and daughter held one another, there was understanding… and at long last, peace.

CHAPTER 18

Show no mercy when bringing a traitor or criminal to justice.
Article XVIII: The Brethren of the Lords

THE BRETHREN HAD NO FEWER than sixty residences and offices scattered in various locations about England. It had been a redesign implemented by a former Sovereign, the Duke of Aubrey, after a misstep had seen his role discovered, and his first wife killed. From then on, the organization had followed a strategy of conducting business in no one location, but within many.

Nathaniel had ridden his horse to exhaustion to reach the Brethren's estates, Aldenham Lodge, on the west side of Watling Street. He now stood, with his arms clasped at his back, awaiting his visitor.

The summons sent 'round by Bennett upon Nathaniel's departure for Radlett Village should see the Marquess of Tennyson arrive at any moment. A *rake* who gambled too much and warmed the beds of countless widows, ladies, and whores, Polite Society would never expect punctuality from the lord.

Nathaniel, however, had read accountings of the gentleman's work and had enough meetings to know there was far more to Tennyson than the world could ever see. A cup of coffee in hand, Nathaniel consulted the ormolu clock atop the mantel.

A knock sounded at the door.

Punctual, as always. "Enter," he called out.

Wright, the lord who oversaw the operations in Radlett opened the door. "Tennyson," he said in a laconic announcement.

Inclining his head, Nathaniel waited until Wright had gone before speaking. "Tennyson," he greeted, pointing to a nearby chair.

The tall, wiry marquess' face was a carved mask, revealing nothing. Wordlessly, he took the indicated seat and waited.

Taking a sip of his coffee, he set it down on the table beside him and picked up the Waters folder. "What were your dealings with Waters?" He tossed it down on the table between them.

A muscle ticked at the corner of the marquess' hard mouth. "I was in the midst of bedding a delectable widow and you would call me away to ask me questions I've already answered?" It spoke either to the man's courage or his stupidity that he'd challenge Nathaniel.

However, the jaded edge was one he recognized. It came from too many years of service where a person lost parts of themselves to the identity they'd crafted. Only being far removed from what had shaped a man, restored him to his former self—if one could ever be fully restored. "I've learned that you, in fact, have more information," he said warningly.

"I gave over everything I had and know about Waters' murder to Fitzwalter. You could have spared us both a trip to this godforsaken part of the country by speaking with him."

That low growl gave him pause. So, Tennyson took umbrage with Nathaniel's first assistant. He sat forward in the Empire gilt-wood armchair. "Ah, but I did not wish to speak to Fitzwalter. I wished to speak to you." Surprise glinted in the marquess' eyes. "Do you believe I don't place the same weight in your findings as an agent?"

Tennyson rolled his shoulders. "The order within the Brethren is quite clear. Rank and file drives all."

That had been the way of the previous Sovereigns. Nathaniel, however, wasn't one who adhered to the old, dead ways that had existed within the order for years. Except that wasn't altogether true. In his inability to form attachments, he'd done precisely what the Brethren drilled into its members—keep all out. That realization hit him square between the eyes with its clarity. His skin pricked with the feel of Tennyson's clever stare on him and

Nathaniel wrestled with control of his thoughts. "I want to know everything: from your courtship of Lady Huntly to your dealings with the late viscount, and Donaldson," Nathaniel said gravely, setting aside his coffee. "I want to know about Donaldson."

The mask of indolent rake lifted and Tennyson's features settled into an impenetrable mask. "As I told you, I was assigned to make myself close to Waters, because of suspicions of his links to the Cato Street Conspiracy."

Nathaniel caught his chin between his thumb and forefinger and rubbed distractedly. "The Cato Event was a product of the London Irish community and trade societies."

Tennyson stretched his long legs out, looping them at the ankles. "That is what the Brethren believes."

"But you do not."

The marquess let his silence serve as his affirmation.

Resting his elbows on his knees, Nathaniel leaned forward. "What was your opinion on the plot?"

Tennyson looked about the room. His gaze alighted on the sideboard. Shoving to his feet, he strolled over and, just like in their last exchange, he availed himself of the contents there. "It is my opinion the Cato Street Conspiracy is more than a scheme concocted by commoners and merchants." Perching his hip on the sideboard, he took a long swallow. "It is someone from within the peerage."

Nathaniel sank back in his seat, incredulous. *Impossible.* His mind raced. Why would noblemen involve themselves in the protests and uprising being led by the masses? While the marquess continued to sip his drink, Nathaniel sought to puzzle through it.

Over the rim of his snifter, Tennyson grinned, an empty, mirthless smile. "Fitzwalter was of a like opinion. Impossible."

Fitzwalter was skilled in his role as Delegator, but every person, regardless of station, was capable of missteps. "You are of a different thought," he hazarded. "Tell me yours."

The marquess set his empty glass down with a *thunk.* "It all stems from the Six Acts."

Those acts, viewed oppressive, which had come after the Peterloo Massacre, outlawed public meetings, restricted press, and banned further actions that might sow political reform. That legislation, however, had also come nearly a year before the Cato Event. "How do you explain the timing?" he put to Tennyson.

"And also the connection between the gentlemen involved and the Six Acts?"

"There are nobles who sought support of the legislation. To have that support, the Tories needed a situation that justified their oppressive agenda."

"What proof do you have?" Nathaniel pressed.

"None. My suspicions were based solely on the timeline of events." Tennyson tightened his mouth. "I was investigating Waters for a possible connection."

Nathaniel sat up in his chair, urging the other man on with his gaze.

"Waters continued to show up at the Coaxing Tom. He sometimes sat down to cards and drinks with Ings and Brunt." Two members of the conspiracy who'd been hanged for treason.

"What happened?"

Sneering, Tennyson lifted his shoulders in a negligent shrug. "I was removed from anything to do with the Cato Street Conspiracy after the hangings." He scoffed. "The matter was done," he said in an expert rendition of Fitzwalter's clipped tones.

Nathaniel filed those details away, making a silent note to question his Delegator's outright dismissal. "How did your courtship of Lady Huntly connect to that case?"

"If there was an attempt at the formation of a political dynasty, he'd certainly never have sold his last unwed daughter to a rake, simply to settle debts."

Frustration took hold. He was no closer to any information about Waters' murder. "How does Donaldson connect to," Nathaniel waved his hand, "all this?"

"Initially, I investigated the pair as a possible link to the plot." Which had yielded nothing. "I did, however, find something of interest on that score."

Nathaniel stitched his eyebrows into a single line. "You've continued your investigation, anyway," he said crisply. It was an offense that should result in Tennyson's dismissal. The smug grin on the marquess' lips, however, gave him pause. Hope stirred. "What did you find?"

"Waters had an entire family with Donaldson's daughter. Lived a separate life, with a wife and three children" Tennyson chuckled, the mirthless sound of cynicism set Nathaniel's teeth on edge.

"That is, three *more* children."

Then the implications of that pronouncement slammed into him with all the force of a fast-moving carriage. "He was a bigamist."

At Tennyson's confirming nod, Nathaniel's cut clenched. "When—?"

"His marriage to Viscountess Waters, came first." Another chuckle escaped the marquess. "Or, that is, the viscountess as the *ton* knows of her."

Ignoring the other man's perverse hilarity, Nathaniel let the revelations sink around his mind. The words whoremonger, drunk, and lecher, had been carved upon Waters' body. Someone had hated the bastard so much that they'd left him marked, to deny him even the simple dignity of a proper funeral. Someone who had discovered the extent of his duplicity. "There is cause," he breathed. Jumping up, he rushed to Tennyson and gripped him by the lapels. "Did Donaldson know?" When the marquess manufactured another one of those infuriating grins, Nathaniel gave him a hard shake. "Did Donaldson know?"

"He did."

Donaldson. Donaldson was the piece. The man was the one who had the power to absolve Victoria's son of any wrongdoing. He lowered his brow. "You have had this information for how long and you've said nothing?"

The marquess gave a lazy shrug. "It did not advance the case I had been investigating." Vindication. He'd been so focused on his own individual absolution, he had put it before the organization. Nathaniel abruptly released Tennyson and pointed to the desk at the center of the room. "I want it all: names, dates, the residence." Nathaniel firmed his jaw. "Where I can find him now."

12 hours later
Luton

YEARS EARLIER, HASTE HAD MARKED Nathaniel's downfall. Hungering to have his mission completed and the evidence in hand to incriminate Fox and Hunter so he could at last return to London and to Victoria, he'd foregone meals… and made the mistake of sitting down to drink with Hunter.

A drug expertly placed in his brandy, and his tongue heavy and careless, he'd made one slip that had revealed his role as a spy. And his life had been forever altered.

As such, after a night's sleep and a full meal in his belly, Nathaniel reached Luton the following morn. With Chapman and Hill, two of his more seasoned officers close behind, he dismounted before the stone cottage. With its thatched roof and floral-lined walk leading to the door, it hinted at the modest origins of its owner. Looping the reins about a nearby sycamore, Nathaniel doffed his hat and glanced about. It was early enough that a shopkeeper would be awake, but not yet at their business, necessarily. And given Donaldson was the owner of this thriving establishment, there would be a foreman to oversee the earliest morning affairs.

A small boy rushed down the drive. "Who are you?" Excitement filled his cherub's face; those chubby cheeks stained with dirt.

Nathaniel assessed the child, not older than six or seven years and sank to a knee beside him. "I'm looking to meet with your father? Is he around?"

The boy giggled and wiped the back of his sleeve over his nose. "My da does not live here. He lives in—"

"Freddie!"

Freddie? Chester Barrett's son. A young woman came sprinting down the graveled path. Her crimson plait flapped wildly about, as she skidded to a stop before him. She positioned the child behind her slender frame. "May I help you?" she asked in cultured tones.

"We have a visitor, Mama. He asked to see Papa, but I was telling him—"

"Enough, Freddie," she ordered and tears instantly filled the boy's eyes.

So, this was the Viscount Waters' other wife and son. Nathaniel had borne witness to the basest levels of evil, but the sight of this pair, ruined by that reprobate, sent nausea roiling in his belly. How many people had been hurt by Waters? "I am here to speak with Mr. Donaldson, Mrs…?"

"Miss Donaldson," she snapped. "Who are you?"

Surprise filled him. She still went by her maiden name. Nathaniel fished a calling card from his jacket and held it out. "Lord Exeter.

I've come on a matter of business." When the woman made no move to take the article, he tucked it back inside his jacket.

Freddie peeked out from around the young woman's waist. She reached behind her, tucking him back into place. "Business takes place in town. You're best served meeting him there." She whipped about and then, grabbing the boy by the hand, marched ahead.

"I am here to ask several questions about Viscount Waters."

The young woman swayed. When she faced him, all earlier resolve was gone; the color leeched from her cheeks. She leaned down and whispered something into the boy's ear. He nodded and then darted off, his little feet kicking up gravel as he went. Miss Donaldson folded her arms at her chest, revealing no trace of her earlier vulnerability. "What manner of questions?"

"The viscount was recently murdered." He searched her face for a hint of a reaction, but her gaunt features remained a set mask. "It is my understanding your father and the viscount met frequently in London and I would speak to Mr. Donaldson about the nature of those exchanges."

"My father is busy," she said tightly. "Perhaps you may try return-ing at a later time." She gave him an arched look. "*When* you've scheduled a meeting."

"Miss Donaldson, I have no intention of leaving until I speak with him," he called after her. They locked eyes in a silent battle. The girl's shoulders sagged slightly. Crooking her chin, she started onward. "How well did you know the viscount?" he asked, falling into step beside her.

"Were your questions for me? Or my father?" she asked through tight lips.

"Mayhap both." Again, the color bled from her cheeks. Not another word was spoken between them as they entered the front door. She guided him through a cheerfully bright home and then stopped.

Lifting her hand, she knocked once on an oak door.

"Enter!"

Miss Donaldson pressed the handle. "You have a visitor."

The rotund figure with rosy-red cheeks, humming a happy tune, gave Nathaniel pause. Donaldson fit not at all with the ruthless sort he had in mind as having dealings with the viscount. "A vis-itor you say, gel?"

Miss Donaldson looked to him. "Yes, Papa."

Papa. Having come here, Donaldson had existed as nothing more than a suspect who might prove the key to absolving Victoria's son. In this instance, studying the tenderness between father and daughter, Nathaniel was humbled by his own ruthlessness. Once he'd expected that to be an inherent part of him, necessary for his work. He'd ceased to see people… as people. Having Victoria back in his life had reminded him of what a bond was between lovers and family…

"Tea and pastries, Marti," Donaldson was saying. "The cherry ones with the powdered edges."

Donaldson's daughter looked back and forth between Nathaniel and her father. Then with stiff strides, she marched out.

Nathaniel pulled the door shut behind them. Still, the hat maker scribbled away at the ledger spread open on his desk. Nathaniel used the older man's distractedness as an opportunity to further study him. He swept his gaze around the room, taking in every detail. His study tidy, children's drawings hung up about the room, this was hardly the office one would take for a monster's. And yet, he had dealt with enough men and women of great evil where he'd not be lulled by a Scottish folksong. His gaze lingered on the field of flowers painting above Donaldson's desk.

"Lovely, isn't it?" The older man, not many years older than him, finally ceased working. He pointed the tip of his pen at the gilded frame behind him.

"Indeed," Nathaniel murmured, taking the question as an invitation to wander over.

"My Marti did it. Quite the artist my girl always was. My three grandbabes also show signs of their mother's talent."

"I've come with questions about Viscount Waters," he announced quietly.

The deep-dimpled smile remained firmly in place. "Of course, you have. Of course." Donaldson leaned back and rested his folded hands atop his big belly.

Taking the chair nearest the desk that also kept a windowless wall at his back, Nathaniel sat.

"You are him, then?" Donaldson raised a monocle to his left eye. "The gentleman asking questions about me in London?"

"Do you trust there is only one?" he evaded.

CHRISTI CALDWELL

"I had... hoped." Leaning down, Donaldson drew open the bottom desk drawer. "I'm an optimist. However, I'm not a lackwit."

Nathaniel withdrew his pistol, training it on the man across from him.

Giving no outward reaction to the sudden appearance of Nathaniel's gun, the crimson-haired gentleman set a decanter down. Two glasses joined beside it. "Do you have children, my lord?" The clink of crystal touching crystal filled the quiet, followed by the steady stream of liquid as Donaldson poured a drink.

They may as well have been two strangers greeting at White's striking up a comfortable discourse. "I..." How to answer that for a stranger?

The other man waggled bushy eyebrows. "You either do or you do not?" he pointed out, shoving a glass across the desk.

Nathaniel ignored that offering. The last drink he ever taken with a stranger had been Hunter.

"I have one daughter," Donaldson went on, when only stony silence met his prodding. "Marti. Romantic girl. Clever. Talented. Did all these paintings," he took a sip and then motioned with the full glass to those frames hanging about the room. "Introduced her one day to a nobleman and the man was smitten. I figured he was a clever man to appreciate my clever girl." And Nathaniel was apparently far more capable of pity and compunction than he'd credited for those emotions swirled in his chest, even before the man went on. For he knew what was coming. "My girl deserved the best. Her mum died early and it was just Marti and me. I would have bought her the moon if she wished," he said, lifting his glass to the sky. His face crumpled. "Instead, I bought her a nobleman."

"Waters," he supplied.

"Waters," Donaldson confirmed. "Told myself it was fine he wasn't wise with money, I had plenty of it. What I didn't have for my daughter..."

"Was a title," he supplied.

The other man punctuated the air with his finger. "Precisely. I never questioned why he preferred to keep my girl in the country. They are odd sorts, the nobles, keeping their separate chambers and Town life and country life... hard to sort it all out." With a sigh, he took a sip of his brandy. "I have made many mistakes in my life: introducing Marti to that reprobate, for not having been wise enough to see precisely what was going on, until it was too late. For not being there for her in the future." He met Nathaniel's gaze, giving him a watery smile. "But I do not regret for one moment having him killed."

There should be a greater sense of triumph. Victoria's son was free and the Barretts could now resume their normal life. But how could there be triumph in any of this? Waters had left a stream of sorrow and pain in his wake.

"What will happen to my family?" Donaldson whispered.

His family. He did not, like the lowest of criminals, worry after his own fate or future. He spoke of his daughter and grandchildren. And yet, for a life hardened by what he'd witnessed, done, and experienced, Nathaniel could not see another family broken—not for a bastard like the late viscount. "Mr. Donaldson, I will do everything within my power," which was considerable, "to secure a lesser charge for you," he promised in solemn tones. As he, who'd only seen the world as distinctly black and white, recognized the various shades of gray. "I'll see that your family's fortune remains in their hands."

Donaldson's throat bobbed. "Why would you do this?" Because Waters had deserved killing. "You do not even know me."

"No," he acknowledged. "But I did gather the type of man Waters was. You will need to accompany me, Mr. Donaldson," he said softly.

The man nodded, downing his drink. "Now? Or might I suggest...later?"

An image flitted in of the small boy, rushing over to his mother: innocence in his brown eyes and a joyful smile on his lips. "After you make your goodbyes to your family." He paused. "I will see one of my men returns to look after them until your circumstances are settled." He'd see that the man did not hang, but there would be some punishment that kept the man from his kin.

Donaldson sighed. "Very well." He set his glass aside and stood. His hands clasped behind him, the small, rotund man started for the door.

"Mr. Donaldson?"

The merchant looked back, over his shoulder. *I am so sorry.* "You are correct. Waters deserved to die."

Donaldson tipped his head. "Thank you."

Together, they made their way from the room.

It was done.

The following evening, Nathaniel, neatly groomed and in a proper change of garments, entered through the front doors of his London offices.

His staff paused, dropping bows. Quiet clapping trailed his footsteps.

Once, there'd been no greater sense of satisfaction than the completion of a mission.

Not this time, however.

His assistant, with a wide grin, fell into step beside him. "I understand congratulations are in order, my lord."

He didn't want congratulations. "Do you think there is anything celebratory about this?" he countered. Bennett's smile faded.

"No, my lord. No. I… my apologies."

Even having secured assurances that Donaldson wouldn't hang, the older man would still find himself in Marshalsea. The man's family, as he'd known from his arrival in the countryside, had been destroyed by Waters.

"I'll draft a public statement for Bow Street and the papers this morn," Nathaniel said, loosening his cravat as he walked. "I don't want a single word breathed outside these walls until," *I speak with Victoria,* "I indicate it is time to do so."

Surprise filled the other man's eyes. "Of course not, my lord. I trust our agents would know better."

"Never make presumptions, Bennett," he reminded. A flush stained Bennett's cheeks. To soften that slight chastisement, he slapped the younger man on the back.

They reached Nathaniel's office. "Call a meeting with the men. Inform them of my wishes."

"Yes, my lord." Dropping a bow, Bennett scurried back in the opposite direction and Nathaniel entered his offices.

As soon as he was alone, he closed the door. Shutting himself inside, he leaned against the door.

Alone.

Just as he'd been after every mission. But with the finality of the

Waters case, everything had changed.

Victoria's son would be exonerated. The gossip would persist because, frankly, that was the way of London and it would always be—until the next juicy morsel presented itself.

Nathaniel rubbed his hands over his face. And then, what happened from here? To the two of them, together? He and Victoria? Restless, he wandered over to the windows. He drew back the thick, brocade fabric and stared down into the dark, empty streets below.

She'd married a bigamist.

The horror of that discovery had not lessened the knot in Nathaniel's belly.

She'd deserved so much more from life. She'd deserved laughter and the love of a good, honorable man. His throat clogged with emotion. And to travel. That had been another gift that should have been hers. Spirited, adventurous Victoria Tremaine should have sailed the globe, exploring all those places she'd dreamed about. Nay, the places they'd dreamed of—together.

Nathaniel rested his forehead against the windowpane; the glass cool against his skin.

I want to be that man for her. The man who journeyed beside her, and loved her, and teased her. *I want to begin again.*

So why couldn't they?

He jerked. His heart slowed and then sped up. Why couldn't they? Why couldn't he offer Victoria marriage as he should have when they'd been a young lady and gentleman with the world laid out before them?

For more than twenty years he'd solidified in his mind his own importance to the Brethren. Yet, he'd come to appreciate, accept, and understand that there would always be the next, great Sovereign to fill in the position. The Brethren was more than Nathaniel and, as such, would not only survive were he to leave it, but would thrive.

But what of Victoria? What could he possibly offer her now? He'd been away from Society for so long, all he knew was the Brethren. The work he'd done for the Home Office had secured any number of enemies. If they married, he'd open her to a greater threat than she'd ever known with her late bastard of a husband.

Then I'd be no different than Waters.

In the crystal panes, his agonized smile reflected back. He'd brought nothing but hurt to her before, he could not do that to her again.

Nathaniel knocked his head against the crystal pane. He wished he'd done so much differently and knew well that nothing had ever come from wishing or hoping.

CHAPTER 19

An agent's mission drives his or her schedule.
Article XIX: The Brethren of the Lords

HE'D BEEN GONE A WEEK.

It was just seven days. And yet, where Nathaniel Archer was concerned and with the work he did for the Crown, Victoria well-understood the significance of a passing day. He'd been gone a week, when he'd vowed to see her in a day's time.

Kneeling on the ground in her gardens, she wrestled the weeds free of the earth. The tug of the roots as they pulled free, usually so satisfying, offered little distraction. Dusting the back of her hand across her damp brow, she tossed aside the weeds in her fingers atop a growing pile at her back.

Phoebe had been wrong. Nathaniel was not a man who'd ever have deceived a woman to obtain information.

And yet, with his continued absence, she almost wanted Phoebe to be correct. For then it would mean Nathaniel was safe and that he was not missing, again captured—

A sob caught in her throat and she renewed her efforts, pulling those weeds free in a flourish. God, how she despised the Brethren. She hated it for taking him away from her always. For stealing more than twenty years of happiness from them. And for the grip it had and would always have upon him. "Bloody, bloody bastard," she rasped. Gripping a root, she wrestled it back and forth.

Why could she not be enough for him? Why—?

"Is it too much to hope that you are talking about that bothersome weed there and not me?"

She reeled back with such force that the root ripped free. It slipped from her suddenly weak grasp and sailed behind her, landing with a thump upon Nathaniel's chest. Victoria scrambled to her feet. Touching a mud-stained glove to her mouth, she stared back at his beloved visage. But for the smattering of dirt staining the lapel of his jacket, he embodied masculine elegance and perfection. "It was a root," she whispered.

He smiled slowly. As quickly as it came, it faded. Suddenly, it was like a cloud covering the sun, leaving in its place only darkness.

"You came back," she said, hugging herself in a lonely embrace.
"I—"

Nathaniel held out a folded sheet of parchment.

Tugging free her gloves, she took several hesitant steps closer, stopping when two paces divided them. "What is this?" she ventured, dropping her gloves and accepting the proffered page.

"It is a confession."

She froze. The earth was suspended; unmoving. Surely, she'd misheard him. "Andrew?"

"Is free. Mr. Donaldson, in fact, coordinated the murder." While he spoke, she read every last horrifying detail of her husband's sins and crimes.

Bile stung her throat. She'd known he was a monster, but never the true depth of his evil. "My God." Only there was no God in any of this...

Nathaniel doffed his hat, beating it against his leg. "I am sorry, Victoria. So very sorry."

Her gaze fell once more to the sheet. "Do you know, I spent my entire marriage hoping he'd make me a widow? And I cannot be moved to any feeling except heartbreak for the young woman so wronged by... by him." Meticulously folding the sheet, she handed it back. "What happens now, Nathaniel?" *To us.* What future awaited them? Or is this all they would ever have? A shared past and a fleeting time together, before his work called him on to the next important mission.

"Reports are currently being prepared and sent off to all the major newspapers and gossip pages. The Runners and constables are being informed of the findings and will mark the case closed."

It was not what she had meant. But how to say as much? How to ask the real questions that she had for him… about them? Victoria held her hand out. "Thank you," she said softly. "There is no one I would have trusted more with my family." And he had proven her so very right.

Nathaniel eyed her fingers a long moment and then enfolded her palm in his. The heat singed her, causing those same delicious shivers. He released her too fast. "I have a meeting."

"Of course," she said hurriedly, backing away. "Of course. You are busy. I appreciate your—" Her words ended on a startled shriek as he closed the distance between them in two long strides.

"I do not want us to be like this," he implored. "Stilted strangers at a loss for words." That had never been them.

"I do not know how to be," she said hoarsely, turning her palms up. "I do not know what we are beyond the time we had together and…" She indicated the folded sheet she'd returned to him. "This. You are your organization and I…" Victoria sucked in a breath. "I want all of you, Nathaniel. I want all of you or nothing. And I'm not selfish enough to ask you to make that sacrifice for me and you should not be so selfish that you expect me to accept anything less." Although she wanted to. Wanted to rail at him and demand to know why she hadn't ever been enough.

"Mother?"

They jumped apart.

Andrew stood at the entrance of the gardens, his eyes clouded with confusion as he looked between them.

She cleared her throat. "L-Lord Exeter arrived with news of your case."

"Did he?" Andrew asked, sounding hopelessly bored.

Nathaniel held out that same scrap. "We have located the man responsible for the murder of your father."

Victoria searched her son for some response; relief, gratitude… anything.

"How incredibly generous of you to bring that information… first to my mother."

He knew. Her son, who she'd always taken to be too self-absorbed to note so much as her presence, had gathered the details to know that something was there between her and Nathaniel.

"If you will excuse me… my lord," she added that last part for Andrew's benefit.

Nathaniel jammed his hat on. "Of course."

Their gazes locked.

We are in hiding, even now. Our entire life has been one clandestine secret known only by us and kept from the world.

And she despised it… with every fiber of her being.

Nathaniel took his leave.

After he'd gone, Victoria proceeded to gather her tools.

"I don't like him." Andrew's voice slashed across the quiet.

She stiffened. "That gentleman you do not like is responsible for your freedom."

"And should I care about that more than I should the fact that he's been panting after you?"

Victoria gasped, whipping about. "Andrew."

"He is the one, isn't he?" he asked bluntly, that question as unexpected as a punch to the gut. "The gent who left you with a babe in your belly and a reason to be grateful for all Father offered you."

"How do you know that?" the question slipped out before she could call it back.

"You always took me for being as self-absorbed as the man who sired me, that you didn't believe me capable of hearing all the hateful words he spewed at you."

"That is not true, Andrew," she said, wincing at the blow he'd landed.

"And I was," he went on as though she hadn't spoken. "Because I never did anything to stop him."

She stormed over, gathering his hands in hers. "You could not." Only death could have compelled Chester to cease his brutalizing. Victoria wrapped her arms about her son, holding him, tightening her grip when he attempted to slip free. "I love you, Andrew," she said simply, giving him the words he needed to hear.

"I should have protected you," he sobbed against her shoulder.

Victoria gently stroked his back, allowing him to cry those healing drops. Wanting him to forgive himself… needing him to. "It is not a child's role to protect one's parent. It was my role as your mother to keep you from hurt." Life, however, had proven that there was some suffering that was beyond the grasp of any devoted mama. "Someday, when you have babes of your own, you will understand that."

He stiffened. Andrew wiped his nose with his kerchief, carefully avoiding her eyes. "I still believe Exeter is undeserving of you."

"You are wrong," she said solemnly, her heart twisting. "Either way, he's not offered me any arrangement, either respectable or otherwise."

"Which proves him the fool I take him for."

Despite the pain of losing Nathaniel and her own son's heartache, a smile formed on her lips. "I love you, Andrew."

He ducked his head. "I love you, too." Then smoothing his palms down his jacket front, he rocked on his heels. "I am off to my clubs." He grinned lazily. "Not every day a man is exonerated for murder."

"Andrew," she warned. "Be careful—"

"White's. I was going to visit White's and see if Edmund and Nick care to join me."

She patted his cheek. "That is a splendid idea." How very much he'd missed the influence of good, honorable men.

After he'd gone, Victoria remained in the gardens, rooted precisely where she'd been when Nathaniel arrived. Silence pealed around the gardens, only broken by the occasional cry of a swallow.

And with her daughters gone and Andrew living for his own life, she was truly alone. Only this was far worse than even before. Before Nathaniel's return, she'd convinced herself that she was perfectly contented and that her grandchildren were enough. That living vicariously through Phoebe and Justina's joyous unions and journeys would fill her life so that there were never regrets.

I want it all. I want to travel the world and see the Sandwich Islands, feel the sand under my toes and make love under the sunset and—

Victoria gave her head a hard shake, dislodging her regrets. Abandoning her efforts in the gardens, she made her way inside. The halls that had once rung with Phoebe, Justina, and Andrew's laughter and teasing, now silent. Climbing the stairs, she shed her apron as she walked the same path she had more times than she could count, finding her rooms.

Pressing the handle, she let herself inside—and stopped. Her heart skipped a beat. Through the crack in the window, the curtains danced softly in the breeze. And she knew… before he even spoke. Victoria slowly turned. *Nathaniel.*

"Long ago, I convinced myself that the Brethren was enough. I could not have you. So instead, I had an organization that kept me distracted from all I had lost. It was a poor replacement for what I truly wanted in my life—you." Nathaniel closed the door, coming closer. "All I have known is responsibility…"

"I know that, Nathaniel." It was why he couldn't offer her more.

"But I want more. You convinced me that I deserve more. I want to see the world, with you at my side."

Tears filled her eyes.

"I want to show you the places I've been, but truly see them for the first time because it is with you."

"But the Brethren?"

He shook his head. "I gave my life to it; it is time for someone else to fill that role. We lost so much, Victoria. So much damned time. I do not want to lose any more." Nathaniel held his hand out.

Victoria eyed those beloved fingers. "What…?"

"Come with me. Let us go explore the world together."

Her mouth opened and closed of its own volition. He spoke of just… leaving. There were her children and grandchildren and—

He sank to a knee and fished inside his jacket, pulling out a folded sheet.

She stifled a gasp with her fingers.

"It is a special license," he explained hoarsely. "I would not come to you until I'd set Andrew's life to rights, and until I'd spoken to the archbishop. Marry me, Victoria. See the world with me." His throat worked. "Love me."

A half-laugh, half-sob burst forth as she launched herself into his arms. He easily caught her to him, righting them before they faltered. "Yes. Yes. And always." She cupped his face between her palms. "I will always love you."

Nathaniel grinned and took her mouth under his. She melted against him, turning herself over to his embrace.

"Are we to sneak through the window as we go, Mr. Archer?" she whispered against his mouth, when he'd ended that kiss.

He dropped his brow to hers. "No more windows. No more sneaking." He held his elbow out. "Shall we?"

Victoria slipped her arm through his and they stepped out of her room—together.

EPILOGUE

3 months later

THEY WERE IN TROUBLE.

And it was not every day that a man of five and forty years and a woman of three and forty found themselves so thoroughly disciplined, and thus far with nothing more than a disapproving look.

Or in this case, five of them.

Seated side by side on Edmund and Phoebe's white satin sofa, with her three children and two sons-in-law looming over them, Victoria felt very much like the once-naughty girl she'd been. And just like when she'd been a girl, Victoria had never been one to wait overly long in silence for someone else to make the first advance. She offered a beaming smile. "We missed you?" But then, she'd been smiling since she and Nathaniel had exchanged vows and begun anew… only this time as husband and wife.

Justina crossed her arms at her middle. "Is that a question?"

Oh, dear. Victoria considered her words. Given the glowers trained on her and Nathaniel, she ultimately decided for none.

"Humph." Andrew nodded. "Certainly a question. Heard it clearly myself."

At her side, Nathaniel's broad shoulders shook slightly.

Her heart somersaulted in her chest at the half-grin on his lips. The grimness that had been etched on his person and features more than three months ago had since faded, leaving in its place, the smiling, teasing man who'd first stolen her heart.

"Is there something amusing about this, Exeter?" Edmund whispered in steely tones that would have had any other man quaking. Nathaniel, however, had faced down devils and, as such, their gruff, but loving son-in-law would never instill fear.

He did offer the benefit of a sheepish look. "Er…"

Victoria rolled her eyes. "There is nothing shamefaced about you, Nathaniel Archer."

Her husband gathered her fingers and brought them to his mouth. His breath fanned her skin. "Are you accusing me of being poor in ways of stratagem?" he whispered close to her ear. He brushed a kiss along her knuckles and a delicious shiver burned at that contact.

"Never," she said, her voice husky. All these years, she'd believed herself a mother to grown children… a grandmother, incapable of feeling and knowing passion. Nathaniel had reminded her of the power of her femininity and she reveled in it. "I could never doubt you." Not again. Never again.

"Exeter," Edmund barked. Nathaniel instantly reapplied that false contrition.

"My apologies," he said in somber tones. Their son-in-law's eyes formed thin slits upon Nathaniel. "You were saying?" he drawled.

Victoria pinched him in the side. "Do not bait—"

"You simply… *left*," Phoebe charged, throwing her arms up in exasperation.

Andrew and Justina spoke in unison.

"Without a word."

"Without a note."

"See what you've done," Victoria muttered. Her daughters had always been the protective sorts… and Andrew had recently adopted that same concern. As such, Victoria was torn between amusement at being lectured by a room full of her children and pride for having raised children who would worry after her.

"What have I done?" Nathaniel challenged. "Made you deliriously happy?" He followed that with a slow wink that earned a husky laugh from her.

"Hullo," Andrew barked. He waved his hand. "Might I remind you both that we are in the middle of a family discussion?"

"I would hardly call this a discussion," Nathaniel pointed out. "It seems more in line with the questioning of the Home Off—"

Victoria stuck another elbow in his side. "Oomph." He winced.

Nick cleared his throat. "I would be remiss if I failed to point out that they are both adults, capable of making their own decisions, and entitled to it, as well."

Four sets of displeased stares moved from Victoria and Nathaniel over to the young duke.

Grateful for his intervention, Victoria favored her son-in-law with a smile, which dipped at his next words.

"Though, at the very least, a note would have been welcome."

"Yes, we certainly owed you that at the very least," Nathaniel spoke in solemn tones.

Victoria's lips twitched. Near in age to her own, he no doubt appreciated being expected to answer to a room full of family many years their junior.

From the corner of her eye she caught a look pass between Nathaniel and Phoebe. Their stares, so very much alike, twinkled.

Understanding dawned. For Phoebe's impressive display of outrage, she'd…*known* of their marriage.

Nathaniel shifted his focus back over to Victoria. "I could not whisk away her mother without speaking to her. Without asking her for your…" *hand*…

Her heart flipped over itself with warmth. He loved Phoebe enough, cared so much, that he'd spoken to her before asking for Victoria's hand. "She has your skill of subterfuge," Victoria said, pride creeping in.

"What are you whispering about over there?" Andrew snapped.

"At the very least, act contrite," Nathaniel whispered against her ear, his breath tickled the sensitive flesh where her neck met her lobe and she giggled.

"I am *not* contrite." Before he'd reentered her life, she would have been. She would have never scandalized her family and would have certainly never sat before them grinning like a debutante just out on the Market. However, she'd tired of pretending to be someone other than who or what she was. Nathaniel had helped free her in that way. "I *am* deliriously happy despite my children's clear displeasure."

"Why… why… you are not even paying attention." Shock underlined Justina's observation.

"Uh—we are?" Victoria vowed.

Andrew snorted. "*Another* question."

Justina ticked off their grievances on her fingers. "First, you marry without including any of us at your ceremony." No, they hadn't. They had lost so much time. In their haste to wed, nothing else had mattered except sealing the vows they'd delayed making too many times. It was something her children could not understand. "Then, you disappear for three months. *Three months* without a word. And suddenly you just reappear?"

As Victoria wasn't wholly certain there was a question there, she chose continued silence.

"Where were you?" Phoebe asked. In place of her earlier annoyance, there was a curiosity now there.

And her firstborn child, who'd hungered to know a taste of Captain Cook's adventures, would understand. Victoria knew that implicitly. "We were journeying to the Sandwich Islands," she said softly.

Who knew just a handful of words could so effectively silence her children?

"But... but... that is on the other side of the world," Justina sputtered.

"I did not say we *reached* them," Victoria pointed out. Had they continued on, it would have taken close to a year.

Her eldest daughter's face fell. "You never made it."

Nathaniel coughed into his fist. "We did not. We thought it wise to return."

Victoria cleared her throat, carefully measuring her words. "I... fell ill." Which was not altogether an untruth.

"Mother?" Phoebe croaked.

The room exploded in a flurry of questions and worry.

Victoria held a staying hand up. "I assure you," she spoke quickly. "I am not dying." Warmth filled every corner of her person as she dropped a hand to her gently rounding belly. "We are with child." *Again.*

The room went silent.

Andrew recoiled. "Good God. *What?*"

"A babe," Nathaniel murmured. Collecting Victoria's fingers, he raised them to his mouth for a gentle kiss. "We are expecting a babe."

"But... but... you are a grandmother," Andrew protested.

Victoria smiled. "And a mother… *again*…"

And while Edmund and Nick came over to shake Nathaniel's hand and her daughters hugged her, Victoria glanced over the tops of their heads to her husband.

Nathaniel's eyes twinkled. *I love you*, he mouthed.

Her heart swelled. She'd come full circle in life: with another child, conceived in love. Victoria smiled. "And I love you," she whispered back, ready for the beginning of the rest of their life—together.

THE END

If you enjoyed *The Spy Who Seduced Her*, Book 1 in
The Brethren series, check out Christi Caldwell's Sinful Brides
series by Montlake Romance. In the latest installment,
Book 3, *The Lady's Guard*, a kingpin of London's underbelly
risks his heart on the woman he's hired to protect.

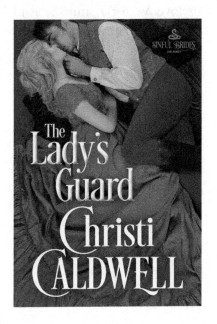

London, 1822

AT THE NOTORIOUS HELL AND Sin Club nestled in London's dark streets, Niall Marksman relishes taking the fortunes of the very same society that once disregarded his existence. Oh yes, Niall has sold his soul to the devil and paid *dearly*. It's only when Lady Diana Verney appears at the gaming club looking for help that Niall knows that the devil has finally come to collect…by forcing him to protect the duke's pampered daughter.

Disdained by the peerage and ignored by her father, Diana knows that someone wants to harm her. Her only protection is Niall, a scarred, intense man who lives and dies by the knife. Now her life and safety are in the hands of the most dangerous man in London. But a man raised on the city's mercenary streets is adept at stealing anything he wishes—including a lady's reputation *and* her heart.

OTHER BOOKS BY CHRISTI CALDWELL

TO ENCHANT A WICKED DUKE
Book 13 in the "Heart of a Duke" Series by Christi Caldwell

A Devil in Disguise

Years ago, when Nick Tallings, the recent Duke of Huntly, watched his family destroyed at the hands of a merciless nobleman, he vowed revenge. But his efforts had been futile, as his enemy, Lord Rutland is without weakness.

Until now…

With his rival finally happily married, Nick is able to set his ruthless scheme into motion. His plot hinges upon Lord Rutland's innocent, empty-headed sister-in-law, Justina Barrett. Nick will ruin her, marry her, and then leave her brokenhearted.

A Lady Dreaming of Love

From the moment Justina Barrett makes her Come Out, she is labeled a Diamond. Even with her ruthless father determined to sell her off to the highest bidder, Justina never gives up on her hope for a good, honorable gentleman who values her wit more than her looks.

A Not-So-Chance Meeting

Nick's ploy to ensnare Justina falls neatly into place in the streets of London. With each carefully orchestrated encounter, he slips further and further inside the lady's heart, never anticipating that Justina, with her quick wit and strength, will break down his own defenses. As Nick's plans begins to unravel, he's left to determine which is more important—Justina's love or his vow for vengeance. But can Justina ever forgive the duke who deceived her?

One Winter with a Baron

Book 12 in the "Heart of a Duke" Series by Christi Caldwell

A clever spinster:

Content with her spinster lifestyle, Miss Sybil Cunning wants to prove that a future as an unmarried woman is the only life for her. As a bluestocking who values hard, empirical data, Sybil needs help with her research. Nolan Pratt, Baron Webb, one of society's most scandalous rakes, is the perfect gentleman to help her. After all, he inspires fear in proper mothers and desire within their daughters.

A notorious rake:

Society may be aware of Nolan Pratt, Baron's Webb's wicked ways, but what he has carefully hidden is his miserable handling of his family's finances. When Sybil presents him the opportunity to earn much-needed funds, he can't refuse.

A winter to remember:

However, what begins as a business arrangement becomes something more and with every meeting, Sybil slips inside his heart. Can this clever woman look beneath the veneer of a coldhearted rake to see the man Nolan truly is?

To Redeem a Rake

Book 11 in the "Heart of a Duke" Series by Christi Caldwell

He's spent years scandalizing society.
Now, this rake must change his ways.

Society's most infamous scoundrel, Daniel Winterbourne, the Earl of Montfort, has been promised a small fortune if he can relinquish his wayward, carousing lifestyle. And behaving means he must also help find a respectable companion for his youngest sister—someone who will guide her and whom she can emulate. However, Daniel knows no such woman. But when he encounters a childhood friend, Daniel believes she may just be the answer to all of his problems.

Having been secretly humiliated by an unscrupulous blackguard years earlier, Miss Daphne Smith dreams of finding work at Ladies of Hope, an institution that provides an education for disabled women. With her sordid past and a disfigured leg, few opportunities arise for a woman such as she. Knowing Daniel's history, she wishes to avoid him, but working for his sister is exactly the stepping stone she needs.

Their attraction intensifies as Daniel and Daphne grow closer, preparing his sister for the London Season. But Daniel must resist his desire for a woman tarnished by scandal while Daphne is reminded of the boy she once knew. Can society's most notorious rake redeem his reputation and become the man Daphne deserves?

To Woo a Widow
Book 10 in the "Heart of a Duke" Series by Christi Caldwell

They see a brokenhearted widow.
She's far from shattered.

Lady Philippa Winston is never marrying again. After her late husband's cruelty that she kept so well hidden, she has no desire to search for love.

Years ago, Miles Brookfield, the Marquess of Guilford, made a frivolous vow he never thought would come to fruition—he promised to marry his mother's goddaughter if he was unwed by the age of thirty. Now, to his dismay, he's faced with honoring that pledge. But when he encounters the beautiful and intriguing Lady Philippa, Miles knows his true path in life. It's up to him to break down every belief Philippa carries about gentlemen, proving that not only is love real, but that he is the man deserving of her sheltered heart.

Will Philippa let down her guard and allow Miles to woo a widow in desperate need of his love?

THE LURE OF A RAKE
Book 9 in the "Heart of a Duke" Series by Christi Caldwell

A Lady Dreaming of Love

Lady Genevieve Farendale has a scandalous past. Jilted at the altar years earlier and exiled by her family, she's now returned to London to prove she can be a proper lady. Even though she's not given up on the hope of marrying for love, she's wary of trusting again. Then she meets Cedric Falcot, the Marquess of St. Albans whose seductive ways set her heart aflutter. But with her sordid history, Genevieve knows a rake can also easily destroy her.

An Unlikely Pairing

What begins as a chance encounter between Cedric and Genevieve becomes something more. As they continue to meet, passions stir. But with Genevieve's hope for true love, she fears Cedric will be unable to give up his wayward lifestyle. After all, Cedric has spent years protecting his heart, and keeping everyone out. Slowly, she chips away at all the walls he's built, but when he falters, Genevieve can't offer him redemption. Now, it's up to Cedric to prove to Genevieve that the love of a man is far more powerful than the lure of a rake.

TO TRUST A ROGUE
Book 8 in the "Heart of a Duke" Series by Christi Caldwell

A rogue

Marcus, the Viscount Wessex has carefully crafted the image of rogue and charmer for Polite Society. Under that façade, however, dwells a man whose dreams were shattered almost eight years earlier by a young lady who captured his heart, pledged her love, and then left him, with nothing more than a curt note.

A widow

Eight years earlier, faced with no other choice, Mrs. Eleanor Collins, fled London and the only man she ever loved, Marcus, Viscount Wessex. She has now returned to serve as a companion for her elderly aunt with a daughter in tow. Even though they're next door neighbors, there is little reason for her to move in the same circles as Marcus, just in case, she vows to avoid him, for he reminds her of all she lost when she left.

Reunited

As their paths continue to cross, Marcus finds his desire for Eleanor just as strong, but he learned long ago she's not to be trusted. He will offer her a place in his bed, but not anything more. Only, Eleanor has no interest in this new, roguish man. The more time they spend together, the protective wall they've constructed to keep the other out, begin to break. With all the betrayals and secrets between them, Marcus has to open his heart again. And Eleanor must decide if it's ever safe to trust a rogue.

To Wed His Christmas Lady
Book 7 in the "Heart of a Duke" Series by Christi Caldwell

She's longing to be loved:

Lady Cara Falcot has only served one purpose to her loathsome father—to increase his power through a marriage to the future Duke of Billingsley. As such, she's built protective walls about her heart, and presents an icy facade to the world around her. Journeying home from her finishing school for the Christmas holidays, Cara's carriage is stranded during a winter storm. She's forced to tarry at a ramshackle inn, where she immediately antagonizes another patron—William.

He's avoiding his duty in favor of one last adventure:

William Hargrove, the Marquess of Grafton has wanted only one thing in life—to avoid the future match his parents would have him make to a cold, duke's daughter. He's returning home from a blissful eight years of traveling the world to see to his responsibilities. But when a winter storm interrupts his trip and lands him at a falling-down inn, he's forced to share company with a commanding Lady Cara who initially reminds him exactly of the woman he so desperately wants to avoid.

A Christmas snowstorm ushers in the spirit of the season:

At the holiday time, these two people who despise each other due to first perceptions are offered renewed beginnings and fresh starts. As this gruff stranger breaks down the walls she's built about herself, Cara has to determine whether she can truly open her heart to trusting that any man is capable of good and that she herself is capable of love. And William has to set aside all previous thoughts he's carried of the polished ladies like Cara, to be the man to show her that love.

THE HEART OF A SCOUNDREL
Book 6 in the "Heart of a Duke" Series by Christi Caldwell

Ruthless, wicked, and dark, the Marquess of Rutland rouses terror in the breast of ladies and nobleman alike. All Edmund wants in life is power. After he was publically humiliated by his one love Lady Margaret, he vowed vengeance, using Margaret's niece, as his pawn. Except, he's thwarted by another, more enticing target—Miss Phoebe Barrett.

Miss Phoebe Barrett knows precisely the shame she's been born to. Because her father is a shocking letch she's learned to form her own opinions on a person's worth. After a chance meeting with the Marquess of Rutland, she is captivated by the mysterious man. He, too, is a victim of society's scorn, but the more encounters she has with Edmund, the more she knows there is powerful depth and emotion to the jaded marquess.

The lady wreaks havoc on Edmund's plans for revenge and he finds he wants Phoebe, at all costs. As she's drawn into the darkness of his world, Phoebe risks being destroyed by Edmund's ruthlessness. And Phoebe who desires love at all costs, has to determine if she can ever truly trust the heart of a scoundrel.

TO LOVE A LORD
Book 5 in the "Heart of a Duke" Series by Christi Caldwell

All she wants is security:

The last place finishing school instructor Mrs. Jane Munroe belongs, is in polite Society. Vowing to never wed, she's been scuttled around from post to post. Now she finds herself in the Marquess of Waverly's household. She's never met a nobleman she liked, and when she meets the pompous, arrogant marquess, she remembers why. But soon, she discovers Gabriel is unlike any gentleman she's ever known.

All he wants is a companion for his sister:

What Gabriel finds himself with instead, is a fiery spirited, bespectacled woman who entices him at every corner and challenges his age-old vow to never trust his heart to a woman. But… there is something suspicious about his sister's companion. And he is determined to find out just what it is.

All they need is each other:

As Gabriel and Jane confront the truth of their feelings, the lies and secrets between them begin to unravel. And Jane is left to decide whether or not it is ever truly safe to love a lord.

LOVED BY A DUKE
Book 4 in the "Heart of a Duke" Series by Christi Caldwell

For ten years, Lady Daisy Meadows has been in love with Auric, the Duke of Crawford. Ever since his gallant rescue years earlier, Daisy knew she was destined to be his Duchess. Unfortunately, Auric sees her as his best friend's sister and nothing more. But perhaps, if she can manage to find the fabled heart of a duke pendant, she will win over the heart of her duke.

Auric, the Duke of Crawford enjoys Daisy's company. The last thing he is interested in however, is pursuing a romance with a woman he's known since she was in leading strings. This season, Daisy is turning up in the oddest places and he cannot help but notice that she is no longer a girl. But Auric wouldn't do something as foolhardy as to fall in love with Daisy. He couldn't. Not with the guilt he carries over his past sins… Not when he has no right to her heart…But perhaps, just perhaps, she can forgive the past and trust that he'd forever cherish her heart—but will she let him?

THE LOVE OF A ROGUE
Book 3 in the "Heart of a Duke" Series by Christi Caldwell

Lady Imogen Moore hasn't had an easy time of it since she made her Come Out. With her betrothed, a powerful duke breaking it off to wed her sister, she's become the *tons* favorite piece of gossip. Never again wanting to experience the pain of a broken heart, she's resolved to make a match with a polite, respectable gentleman. The last thing she wants is another reckless rogue.

Lord Alex Edgerton has a problem. His brother, tired of Alex's carousing has charged him with chaperoning their remaining, unwed sister about *ton* events. Shopping? No, thank you. Attending the theatre? He'd rather be at Forbidden Pleasures with a scantily clad beauty upon his lap. The task of *chaperone* becomes even more of a bother when his sister drags along her dearest friend, Lady Imogen to social functions. The last thing he wants in his life is a young, innocent English miss.

Except, as Alex and Imogen are thrown together, passions flare and Alex comes to find he not only wants Imogen in his bed, but also in his heart. Yet now he must convince Imogen to risk all, on the heart of a rogue.

More Than a Duke
Book 2 in the "Heart of a Duke" Series by Christi Caldwell

Polite Society doesn't take Lady Anne Adamson seriously. However, Anne isn't just another pretty young miss. When she discovers her father betrayed her mother's love and her family descended into poverty, Anne comes up with a plan to marry a respectable, powerful, and honorable gentleman—a man nothing like her philandering father.

Armed with the heart of a duke pendant, fabled to land the wearer a duke's heart, she decides to enlist the aid of the notorious Harry, 6th Earl of Stanhope. A scoundrel with a scandalous past, he is the last gentleman she'd ever wed…however, his reputation marks him the perfect man to school her in the art of seduction so she might ensnare the illustrious Duke of Crawford.

Harry, the Earl of Stanhope is a jaded, cynical rogue who lives for his own pleasures. Having been thrown over by the only woman he ever loved so she could wed a duke, he's not at all surprised when Lady Anne approaches him with her scheme to capture another duke's affection. He's come to appreciate that all women are in fact greedy, title-grasping, self-indulgent creatures. And with Anne's history of grating on his every last nerve, she is the last woman he'd ever agree to school in the art of seduction. Only his friendship with the lady's sister compels him to help.

What begins as a pretend courtship, born of lessons on seduction, becomes something more leaving Anne to decide if she can give her heart to a reckless rogue, and Harry must decide if he's willing to again trust in a lady's love.

FOR LOVE OF THE DUKE
First Full-Length Book in the "Heart of a Duke" Series
by Christi Caldwell

After the tragic death of his wife, Jasper, the 8th Duke of Bainbridge buried himself away in the dark cold walls of his home, Castle Blackwood. When he's coaxed out of his self-imposed exile to attend the amusements of the Frost Fair, his life is irrevocably changed by his fateful meeting with Lady Katherine Adamson.

With her tight brown ringlets and silly white-ruffled gowns, Lady Katherine Adamson has found her dance card empty for two Seasons. After her father's passing, Katherine learned the unreliability of men, and is determined to depend on no one, except herself. Until she meets Jasper…

In a desperate bid to avoid a match arranged by her family, Katherine makes the Duke of Bainbridge a shocking proposition—one that he accepts.

Only, as Katherine begins to love Jasper, she finds the arrangement agreed upon is not enough. And Jasper is left to decide if protecting his heart is more important than fighting for Katherine's love.

IN NEED OF A DUKE
A Prequel Novella to "The Heart of a Duke" Series
by Christi Caldwell

In Need of a Duke: (Author's Note: This is a prequel novella to "The Heart of a Duke" series by Christi Caldwell. It was originally available in "The Heart of a Duke" Collection and is now being published as an individual novella.

~★~

It features a new prologue and epilogue.

Years earlier, a gypsy woman passed to Lady Aldora Adamson and her friends a heart pendant that promised them each the heart of a duke.

Now, a young lady, with her family facing ruin and scandal, Lady Aldora doesn't have time for mythical stories about cheap baubles. She needs to save her sisters and brother by marrying a titled gentleman with wealth and power to his name. She sets her bespectacled sights upon the Marquess of St. James.

Turned out by his father after a tragic scandal, Lord Michael Knightly has grown into a powerful, but self-made man. With the whispers and stares that still follow him, he would rather be anywhere but London…

Until he meets Lady Aldora, a young woman who mistakes him for his brother, the Marquess of St. James. The connection between Aldora and Michael is immediate and as they come to know one another, Aldora's feelings for Michael war with her sisterly responsibilities. With her family's dire situation, a man of Michael's scandalous past will never do.

Ultimately, Aldora must choose between her responsibilities as a sister and her love for Michael.

ONCE A WALLFLOWER, AT LAST HIS LOVE
Book 6 in the Scandalous Seasons Series

Responsible, practical Miss Hermione Rogers, has been crafting stories as the notorious Mr. Michael Michaelmas and selling them for a meager wage to support her siblings. The only real way to ensure her family's ruinous debts are paid, however, is to marry. Tall, thin, and plain, she has no expectation of success. In London for her first Season she seizes the chance to write the tale of a brooding duke. In her research, she finds Sebastian Fitzhugh, the 5th Duke of Mallen, who unfortunately is perfectly affable, charming, and so nicely… configured… he takes her breath away. He lacks all the character traits she needs for her story, but alas, any duke will have to do.

Sebastian Fitzhugh, the 5th Duke of Mallen has been deceived so many times during the high-stakes game of courtship, he's lost faith in Society women. Yet, after a chance encounter with Hermione, he finds himself intrigued. Not a woman he'd normally consider beautiful, the young lady's practical bent, her forthright nature and her tendency to turn up in the oddest places has his interests… roused. He'd like to trust her, he'd like to do a whole lot more with her too, but should he?

A Marquess For Christmas
Book 5 in the Scandalous Seasons Series

Lady Patrina Tidemore gave up on the ridiculous notion of true love after having her heart shattered and her trust destroyed by a black-hearted cad. Used as a pawn in a game of revenge against her brother, Patrina returns to London from a failed elopement with a tattered reputation and little hope for a respectable match. The only peace she finds is in her solitude on the cold winter days at Hyde Park. And even that is yanked from her by two little hellions who just happen to have a devastatingly handsome, but coldly aloof father, the Marquess of Beaufort. Something about the lord stirs the dreams she'd once carried for an honorable gentleman's love.

Weston Aldridge, the 4th Marquess of Beaufort was deceived and betrayed by his late wife. In her faithlessness, he's come to view women as self-serving, indulgent creatures. Except, after a series of chance encounters with Patrina, he comes to appreciate how uniquely different she is than all women he's ever known.

At the Christmastide season, a time of hope and new beginnings, Patrina and Weston, unexpectedly learn true love in one another. However, as Patrina's scandalous past threatens their future and the happiness of his children, they are both left to determine if love is enough.

Always a Rogue, Forever Her Love
Book 4 in the Scandalous Seasons Series

Miss Juliet Marshville is spitting mad. With one guardian missing, and the other singularly uninterested in her fate, she is at the mercy of her wastrel brother who loses her beloved childhood home to a man known as Sin. Determined to reclaim control of Rosecliff Cottage and her own fate, Juliet arranges a meeting with the notorious rogue and demands the return of her property.

Jonathan Tidemore, 5th Earl of Sinclair, known to the *ton* as Sin, is exceptionally lucky in life and at the gaming tables. He has just one problem. Well…four, really. His incorrigible sisters have driven off yet another governess. This time, however, his mother demands he find an appropriate replacement.

When Miss Juliet Marshville boldly demands the return of her precious cottage, he takes advantage of his sudden good fortune and puts an offer to her; turn his sisters into proper English ladies, and he'll return Rosecliff Cottage to Juliet's possession.

Jonathan comes to appreciate Juliet's spirit, courage, and clever wit, and decides to claim the fiery beauty as his mistress. Juliet, however, will be mistress for no man. Nor could she ever love a man who callously stole her home in a game of cards. As Jonathan begins to see Juliet as more than a spirited beauty to warm his bed, he realizes she could be a lady he could love the rest of his life, if only he can convince the proud Juliet that he's worthy of her hand and heart.

Always Proper, Suddenly Scandalous
Book 3 in the Scandalous Seasons Series

Geoffrey Winters, Viscount Redbrooke was not always the hard, unrelenting lord driven by propriety. After a tragic mistake, he resolved to honor his responsibility to the Redbrooke line and live a life, free of scandal. Knowing his duty is to wed a proper, respectable English miss, he selects Lady Beatrice Dennington, daughter of the Duke of Somerset, the perfect woman for him. Until he meets Miss Abigail Stone…

To distance herself from a personal scandal, Abigail Stone flees America to visit her uncle, the Duke of Somerset. Determined to never trust a man again, she is helplessly intrigued by the hard, too-proper Geoffrey. With his strict appreciation for decorum and order, he is nothing like the man' she's always dreamed of.

Abigail is everything Geoffrey does not need. She upends his carefully ordered world at every encounter. As they begin to care for one another, Abigail carefully guards the secret that resulted in her journey to England.

Only, if Geoffrey learns the truth about Abigail, he must decide which he holds most dear: his place in Society or Abigail's place in his heart.

NEVER COURTED, SUDDENLY WED
Book 2 in the Scandalous Seasons Series

Christopher Ansley, Earl of Waxham, has constructed a perfect image for the *ton*–the ladies love him and his company is desired by all. Only two people know the truth about Waxham's secret. Unfortunately, one of them is Miss Sophie Winters.

Sophie Winters has known Christopher since she was in leading strings. As children, they delighted in tormenting each other. Now at two and twenty, she still has a tendency to find herself in scrapes, and her marital prospects are slim.

When his father threatens to expose his shame to the *ton*, unless he weds Sophie for her dowry, Christopher concocts a plan to remain a bachelor. What he didn't plan on was falling in love with the lively, impetuous Sophie. As secrets are exposed, will Christopher's love be enough when she discovers his role in his father's scheme?

FOREVER BETROTHED, NEVER THE BRIDE
Book 1 in the Scandalous Seasons Series

Hopeless romantic Lady Emmaline Fitzhugh is tired of sitting with the wallflowers, waiting for her betrothed to come to his senses and marry her. When Emmaline reads one too many reports of his scandalous liaisons in the gossip rags, she takes matters into her own hands.

War-torn veteran Lord Drake devotes himself to forgetting his days on the Peninsula through an endless round of meaningless associations. He no longer wants to feel anything, but Lady Emmaline is making it hard to maintain a state of numbness. With her zest for life, she awakens his passion and desire for love.

The one woman Drake has spent the better part of his life avoiding is now the only woman he needs, but he is no longer a man worthy of his Emmaline. It is up to her to show him the healing power of love.

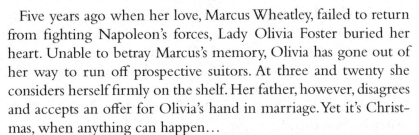

A SEASON OF HOPE
A Danby Novella

Five years ago when her love, Marcus Wheatley, failed to return from fighting Napoleon's forces, Lady Olivia Foster buried her heart. Unable to betray Marcus's memory, Olivia has gone out of her way to run off prospective suitors. At three and twenty she considers herself firmly on the shelf. Her father, however, disagrees and accepts an offer for Olivia's hand in marriage. Yet it's Christmas, when anything can happen…

Olivia receives a well-timed summons from her grandfather, the Duke of Danby, and eagerly embraces the reprieve from her betrothal.

Only, when Olivia arrives at Danby Castle she realizes the Christmas season represents hope, second chances, and even miracles.

"Winning a Lady's Heart"
A Danby Novella

Author's Note: This is a novella that was originally available in A Summons From The Castle (The Regency Christmas Summons Collection). It is being published as an individual novella.

~★~

For Lady Alexandra, being the source of a cold, calculated wager is bad enough…but when it is waged by Nathaniel Michael Winters, 5th Earl of Pembroke, the man she's in love with, it results in a broken heart, the scandal of the season, and a summons from her grandfather – the Duke of Danby.

To escape Society's gossip, she hurries to her meeting with the duke, determined to put memories of the earl far behind. Except the duke has other plans for Alexandra…plans which include the 5th Earl of Pembroke!

Tempted by a Lady's Smile
Book 4 in the "Lords of Honor" Series

Richard Jonas has loved but one woman—a woman who belongs to his brother. Refusing to suffer any longer, he evades his family in order to barricade his heart from unrequited love. While attending a friend's summer party, Richard's approach to love is changed after sharing a passionate and life-altering kiss with a vibrant and mysterious woman. Believing he was incapable of loving again, Richard finds himself tempted by a young lady determined to marry his best friend.

Gemma Reed has not been treated kindly by the *ton*. Often disregarded for her appearance and interests unlike those of a proper lady, Gemma heads to house party to win the heart of Lord Westfield, the man she's loved for years. But her plan is set off course by the tempting and intriguing, Richard Jonas.

A chance meeting creates a new path for Richard and Gemma to forage—but can two people, scorned and shunned by those they've loved from afar, let down their guards to find true happiness?

"Rescued By A Lady's Love"
Book 3 in the "Lords of Honor" Series

Destitute and determined to finally be free of any man's shackles, Lily Benedict sets out to salvage her honor. With no choice but to commit a crime that will save her from her past, she enters the home of the recluse, Derek Winters, the new Duke of Blackthorne. But entering the "Beast of Blackthorne's" lair proves more threatening than she ever imagined.

With half a face and a mangled leg, Derek—once rugged and charming—only exists within the confines of his home. Shunned by society, Derek is leery of the hauntingly beautiful Lily Benedict. As time passes, she slips past his defenses, reminding him how to live again. But when Lily's sordid past comes back, threatening her life, it's up to Derek to find the strength to become the hero he once was. Can they overcome the darkness of their sins to find a life of love and redemption?

Captivated by a Lady's Charm
Book 2 in the "Lords of Honor" Series

In need of a wife...

Christian Villiers, the Marquess of St. Cyr, despises the role he's been cast into as fortune hunter but requires the funds to keep his marquisate solvent. Yet, the sins of his past cloud his future, preventing him from seeing beyond his fateful actions at the Battle of Toulouse. For he knows inevitably it will catch up with him, and everyone will remember his actions on the battlefield that cost so many so much—particularly his best friend.

In want of a husband…

Lady Prudence Tidemore's life is plagued by familial scandals, which makes her own marital prospects rather grim. Surely there is one gentleman of the ton who can look past her family and see just her and all she has to offer?

When Prudence runs into Christian on a London street, the charming, roguish gentleman immediately captures her attention. But then a chance meeting becomes a waltz, and now…

A Perfect Match…

All she must do is convince Christian to forget the cold requirements he has for his future marchioness. But the demons in his past prevent him from turning himself over to love. One thing is certain—Prudence wants the marquess and is determined to have him in her life, now and forever. It's just a matter of convincing Christian he wants the same.

Seduced By a Lady's Heart
Book 1 in the "Lords of Honor" Series

You met Lieutenant Lucien Jones in "Forever Betrothed, Never the Bride" when he was a broken soldier returned from fighting Boney's forces. This is his story of triumph and happily-ever-after!

~★~

Lieutenant Lucien Jones, son of a viscount, returned from war, to find his wife and child dead. Blaming his father for the commission that sent him off to fight Boney's forces, he was content to languish at London Hospital… until offered employment on the Marquess of Drake's staff. Through his position, Lucien found purpose in life and is content to keep his past buried.

Lady Eloise Yardley has loved Lucien since they were children. Having long ago given up on the dream of him, she married another. Years later, she is a young, lonely widow who does not fit in with the ton. When Lucien's family enlists her aid to reunite father and son, she leaps at the opportunity to not only aid her former friend, but to also escape London.

Lucien doesn't know what scheme Eloise has concocted, but

knowing her as he does, when she pays a visit to his employer, he knows she's up to something. The last thing he wants is the temptation that this new, older, mature Eloise presents; a tantalizing reminder of happier times and peace.

Yet Eloise is determined to win Lucien's love once and for all… if only Lucien can set aside the pain of his past and risk all on a lady's heart.

ONLY FOR THEIR LOVE
Book 3 in the "The Theodosia Sword" Series

Miss Carol Cresswall bore witness to her parents' loveless union and is determined to avoid that same miserable fate. Her mother has altogether different plans—plans that include a match between Carol and Lord Gregory Renshaw. Despite his wealth and power, Carol has no interest in marrying a pompous man who goes out of his way to ignore her. Now, with their families coming together for the Christmastide season it's her mother's last-ditch effort to get them together. And Carol plans to avoid Gregory at all costs.

Lord Gregory Renshaw has no intentions of falling prey to his mother's schemes to marry him off to a proper debutante she's picked out. Over the years, he has carefully sidestepped all endeavors to be matched with any of the grasping ladies.

But a sudden Christmastide Scandal has the potential show Carol and Gregory that they've spent years running from the one thing they've always needed.

ONLY FOR HER HONOR
Book 2 in the "The Theodosia Sword" Series

A wounded soldier:

When Captain Lucas Rayne returned from fighting Boney's forces, he was a shell of a man. A recluse who doesn't leave his family's estate, he's content to shut himself away. Until he meets Eve...

A woman alone in the world:

Eve Ormond spent most of her life following the drum alongside her late father. When his shameful actions bring death and pain to English soldiers, Eve is forced back to England, an outcast. With no family or marital prospects she needs employment and finds it in Captain Lucas Rayne's home. A man whose life was ruined by her father, Eve has no place inside his household. With few options available, however, Eve takes the post. What she never anticipates is how with their every meeting, this honorable, hurting soldier slips inside her heart.

The Secrets Between Them:

The more time Lucas spends with Eve, he remembers what it is to be alive and he lets the walls protecting his heart down. When the secrets between them come to light will their love be enough? Or are they two destined for heartbreak?

ONLY FOR HIS LADY
Book 1 in the "The Theodosia Sword" Series

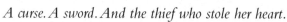

A curse. A sword. And the thief who stole her heart.

The Rayne family is trapped in a rut of bad luck. And now, it's up to Lady Theodosia Rayne to steal back the Theodosia sword, a gladius that was pilfered by the rival, loathed Renshaw family. Hopefully, recovering the stolen sword will break the cycle and reverse her family's fate.

Damian Renshaw, the Duke of Devlin, is feared by all—all, that is, except Lady Theodosia, the brazen spitfire who enters his home and wrestles an ancient relic from his wall. Intrigued by the vivacious woman, Devlin has no intentions of relinquishing the sword to her.

As Theodosia and Damian battle for ownership, passion ignites. Now, they are torn between their age-old feud and the fire that burns between them. Can two forbidden lovers find a way to make amends before their families' war tears them apart?

MY LADY OF DECEPTION
Book 1 in the "Brethren of the Lords" Series

This dark, sweeping Regency novel was previously only offered as part of the limited edition box sets: "From the Ballroom and Beyond", "Romancing the Rogue", and "Dark Deceptions". Now, available for the first time on its own, exclusively through Amazon is "My Lady of Deception".

~★~

Everybody has a secret. Some are more dangerous than others.

For Georgina Wilcox, only child of the notorious traitor known as "The Fox", there are too many secrets to count. However, after her interference results in great tragedy, she resolves to never help another... until she meets Adam Markham.

Lord Adam Markham is captured by The Fox. Imprisoned, Adam loses everything he holds dear. As his days in captivity grow, he finds himself fascinated by the young maid, Georgina, who cares for him.

When the carefully crafted lies she's built between them begin to crumble, Georgina realizes she will do anything to prove her love and loyalty to Adam—even it means at the expense of her own life.

NON-FICTION WORKS BY
CHRISTI CALDWELL

Uninterrupted Joy: Memoir: My Journey through Infertility, Pregnancy, and Special Needs

The following journey was never intended for publication. It was written from a mother, to her unborn child. The words detailed her struggle through infertility and the joy of finally being pregnant. A stunning revelation at her son's birth opened a world of both fear and discovery. This is the story of one mother's love and hope and…her quest for uninterrupted joy.

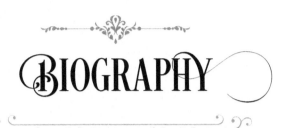

BIOGRAPHY

Christi Caldwell is the bestselling author of historical romance novels set in the Regency era. Christi blames Judith McNaught's "Whitney, My Love," for luring her into the world of historical romance. While sitting in her graduate school apartment at the University of Connecticut, Christi decided to set aside her notes and try her hand at writing romance. She believes the most perfect heroes and heroines have imperfections and rather enjoys tormenting them before crafting a well-deserved happily ever after!

When Christi isn't writing the stories of flawed heroes and heroines, she can be found in her Southern Connecticut home chasing around her eight-year-old son, and caring for twin princesses-in-training!

Visit *www.christicaldwellauthor.com* to learn more about what Christi is working on, or join her on Facebook at Christi Caldwell Author, and Twitter *@ChristiCaldwell*

Made in the USA
Middletown, DE
16 February 2019